FIVE ON A SECRET TRAIL

FIVE ON
A SECRET TRAIL

ENID BLYTON

Hodder
Children's
Books

a division of Hachette Children's Books

First published in Great Britain in 1956
by Hodder and Stoughton

This edition 2001

The right of Enid Blyton to be identified as the Author of
the Work has been asserted by her in accordance with the
Copyright, Designs and Patents Act 1988.

For further information on Enid Blyton
please contact www.blyton.com

9

A catalogue record for this title is
available from the British Library

ISBN-13: 978 0 340 79629 0

Typeset by Hewer Text UK Ltd, Edinburgh
Printed and bound in Great Britain by
Clays Ltd, St Ives plc

The paper and board used in this paperback by Hodder Children's
Books are natural recyclable products made from wood grown
in sustainable forests. The manufacturing processes conform
to the environmental regulations of the country of origin.

Hodder Children's Books
a division of Hachette Children's Books
338 Euston Road, London NW1 3BH
An Hachette Livre UK Company

Contents

[1]

George is rather difficult

'Mother! Mother, where are you?' shouted George, rushing into the house. 'Mother, quick!'

There was no answer. George's mother was out in the garden at the back of Kirrin Cottage, picking flowers. George yelled again, this time at the top of her very strong voice.

'MOTHER! MOTHER! Where are you? IT'S URGENT.'

A door was flung open nearby and George's father stood there, glaring at her.

'George! What's this row about? Here am I in the middle of some very difficult—'

'Oh Father! Timmy's hurt!' said George. 'He went—'

Her father looked down at Timmy, standing

meekly behind George. He gave a little snort.

'Hurt! He seems all right to me. I suppose he's got a thorn in his paw again – and you think it's the end of the world or something, and come yelling in here and—'

'Timmy *is* hurt!' said George, with tears in her voice. 'Look!'

But her father had gone back into his study again, and the door slammed. George glared at it, looking exactly like her hot-tempered father.

'You're unkind!' she shouted, 'and . . . oh there's MOTHER. MOTHER!'

'Dear me, George, whatever *is* the matter?' said her mother, putting down the flowers. 'I heard your father shouting, and then you.'

'Mother – Timmy's hurt!' said George. 'Look!'

She knelt down by the dog, and gently pulled forward one ear. Behind it was a big cut. Timmy whined. Tears came into George's eyes, and she looked up at her mother.

'Now don't be silly, George,' said Mrs Kirrin. 'It's only a cut. How did he do it?'

'He tried to jump over a ditch, and he didn't see some old barbed wire there,' said George. 'And a rusty piece caught his ear, and ripped that awful cut. I can't stop it bleeding.'

Her mother looked at it. It certainly was quite deep. 'Take him to the vet, George,' she said. 'Perhaps it ought to be stitched. It does look rather deep. Poor old Timmy-boy – well, it's a good thing it wasn't his eye, George.'

'I'll take him to the vet at once,' said George, getting up. 'Will he be in, Mother?'

'Oh yes – it's his surgery hour,' said her mother. 'Take him along now.'

So Timmy was hurried along the country lanes to the pretty little house where the vet lived. George, very anxious indeed, was most relieved to see that the vet seemed quite unconcerned.

'A couple of stitches and that cut will heal well,' he said. 'Hold him, will you, while I do the job? He'll hardly feel it. There, old boy – stand still – that's right.'

In five minutes' time George was thanking the vet wholeheartedly. 'Thank you! I *was* worried! Will he be all right now?'

'Good gracious, yes – but you mustn't let him scratch that wound,' said the vet, washing his hands. 'If he does, it may go wrong.'

'Oh. But how can I stop him?' asked George anxiously. 'Look – he's trying to scratch it now.'

'Well, you must make him a big cardboard collar,' said the vet. 'One that sticks out right round his neck, so that his paw can't get near that cut, however much he tries to reach it.'

'But – but Timmy won't like that a bit,' said George. 'Dogs look silly wearing cardboard collars like great ruffs round their necks. I've seen them. He'll hate one.'

'Well, it's the only way of stopping him from scratching that wound,' said the vet. 'Get along now, George – I've more patients waiting.'

George went home with Timmy. He padded along quietly, pleased at the fuss that George was making of him. When he was nearly home, he suddenly sat down and put up his hind leg to scratch his bad ear.

'No, Timmy! NO!' cried George, in alarm. 'You must NOT scratch. You'll get the plaster off in no time, and break the stitches. NO, Timmy!'

Timmy looked up in surprise. Very well. If scratching was suddenly upsetting George, he would wait till he was alone.

But George could read Timmy's thoughts as easily as he could read hers! She frowned.

'Blow! I'll *have* to make him that cardboard collar. Perhaps Mother will help me.'

Her mother was quite willing to help. George was not good at things of that sort, and she watched her mother cutting out a big cardboard collar, fitting it round the surprised Timmy's head, and then lacing the edges together with thread so that he could not get it off. Timmy was most surprised, but he stood very patiently.

As soon as the collar was finished, and safely round his neck, he walked away. Then he raised his hind leg to scratch at his smarting ear – but, of course, he couldn't get it over the collar, and merely scratched the cardboard.

'Never mind, Timmy,' said George. 'It will only be for a few days.'

The study door nearby opened and her father came out. He saw Timmy in his collar and stopped in surprise. Then he roared with laughter.

'Hey, Timmy – you look like Queen Elizabeth the First in a fine big ruff!' he said.

'Don't laugh at him, Father,' said George. 'You know that dogs can't bear being laughed at.'

Timmy certainly looked offended. He turned his back on George's father and stalked off to the kitchen. A little squeal of laughter came

from there and then a loud guffaw from someone at the kitchen door – the milkman.

'Oh Timmy – whatever have you got that
collar on for?' said the cook's voice. 'You do
look peculiar!'

George was angry. She remained angry all
that day and made everyone most uncomfortable. How *mean* of people to jeer at poor
Timmy! Didn't they realise how terribly uncomfortable a collar like that was – and Timmy
had to wear it night and day! He couldn't even
lie down comfortably. George mooned about
looking so angry and miserable that her mother
felt worried.

'George dear, don't be silly about this. You
will make your father cross. Timmy will have to
wear that collar for at least a week, you know,
and he *does* look a bit comical when you first
see him. He's getting used to it, he soon won't
notice it.'

'Everybody laughs at him,' said George, in
an angry voice. 'He went into the garden and

a lot of kids hung over the wall and laughed like anything. And the postman told me it was cruel. And Father thinks it's funny. And—'

'Oh dear, George, don't get into one of your moods,' said her mother. 'Remember, Anne is coming soon. She won't enjoy things much if you behave like this.'

George bore it for one day more. Then, after two upsets with her father over Timmy, another with a couple of boys who laughed at him, and one with the paper-boy, she decided she wouldn't stay at Kirrin Cottage for one day longer!

'We'll take my little tent, and go off by ourselves somewhere,' she told Timmy. 'Some place where nobody can see you till your ear is better and that hateful collar is off. Don't you think that's a good idea, Timmy?'

'Woof,' said Timmy. He thought that any of George's ideas were good, though the collar puzzled him very much.

'You know the *dogs* laugh at you too, Timmy,' said George, earnestly. 'Did you see how that silly little poodle belonging to Mrs Janes up the lane stood and stared at you? He looked *exactly* as if he was laughing. I won't have you laughed at. I know you hate it.'

Timmy certainly didn't like it, but he really was not as upset about the collar as George seemed to be. He followed her as she went up to her bedroom and watched her as she began to put a few things into a small bag.

'We'll go to that lonely little spot on the common,' she said to him. 'We'll pitch our tent near a little stream, and we'll jolly well stay there till your ear's better. We'll go tonight. I'll take my bike, and strap everything on to the back.'

So, in the middle of the night, when Kirrin Cottage was dark and quiet, George stole downstairs with Timmy. She left a note on the dining-room table, and then went to get her bicycle. She strapped her little tent on it, and the bag containing food and other odds and ends.

'Come on!' she whispered to the surprised Timmy. 'We'll go. I'll ride slowly and you can run beside me. Don't bark for goodness' sake!'

They disappeared into the darkness, Timmy running like a black shadow beside the bicycle. Nobody guessed they were gone. Kirrin Cottage was quiet and undisturbed – except for the creaking of the kitchen door, which George had forgotten to shut.

But in the morning, what a disturbance! Joanna the cook found George's note first and wondered what a letter in George's writing was doing on the dining-room table. She ran straight up to George's room and looked inside.

The bed was empty. There was no George and Timmy's basket was empty. Joanna went to take the note to Mrs Kirrin.

'Oh *dear*! How silly George is!' she said, when she had read it. 'Look, Quentin – such a fuss about Timmy! Now George has gone off with him, goodness knows where!'

Her husband took the note and read it out loud. 'Dear Mother, I'm going off for a few days with Timmy till his ear is better. I've taken my tent and a few things. Don't worry, please. Tell Anne if she wants to join me, to come to the end of Carters Lane on the common and I will show her where I'm camping. Tell her to come at twelve. Love from George.'

'Well, I'm blessed!' said George's father. 'All right, let her stay away if she wants to – I'm tired of her sulky face and Timmy's hang-dog looks. Tell Anne to join George, and maybe I shall have peace for a few days!'

'George should be all right,' said his wife. 'She's quite sensible really – and she's got Timmy. I'll tell Anne to join her when she arrives this morning.'

When Anne arrived at Kirrin Station, and looked out for George and Timmy, they weren't there – only her aunt was there, smiling as usual.

'What's happened?' said Anne. 'Where's George – and Timmy?'

'Oh, George has gone off by herself,' said her Aunt Fanny. 'Come along, and I'll tell you!'

[2]

Anne joins the little camp

Aunt Fanny soon told Anne about Timmy's ear and the big collar of cardboard that had caused all the trouble. Anne couldn't help smiling.

'Oh Aunt Fanny – George is quite crazy about old Tim, isn't she? I'll go and meet her at twelve, and of course I'll camp with her for a day or two. It's lovely weather and I'd like to. I expect Uncle Quentin will be glad to have us out of the house!'

'How are Julian and Dick?' asked her aunt. She was very fond of Anne's two brothers, George's cousins. 'Will they be coming down here at all these holidays?'

'I don't know,' said Anne. 'They're still in France, you know, on a schoolboys' tour. I feel funny without them! George will be cross to hear they probably won't be coming to Kirrin. She'll just have to put up with *me*!'

At twelve o'clock Anne was standing patiently at the end of Carters Lane. It ran to the common and then ended in a small, winding path that led to nowhere in particular. Big gorse bushes grew here and there, and slender birch trees. Anne, her belongings strapped to her back, and a bag in her hand, looked over the common to see if she could spy George coming.

There was no sign of her. 'Blow!' said Anne. 'I suppose she's changed her mind or something. Perhaps her watch has stopped and she doesn't know the time. She ought to, though, by looking at the sun! How long shall I wait?'

She sat down by a big gorse bush, out of the hot sun. She hadn't been there for more than a minute when she heard a hissing sound.

'Pssssst!'

Anne sat up at once. The sound came from

the other side of the bush, and she got up and walked round it. Half-hidden under a prickly branch were George and Timmy!

'Hallo!' said Anne, surprised. 'Didn't you see me when I arrived? Hallo, Tim darling! How's your poor old ear? Oh, doesn't he look a quaint old dear in that collar, George?'

George scrambled out of the bush. 'I hid here just in case Father or Mother should come with you and try to make me come back,' she said. 'I wanted to make quite sure they weren't waiting somewhere a little way away. I'm glad you've come, Anne.'

'Of course I've come,' said Anne. 'I wouldn't stay alone at Kirrin Cottage while you were camping out. Besides, I understand how you feel about Timmy. The collar's a jolly good idea, of course – but it does make him look comical. I think he looks rather a dear in it, I do really.'

George was almost relieved that Anne had not laughed at Timmy as most people had. She smiled at her cousin, and Timmy licked her till Anne really had to push him away.

'Let's go,' said George, scrambling up. 'I've got a lovely camping place, Anne. You'll like it. It's near a little spring too, so there's plenty of water for Timmy to drink – and us too. Did you bring any more food? I didn't really bring much.'

'Yes. I've brought heaps,' said Anne. 'Aunt Fanny made me. She's not cross with you, George. I didn't see your father. He was shut up in his study.'

George's spirits suddenly rose. She gave Anne a friendly punch. 'This is going to be fun! Timmy's ear will soon be better, and he loves camping out as much as we do. I've really found a good place – about the loneliest on the common! Nobody near us for miles!'

They set off together, Timmy at their heels, darting off every now and again when he smelt rabbit.

'When are Julian and Dick coming down?'

asked George. 'In a few days? Timmy's ear will be all right then and we can go back to Kirrin Cottage to welcome the boys, and have some fun there.'

'They may not be coming down at all these hols,' said Anne, and George's face fell at once. She stopped and stared at Anne in dismay.

'Not coming! But they *always* come in the hols – or we go away somewhere together!' she said. 'They *must* come! I shall be miserable without Ju and Dick.'

'Well – they're still in France, on a tour or something,' said Anne. 'We shall hear if they're staying on there or coming down to Kirrin when we get back to the cottage. Don't look so woebegone, George!'

But George felt woebegone. The holidays stretched before her, suddenly seeming long and dreary. Her two boy cousins were always such fun – they had had such wonderful adventures together. And now – now they weren't coming!

'We shan't have any adventures at all if the boys don't come,' she said, in a small voice.

'I shan't mind that,' said Anne. 'I'm the peaceful one, not always on the look-out for something to happen, like you and the boys! Perhaps these holidays will be quite unexciting without even the *smell* of an adventure! Oh George – cheer up! *Don't* look so mournful. You'd better send a letter to Julian and Dick if you feel so badly about it.'

'I've a good mind to!' said George. 'I can't *imagine* hols without the boys. Why – we shan't be the Five – the Famous Five – if they don't come!'

'Woof!' said Timmy, quite agreeing. He sat down and tried to scratch his ear, but the big collar prevented him. He didn't seem to mind and ran off after a rabbit quite happily.

'I think *you* are more upset about that collar than Timmy,' said Anne, as they walked along. 'Are we getting near this place of yours, George? It's a jolly long way.'

'We go up this hill in front of us – and then drop down to a little copse,' said George. 'There's a funny old cottage nearby – quite ruined and empty. At first I thought perhaps people lived there, but when I went nearer I saw that it was ruined. There's a big old rose-rambler climbing all over it, even inside. I suppose the people who used to live there planted it.'

They walked up the little hill and down again, following curving rabbit paths. 'Better look out for adders,' said Anne. 'This is just the kind of place for them. My word, it's hot, George. Is there anywhere to swim near here – a pool or anything?'

'I don't know. We could explore and see,' said George. 'I did bring my swimsuit just in case. Look, you can see part of the old cottage now. My camp is fairly near there. I thought I'd better camp near the spring.'

They were soon at George's rough little camp. Her tent was up, and she had made a bed inside of the springy heather. A mug, a bag of dog biscuits, a few tins, and a loaf of bread were at one end of the tent. It didn't seem to Anne as if George had brought very much, and she felt glad that she had managed to pack such a lot of things.

'Aunt Fanny cut dozens and dozens of sandwiches,' said Anne. 'She said if we kept them in this tin they wouldn't go stale, and would last us a day or two till we went back. I'm hungry. Shall we have some now?'

They sat out in the sun, munching the ham sandwiches. Anne had brought tomatoes too, and they took a bite at a sandwich and then a bite at a tomato. Timmy had to make do with a handful of dog biscuits and half a sandwich every now and again. After a bit he got up and wandered off.

'Where's he going?' asked Anne. 'To look for a rabbit?'

'No. Probably to get a drink,' said George. 'The spring is in the direction he's gone. I'm thirsty too – let's take the mug and get a drink ourselves.'

They went off with the mug, Anne following George through the thick heather. The little spring was a lovely one. It had evidently been used by the people who had once lived in the old cottage, and was built round with big white stones, so that the spring ran through a little stony channel, as clear as crystal.

'Oooh – it's as cold as ice!' said Anne. 'Simply delicious! I could drink gallons of this!'

They lay on the heather out in the sun, talking, when they came back from the spring. Timmy wandered off by himself again.

'It's so peaceful here,' said Anne. 'Nobody near us for miles. Just the birds and the rabbits. This is what I like!'

'There's hardly a sound,' said George, yawning.

And then, just as she said that, there came a noise in the distance. A sharp sound, like metal on stone. It came again and again and then stopped.

'What's that, do you suppose?' said George, sitting up.

'I can't imagine,' said Anne. 'Anyway, it's a long way away – everything is so still that sounds carry from quite a distance.'

The sharp noises began again in a little while and then stopped. The girls shut their eyes, and slept. There wasn't a sound now except the pop-pop-pop of gorse pods exploding in the sun and sending out their little black seeds.

George woke up when Timmy came back. He sat down heavily on her feet and she woke up with a jump.

'Timmy! Don't!' she said. 'Get off my feet, you made me jump!' Timmy obligingly removed himself and then picked up something he had dropped, lay down and began gnawing it. George looked to see what it was.

'Timmy! That's a bone! Where did you get it?' she said. 'Anne, did you bring a bone for Tim?'

'What? What did you say?' said Anne, half asleep. 'A bone. No, I didn't. Why?'

'Because Timmy's found one,' said George, 'and it's a bone that has had cooked meat on it, so it's not a rabbit or anything Timmy's caught. Timmy, where did you get it?'

'Woof,' said Timmy, offering the bone to George, thinking that she too might like a gnaw, as she seemed so interested in it.

'Do you suppose anyone else is camping near us?' asked Anne, sitting up and yawning. 'After all, bones don't grow in the heather. That's quite a good meaty one, too. Timmy, have you stolen it from another dog?'

Timmy thumped his tail on the ground and went on with his bone. He looked pleased with himself.

'It's rather an old bone,' said George. 'It's smelly. Go away, Tim – take it further off.'

The sharp metallic noises suddenly began again and George frowned. 'I believe there *is* someone camping near us, Anne. Come on –

let's do a bit of exploring and find out. I vote we move our camp if there are other people near. Come on, Timmy – that's right, bury that horrible bone! This way Anne!'

[3]

The old cottage – and a surprise

The two girls, with Timmy at their heels, left their camping place and set off in the hot sun. Anne caught sight of the ruined cottage and stopped.

'Let's have a look at it,' she said. 'It must be awfully old, George.'

They went in at the wide doorway. There was no door left, only the stone archway. Inside was a big room, whose floor had once been paved with slabs of white stone. Now grass and other weeds had grown between the cracks, and had actually lifted up some of the slabs so that the whole floor was uneven.

Here and there parts of the walls had fallen

away and the daylight came through. One window was still more or less intact, but the others had fallen out. A small crooked stairway of stone led upwards in one corner.

'To rooms above, I suppose,' said Anne. 'Oh, here's another doorway, leading into a second room – a small one. It's got an old sink in it, look – and this must be the remains of a pump.'

'There's not much to see, really,' said George, looking round. 'The top rooms must be quite ruined, because half the roof is off. Hallo, here's another door – a back door. It's actually a *door* too, not just a doorway.'

She gave a push at the stout wood – and the old door promptly fell off its hinges and crashed outwards into an overgrown yard.

'Goodness!' said George, startled. 'I didn't know it was quite so rotten. It made poor Tim jump almost out of his skin!'

'There are outhouses here – or the remains of

them,' said Anne, exploring the back-yard. 'They must have kept pigs and hens and ducks. Here's a dried-up pond, look.'

Everything was falling to pieces. The best preserved corner of the old place was what must have been a small stable. Rusted mangers were still there and the floor was of stone. An old, old piece of harness hung on a big nail.

'It's got quite a nice "*feel*" about it, this old place,' said Anne. 'Sometimes I don't like the feel of places – they give me an uneasy feeling, a feeling that horrid things may have happened there. But this is quite different. I think people have been happy here, and led peaceful lives. I can almost hear hens clucking and ducks quacking, and pigs gr—'

'Quack, quack, quack! Quack!'

'*Cuck*-cuk-cuk-cuk-cuk! *Cuck*-cuk-cuk-cuk-cuk!'

Anne clutched George and the two girls looked extremely startled to hear the sudden loud noise of quacking and clucking. They stood and listened.

'What was it?' said Anne. 'It *sounded* like hens and ducks – though I'm not quite sure. But there aren't any here, surely. We shall hear a horse whinnying next!'

They didn't hear a whinny – but they heard the snorting of a horse at once. 'Hrrrrr-umph! Hrrrrr-umph!'

Both girls were now quite alarmed. They looked for Timmy. He was nowhere to be seen! Wherever could he have got to?

'*Cuck*-cuk-cuk-cuk-cuk!'

'This is silly,' said George. 'Are we imagining things? Anne, there *must* be hens near. Come round the back of these stables and look. Timmy, where are you? TIMMY!'

She whistled shrilly – and immediately an echo came – or so it seemed!

'Phee-phee-phee-phee-phee!'

'TIMMY!' yelled George, beginning to feel as if she was in a dream.

Timmy appeared, looking rather sheepish. He wagged his tail – and to the girls' enormous amazement, they saw that he had a ribbon tied on it. A ribbon – a bright blue one at that!

'Timmy! Your tail – the ribbon – Timmy, what's all this about?' said George, really startled.

Timmy went to her, still looking sheepish, and George tore the ribbon off his tail. 'Who tied it there?' she demanded. 'Who's here? Timmy, where have you been?'

The two girls searched the old buildings thoroughly, and found nothing and nobody. Not a hen, not a duck, not a pig – and certainly not a horse. Then – what was the explanation? They stared at one another in bewilderment.

'And where did Timmy get that silly ribbon?' said George, exasperated. '*Someone* must have tied it on.'

'Perhaps it was a hiker passing by – perhaps he heard us here and saw Timmy and played a joke,' said Anne. 'But it's strange that old Tim *let* him tie on the ribbon. I mean – Timmy's not overfriendly with strangers, is he?'

The girls gave up the idea of exploring any further and went back to their little camp. Timmy went with them. He lay down – and then suddenly got up again, making for a thick gorse bush. He tried to squirm underneath.

'*Now* what's he after?' said George. 'Really, I think Timmy's gone mad. Timmy, you *can't* get under there with that great collar on. TIMMY, do you hear me!'

Timmy backed out reluctantly, the collar all crooked. After him came a peculiar little mongrel dog with one blind eye and one exceedingly bright and lively one. He was half-white and half-black, and had a ridiculously long thin tail, which he waved about merrily.

'*Well*!' said George, amazed. 'What's that dog doing there? And how did Timmy get so friendly with him? Timmy, I can't make you out.'

'Woof,' said Timmy, and brought the mongrel dog over to Anne and George. He then proceeded to dig up the smelly bone he had buried, and actually offered it to the little dog, who looked away and took no interest in it at all.

'This is all very peculiar,' said Anne. 'I shall expect to see Timmy bring a cat to us next!'

At once there came a pathetic mewing.

'Mee-ew! Mee-ew-ee-ew-ee-ew!'

Both dogs pricked up their ears, and rushed to the bush. Timmy was once again kept back by his big collar and barked furiously.

George got up and marched to the bush. 'If there's a cat there, it won't have much chance against two dogs,' she called to Anne. 'Come away, Tim. Hey, you little dog, come away, too.'

Timmy backed out, and George pulled out the small dog very firmly indeed. 'Hold him, Anne!' she called. 'He's quite friendly. He won't bite. I'm going to find that cat.'

Anne held on to the small mongrel, who gazed at her excitedly with his one good eye and wagged his tail violently. He was a most friendly little fellow. George began to crawl into the bare hollow space under the big gorse bush.

She looked into it, not able to see anything at first, because it was dark there after the bright sunlight. Then she got a tremendous shock.

A round, grinning face stared back at her, a face with very bright eyes and tousled hair falling on to the forehead. The mouth was set in a wide smile, showing very white teeth.

'Mee-ew-ee-ew-ee-ew!' said the face.

George scrambled back at top speed, her heart thumping. 'What is it?' called Anne.

'There's somebody hiding there,' said George. 'Not a cat. An idiot of a boy who is doing the mewing.'

'Mew-ee-ew-ee-ew!'

'Come out!' called Anne. 'Come out and let's see you. You must be crazy.'

There was a scrambling noise and a boy came head first from the hollow space under the bush. He was about twelve or thirteen, short, sturdily built, and with the cheekiest face Anne had ever seen.

Timmy rushed at him and licked him lovingly. George stared in amazement.

'How does my dog know you?' she demanded.

'Well, he came growling at me yesterday when I was in my own camp,' said the boy. 'And I offered him a nice meaty bone. Then he saw my little dog Jet – short for jet-propelled, you know – and made friends with him – and with me too.'

'I see,' said George, still not at all friendly. 'Well, I don't like my dog to take food from strangers.'

'Oh, I couldn't agree more,' said the boy. 'But I thought I'd rather he ate the bone than ate *me*. He's a nice dog, yours. He feels a bit of an idiot wearing that collar, doesn't he? You should have heard Jet laugh when he first saw it!'

George frowned. 'I came here to be alone so that Timmy shouldn't be jeered at,' she said. 'He's got a bad ear. I suppose *you* were the fathead who tied a blue ribbon on his tail?'

'Just for a joke,' said the boy. '*You* like frowning and glaring, I can see. Well, *I* like joking and tricking! Your Timmy didn't mind a bit. He took to my dog right away. But everyone likes Jet! I wanted to find out who owned Timmy – because, like you, *I* don't like strangers messing about when I'm camping out. So I came along.'

'I see. And you did all the clucking and quacking and hrrr-umphing?' said Anne. She liked this idiot of a boy, with his broad friendly grin. 'What are you doing – just camping – or hiking – or botanising?'

'I'm digging,' said the boy. 'My father's an archaeologist – he loves old buildings more than anything else in the world. I take after him, I suppose. There was once an old Roman camp on this common, you know – and I've found a place where part of it must have been, so I'm digging for anything I can find – pottery, weapons, anything like that. See, I found this yesterday – look at the date on it!'

He suddenly thrust an old coin at them – a strange, uneven one, rather heavy to hold.

'Its date is 292,' he said. 'At least, as far as I can make out. So the camp's pretty old, isn't it?'

'We'll come and see it,' said Anne, excited.

'No, don't,' said the boy. 'I don't like people messing round me when I'm doing something serious. Please don't come. I won't bother you again. I promise.'

'All right. We won't come,' said Anne, quite understanding. 'But don't you play any more silly tricks on us, see?'

'I promise,' said the boy. 'I tell you, I won't come near you again. I only wanted to see whose dog this was. Well, I'm off. So long!'

And, whistling to Jet, he set off at a furious pace. George turned to Anne.

'What a peculiar boy!' she said. 'Actually – I'd rather *like* to see him again. Wouldn't you?'

[4]

That night

It was now tea-time, according to Anne's watch
and also according to everyone's feelings, including Timmy's. Timmy felt the heat very
much and was always wandering off to the
little spring to lap the crystal-cold water. Anne
wished that she and George had a big jug that
they could fill – it was such a nuisance to have
to keep running to and fro with just a mug.

They had tea – biscuits, a sandwich each, and
a bar of rather soft chocolate. George examined
Timmy's ear for the hundredth time that day,
and pronounced it very much better.

'Well, don't take off that collar yet,' said
Anne. 'He'll only open the wound by scratching
if you do.'

'I'm not *going* to take it off!' said George,

touchily. 'What shall we do now, Anne? Go for a walk?'

'Yes,' said Anne. 'Listen – you can hear those sharp, metallic noises again – that's the boy at work again, I expect. Funny boy he must be – coming to dig about all on his own with his comical little dog. I wish we could see what he's doing.'

'We promised we wouldn't,' said George. 'So I don't feel that we even ought to go and peep.'

'Of course not!' said Anne. 'Come on – let's go in the opposite direction, George – right away from the boy. I hope we shan't get lost!'

'Not while Timmy's with us, silly!' said George. 'You'd find your way home from the moon, wouldn't you, Tim?'

'Woof,' agreed Timmy.

'He always says yes to whatever you say, George,' said Anne. 'I say – isn't it a lovely evening? I wonder what Julian and Dick are doing?'

George immediately looked downcast. She

felt that her two cousins had no right to go rushing across France when she wanted them at Kirrin. Didn't they like Kirrin? Would they be having magnificent adventures abroad, and not want to spend even a week at Kirrin? She looked so lost in miserable thoughts that Anne laughed at her.

'Cheer up! At least *I* am here with you – though I agree that compared with Ju and Dick I'm very poor company, and not at all adventurous!'

They had a lovely walk, and sat down half-way to watch hordes of rabbits playing together. Timmy was very unhappy about this. Why *sit down* to watch silly rabbits? Rabbits were made to *chase*, weren't they? Why did George always put a restraining hand on his collar when she sat down to watch rabbits? He whined continually, as he watched with her.

'Shut up, Timmy, you ass,' said George. 'You'd only spoil the entertainment if you sent them to their holes.'

They watched for a long while and then got

up to go back to the camp. When they came near, they heard the sound of low whistling. Someone was about that evening, quite near their camp. Who was it?

They came round a big gorse bush, and almost bumped into a boy. He got out of their way politely, but said nothing.

'Why – it's *you*!' said George, in surprise. 'I don't know your name. What are you doing here? You said you wouldn't come near us.'

The boy stared, looking very surprised. His tousled hair fell right across his forehead, and he brushed it back.

'I said nothing of the sort,' he said.

'Oh, you *did*!' said Anne. 'You know you did. Well, if you break your promise, there's no reason for us to keep ours. We shall come and visit *your* camp.'

'I never made you any promise,' said the boy, looking quite startled. 'You're mad!'

'Don't be an idiot!' said George, getting cross. 'I suppose you'll be saying next that you didn't act like a hen, and a duck, and a horse this afternoon . . .'

'And a cat,' said Anne.

'Barmy!' said the boy, looking at them pityingly. 'Quite barmy.'

'Are you coming here again?' demanded George.

'If I want to,' said the boy. 'The water in this spring is better than the one over by my camp.'

'Then we shall come and explore *your* camp,' said George, firmly. 'If you don't keep your promise, we shan't keep ours.'

'By all means come if you want to,' said the boy. 'You seem quite mad, but I daresay you're harmless. But don't bring your dog. He might eat mine.'

'You know he wouldn't eat Jet!' said Anne. 'They're good friends.'

'I don't know anything of the sort,' said the boy, and went off, brushing his hair out of his eyes again.

'What do you make of *that*?' said George,

staring after him. 'Not a bit the same as he was this afternoon. Do you think he really *had* forgotten about his promise and everything?'

'I don't know,' said Anne, puzzled. 'He was so perky and jolly and full of fun before – grinning all the time – but just now he seemed quite serious – not a smile in him!'

'Oh well – perhaps he's a bit crazy,' said George. 'Are you sleepy, Anne? I am, though I can't think why!'

'Not very – but I'd like to lie down on this springy heather and watch the stars gradually come sparkling into the sky,' said Anne. 'I don't think I'll sleep in the tent, George. You'll want Timmy with you, and honestly there's so little room inside the tent that I'm quite sure Timmy would lie on my legs all night long.'

'I'll sleep in the open air as well,' said George. 'I only slept in the tent last night because it looked a bit like rain. Let's get some more heather and make a kind of mattress of it. We can put a rug on top of it, and lie on that.'

The two of them pulled a lot of heather and carried it to their 'bed'. Soon they had a fine pile, and Timmy went to lie on it.

'Hey – it's not for you!' cried George. 'Get off – you'll flatten it right down. Where's the rug, Anne?'

They laid the rug on the heather pile and then went to the spring to wash and clean their teeth. Timmy immediately got on to the heather bed again, and shut his eyes.

'You old fraud!' said George, lugging him off. 'You're not asleep. Keep off our bed! Look – there's a nice soft patch of grass for you. That's your bed!'

George lay down on the rug, and the heathery bed sank a little beneath her weight. 'Very comfortable!' said George. 'Shall we want a rug over us, Anne?'

'Well, I did bring one,' said Anne. 'But I don't think we'll want it, the night's so hot. Look – there is a star already!'

Soon there were six or seven – and then

gradually hundreds more pricked through the evening sky as the twilight deepened. It was a wonderful night.

'Don't the stars look big and bright?' said Anne, sleepily. 'They make me feel very small, they're such millions of miles away. George, are you asleep?'

There was no answer. George hadn't heard a word. She was fast asleep. Her hand fell down the side of the heather and rested on the ground below. Timmy moved a little nearer and gave it a small lick. Then he too fell asleep, and gave some small doggy snores.

The night darkened. There was no moon but the stars shone out well from the midnight sky. It was very quiet out there on the common, far away from streets and villages and towns. Not even an owl hooted.

Anne didn't quite know why she awoke. At first she had no idea where she was, and she lay gazing up at the stars in astonishment, thinking she must still be asleep.

She suddenly felt very thirsty. She groped about in the nearby tent for the mug, couldn't find it and gave it up.

'I'll drink from my cupped hands,' she thought, and set off for the little spring. Timmy wondered whether to follow her. No – he would stay with George. She wouldn't like it if she awoke and found him gone with Anne. So he settled his head down on his paws again and slept, leaving one ear open for Anne.

Anne found the little spring. Its tinkling gurgling sound guided her as soon as she heard it. She sat down on one of the stones nearby, and held out her cupped hands. How very cold the water was – and how delicious to drink on this hot night! She sipped thirstily, slopping some of the water down her front.

She got up to go back, and walked a few steps in the starlight. Then she stopped. Wait – was she going in the right direction? She wasn't sure.

'I *think* I am!' she decided, and went on,

carefully and quietly. Surely she must be near their little camp now?

Then all at once she stood still, and felt herself stiffen. She had suddenly seen a light. It had flashed and disappeared. Ah – there it was again! Whatever could it be?

Then, as her eyes strained through the starlit darkness, she suddenly saw that she *had* taken the wrong way – she had gone in the direction of the old ruined cottage, and not the camp – and the light had come from there!

She didn't dare go any nearer. She felt glued to the grass she was standing on! Now she could hear sounds – whispering sounds – and the noise of a football on the stone floor of the cottage – and then the flash of a light came again! Yes, it *was* from the old cottage!

Anne began to breathe fast. Who was it in the old cottage? She simply dared not go and see. She must go back to George, and to Timmy's protection. As fast and as silently as she could she found her way back to the spring – and then, almost stumbling now, made her way to where George was still lying peacefully asleep.

'Woof,' said Timmy, sleepily, and tried to lick her hand. Anne climbed on to the heathery bed beside George, her heart still beating fast.

'George!' she whispered. 'George, do wake up. I've something strange to tell you!'

[5]
That boy again!

George would not wake up. She grunted when Anne poked her and prodded her, and then she turned over, almost falling off the small heather bed.

'Oh George – *please* do wake!' begged Anne, in a whisper. She was afraid of speaking out loud in case anyone should hear her. Who knew what might happen if she drew attention to their little camp?

George awoke at last and was cross. 'Whatever is it, Anne?' she said, her voice sounding loud in the night.

'Sh!' said Anne. 'Sh!'

'Why? We're all alone here! We can make as much noise as we like!' said George, surprised.

'George, do listen! There's someone in that

old cottage!' said Anne, and at last George heard and understood. She sat up at once.

Anne told her the whole story – though it didn't really seem very much of a tale when she related it. George spoke to Timmy.

'Tim!' she said, keeping her voice low. 'We'll go and do a little exploring, shall we? Come on, then – and keep quiet!'

She slid off the rug and stood up. 'You stay here,' she said to Anne. 'Timmy and I will be very quiet and careful, and see what we can find out.'

'Oh no – I couldn't stay here *alone*!' said Anne in alarm, and got up hurriedly. 'I shall have to come too. I don't mind a bit now Timmy's with us. I wonder he didn't bark at the people in the old cottage, whoever they were.'

'He probably thought it was you messing about,' said George, and Anne nodded. Yes, of course, Timmy must have thought that any noises he heard had been made by her.

They took the path that led to the old cottage. George had Timmy well to heel. He knew he must not push forward unless told to. His ears were pricked now, and he was listening hard.

They came cautiously to the cottage. They could see its dark outline in the starlight, but little else. There was no light flashing there. Nor did there seem to be any noises at all.

All three stood still and quiet for about five minutes. Then Timmy moved restlessly. This was boring! Why wouldn't George let him run forward and explore everywhere if she wanted to know if intruders were about?

'I don't think there's a soul here!' whispered George into Anne's ear. 'They must have gone – unless you dreamed it all, Anne!'

'I didn't!' whispered back Anne indignantly. 'Let's go forward a bit and send Timmy into the cottage. He'll soon bark if there's anyone there.'

George gave Timmy a little shove. 'Go on, then!' she said. 'Find, Timmy, find!'

Timmy gladly shot forward into the darkness. He trotted into the cottage, though it was impossible even to see him go to it. The two girls stood and listened, their heartbeats sounding very loud to them! There was not a sound to be heard, except occasionally the rattle of Timmy's strong claws on a stony slab.

'There can't be anyone there,' said George at last, 'else Timmy would have sniffed them out. You're an ass, Anne – you dreamt it all!'

'I did not!' said Anne, indignant again. 'I *know* there was someone there – in fact, more than one person, because I'm sure I heard whispering!'

George raised her voice. 'Timmy!' she called loudly, making Anne jump violently. 'Timmy! Come along. We've sent you on a silly wild goose chase – but now we'll go back to bed!'

Timmy came trotting out of the cottage and

went obediently to George. She heard him yawn as he stood beside her, and she laughed.

'Anne had a bad dream, that's all, Timmy,' she said.

Anne felt cross – very cross. She said no more and they left the old cottage and went back to their heather bed. Anne climbed on to her side and turned over with her back to George. All right – let George think it was a dream if she liked!

But when Anne awoke in the morning and remembered the happenings of the night before, she too began to wonder uneasily if she *had* dreamed what she had seen and heard in the old cottage.

'After all – Timmy would certainly have caught anyone who was there,' she thought. 'And he wasn't at all excited, so there can't have *been* anyone in the cottage. And anyway, why would they come? It's just silly!'

So, when George talked about Anne's dream-ing in the middle of the night, Anne did not defend herself. She really could *not* be sure that it had really happened. So she stuck out her tongue when George teased her, and said nothing.

'Let's go and see that boy and his camp,' George said when they had eaten a few rather stale sandwiches and some shortbread biscuits. 'I'm beginning to feel bored, aren't you? I wish Timmy's ear would quite heal up. I'd go back home like a shot then.'

They set off in the direction of the camp with Timmy. They heard a chip-chipping noise as they came near, and then something small and hairy shot out from a bush and rushed up, barking a welcome.

'Hallo, Jet!' said Anne. 'Don't you let Timmy have any more of your bones!'

The chipping noise had stopped. The two girls went on and came to a very messy piece of common. It had been well dug over, in some places very deeply. Surely that boy couldn't have done so much excavating by himself?

'Hey! Where are you?' called George. Then she saw the boy below her, examining something in a trench he had dug out. He jumped and looked upwards.

Then he scowled. 'Look – you promised not to come and disturb me!' he shouted. 'You're mean. Just like girls to break a promise.'

'Well! I like *that*!' said George amazed. 'It was *you* who broke yours! Who came messing round *our* camp yesterday evening I'd like to know?'

'Not me!' said the boy at once. 'I always keep my promises. Now go away and keep yours. Girls! Pooh!'

'Well, I can't say we think much of *you*,' said George, disgusted. 'We're going. *We* don't want to see anything of your silly digging. Good-bye!'

'Good-bye and good riddance!' called the boy rudely, and turned back to his work.

'I think he must be *quite* mad,' said Anne. 'First he makes a promise – then last evening he broke his promise and even said he hadn't made one – and now today he says he *did* make a promise and that he'd kept his and we'd broken ours. Idiotic!'

They went up a little rabbit path, and into a small copse of birch trees. Someone was sitting there reading. He looked up as they came.

The two girls stopped in amazement. It was that boy *again*! But how had he got here? They had just left him behind in a trench! Anne looked at the title of the book he was reading. Goodness – what a learned title – something about archaeology.

'Another little trick of yours, I suppose?' said George, sarcastically, stopping in front of him. 'You must be a jolly good runner, I must say, to have got here so quickly. Funny boy, aren't you – very very funny!'

'Good gracious – it's those potty girls again,' groaned the boy. 'Can't you leave me alone? You talked a lot of rubbish yesterday – and now you're talking it again.'

'How did you get here so quickly?' said Anne, puzzled.

'I didn't get here quickly. I came very slowly, reading my book as I went,' said the boy.

'Fibber!' said George. 'You must have run at top speed. Why do you pretend like this? It's only a minute or so ago that we saw you.'

'Now *you're* the fibber!' said the boy. 'I do think you two girls are awful. Go away and leave me alone and never let me see you again!'

Timmy didn't like the tone of the boy's voice and he growled. The boy scowled at him. 'And just you shut up too,' he said.

Anne pulled at George's sleeve. 'Come on,' she said, 'it's no good staying here arguing. The boy's crazy – mad – we'll never get any sense out of him!'

The two girls walked off together, Timmy following. The boy took absolutely no notice. His face was turned to his book and he was quite absorbed in it.

'I've never met anyone *quite* so mad before!' said Anne, rather puzzled. 'By the way, George – you don't suppose it could have been that idiotic boy last night in the cottage?'

'No. I tell you I think you dreamed it,' said George, firmly. 'Though that boy is quite idiot enough to explore an old cottage in the middle of the night. He would probably think it a very good time to do so. Oh Anne, look – there's a pool – in that hollow there. Do you think we could swim in it?'

It certainly shone very temptingly. They went down to have a closer look. 'Yes – we'll have a swim this afternoon,' said George. 'And then I really think, Anne, we ought to go back to Kirrin Cottage and get a few more provisions. The sandwiches we've got left are so dry that we really shan't enjoy eating them – and as Timmy's ear isn't healed, it looks as if we'll have to stay a bit longer.'

'Right!' said Anne, and they went on back to the camp. They changed into their swimsuits in the afternoon and went off to the little pool. It was fairly deep, very warm and quite clean. They spent a lovely hour swimming and basking and swimming again – then they reluctantly dressed and began to think of going off on the long journey to Kirrin Cottage.

George's mother was very surprised to see the two girls and Timmy. She said yes, of course they could have some more food, and sent them to ask Joanna for all she could spare.

'By the way, I've heard from Julian and Dick,' she said. 'They're back from France – and may be here in a day or two! Shall I tell them to join you or will you come back here?'

'Tell them to come and fetch us as soon as they get here!' said George, delighted. Her face shone. Ah – the Five would be together again. How wonderful!

'Leave me directions to give them so that they can find you,' said her mother. 'Then you can all come back – together. The boys can help to carry everything.'

What fun, what fun! Julian and Dick again, now things would be exciting, things would happen, as they always did. What FUN!

[6]

Storm in the night

It was fun to go back to their little camping place again. It was growing dark, as they had stayed to have a good meal at Kirrin Cottage, and Timmy had eaten a most enormous plate of meat, vegetables and gravy. Then he had sat down and sighed as if to say 'That was jolly good! I could do with some more!'

However, nobody took any notice of this, so he trotted off to have a good look round the garden to make sure it was just the same as when he had left it a day or two before. Then it was time to start back to the camping place, and Timmy heard George's whistle.

'Well, nobody laughed at Timmy this evening!' said Anne. 'Not even your father!'

'Oh, I expect Mother had told him not to,'

said George. 'Anyway, I *said* I would stay away till Tim's ear is better, and I mean to.'

'Well, I'm quite willing,' said Anne. 'The only thing I'm a bit worried about is – do you suppose there will be anyone snooping about in that old cottage again?'

'You dreamed it all!' said George. 'You admitted you did!'

'Well, yes, I did wonder if I *had* dreamed it,' said Anne, as they walked up the long Carters Lane to the moor. 'But now that it will soon be dark, I'm beginning to think I *didn't* dream it – and it isn't a very nice feeling.'

'Oh, don't be silly!' said George impatiently. 'You can't chop and change about like that. Anyway, we've got Timmy – no one would dare to upset Timmy! Would they, Tim?'

But Timmy was ahead, hoping against hope that he might for once in a while catch a rabbit. There were so many about on the common at this time of the evening, peeping at him here, making fun of him there, and showing their little white bobtails as soon as he moved in their direction.

The two girls got safely back to their camp. The tent was still up, their heather bed out in the open, covered with the old rug. They put down their loads thankfully, and went to the little spring for a drink.

George yawned. 'I'm tired. Let's get to bed at once, shall we? Or wait – perhaps it would be a good idea to have a look in at that cottage to make sure no one is there to disturb us tonight.'

'Oh no – I don't want to look,' said Anne. 'It's getting dark now.'

'All right – I'll go with Timmy,' said George, and off she went. She came back in about five minutes, her little torch shining in front of her, for it was now almost dark.

'Nothing to report,' she said. 'Nothing whatever – except one bat flying round that big room. Timmy nearly went mad when it flew down and almost touched his nose.'

'Oh. That's when he barked, I suppose,' said

Anne, who was now curled up on the heather bed. 'I heard him. Come on, George – I'm sleepy.'

'I must just look at Timmy's ear once more,' said George and shone her torch on it.

'Well, buck up, then,' said Anne. 'That's about the thousandth time today you've examined it.'

'It does seem much better,' said George, and she patted Timmy. 'I *shall* be glad when I can take this awful collar off him. I'm sure he hates it.'

'I don't believe he even *notices* it now,' said Anne. 'George, are you coming or not? I really can't keep awake one minute more.'

'I'm coming,' said George. 'No, Tim – you are *not* sleeping on our bed. I told you that last night. There's hardly enough room for Anne and me.'

She climbed carefully on to the heather bed, and lay looking up at the twinkling stars. 'I feel happy tonight,' she said, 'because Julian and

Dick are coming. I was down in the dumps when I thought they might not be coming at all these hols. When do you suppose they'll be here, Anne?'

There was no answer. Anne was asleep. George sighed. She would have liked to plan what they were going to do when the boys came. Timmy's ear would surely be all right in a day or two – and the boys could carry everything back from this little camp to Kirrin Cottage – and then long days of swimming and boating and fishing and all kinds of fun could begin – begin – begin – be . . .

And now George was asleep too! She didn't feel a small spider running over her hand, wondering whether or not to spin a web between her finger and thumb. She didn't hear the scramble of a hedgehog not far off – though Timmy did and pricked one ear. It was a very peaceful night indeed.

Next day the girls were very cheerful. They made a good breakfast of some of the food they had brought, and then spent some time getting more heather for their bed, which, under the weight of their two bodies, was now rather flat and uncomfortable.

'Now for a swim!' said George. They put on their swimsuits, threw cardigans over their shoulders and set off to the little pool. On the way they saw Jet, the little mongrel dog, in the distance, and the boy with him. Jet tore up to them and danced round Timmy excitedly.

The boy called to them. 'It's all right, don't worry, I'm not going near your place! I'm still keeping *my* promise! Jet – come here!'

The girls took no notice of the grinning boy, but couldn't resist patting the little one-eyed mongrel. Jet really was like a piece of quick-silver, darting in and out and round about. He shot back to the boy at once.

The girls went on to the pool – and stopped in dismay when they came near. Someone was already there, swimming vigorously!

'Who is it?' said Anne. 'Dear me, this lonely

common seems absolutely *crowded* with people!'

George was staring at the swimmer in utmost amazement. 'Anne – it's that boy!' she said. 'Look – tousled hair and everything! But – but . . .'

'But we've just met him going in the opposite direction!' said Anne, also amazed. 'How extraordinary! No, it *can't* be the boy!'

They went a little nearer. Yes – it *was* the boy. He called out to them. 'I'm just going out. I shan't be a minute!'

'How did you get here?' shouted George. 'We never saw you turn back and run.'

'I've been here for about ten minutes,' shouted back the boy.

'Fibber!' yelled back George at once.

'Ah – barmy as usual!' yelled the boy. 'Same as yesterday!'

He got out and walked off, dripping wet, in the direction of the trenches and pits which he was digging. George looked about for Jet, but she couldn't see him. 'Perhaps he's in the pool too,' she said. 'Come on, Anne – let's swim. I must say that that boy is extraordinary! I suppose he thinks it's funny to meet people, then double back and appear again!'

'He was nicer the first time of all that we saw him,' said Anne. 'I liked him then. I just don't understand him now. Ooooh – isn't this water lovely and warm!'

They had a long swim, got out and basked in the sun, lying on the heather, and then swam again. Then they began to feel hungry and went back to their little camping place.

The day passed quickly. They saw no more of the puzzling boy, or of Jet. They occasionally heard the sharp noise of metal on stone, or of chipping, from the place where the boy was presumably still digging in the old Roman camp.

'Or what he *hopes* is an old Roman camp,' said George. 'Personally I think he's so mad that I don't suppose he would know the difference between a Roman camp and a Boy Scouts' camp!'

They settled down on their heather bed that night but saw no stars twinkling above them this time. Instead there were rather heavy clouds, and it was not nearly so warm.

'Gosh – I hope it's not going to rain!' said George. 'Our tent wouldn't be much good against a real downpour! We could squeeze into it all right, but it's not a proper water-proof tent. Do you think it's going to rain, Anne?'

'No,' said Anne, sleepily. 'Anyway, I'm not getting up till I have to! I'm tired.'

She went to sleep, and so did George. Timmy didn't, though. He had heard the far-off growl of thunder, and he was uneasy. Timmy was not afraid of thunderstorms, but he didn't like them. They were things that growled like enormous dogs in the sky, and flashed angrily – but he never could get at them, or frighten them!

He closed both eyes, and put down one ear, leaving the other one up, listening.

Another thunder growl came, and one large and heavy drop of rain fell on Timmy's black nose. Then another fell on his cardboard collar and made a very loud noise indeed, startling him. He sat up, growling.

The rain came closer, and soon large drops, the size of ten-penny pieces, peppered the faces of the two sleeping girls. Then came such a crash of thunder that they both awoke in a fright.

'Blow! It's a thunderstorm!' said George. 'And pouring rain too. We shall be soaked.'

'Better get into the tent,' said Anne, as a flash of lightning forked down the sky and lit up everything with a quick brilliance.

'No good,' said George. 'It's soaked already. There's nothing for it but to get into the cottage, Anne. At least we'll have a roof over our heads or rather, a ceiling, for the roof's gone. Come on.'

Anne didn't in the least want to shelter in the old cottage, but there was absolutely nothing else to do. The girls grabbed their rug and ran through the rain, George flashing her torch to guide them. Timmy ran too, barking.

They came to the doorway of the cottage and went inside. What a relief to get out of the rain! The two girls huddled down into a corner, the rug round them – but soon they were too hot and threw it off.

The storm passed overhead with a few terrific crashes and much lightning. Gradually the rain grew less and soon stopped. One star came out, and then others followed as the thunder-clouds swept away in the wind.

'We can't go back to the tent – we'll have to stay here,' said George. 'I'll go and get our bags for pillows. We can lie on the rug.'

Anne went with her, and carried a bag back too. Soon the girls were lying in a corner of the rug, their heads on the bags, and Timmy close beside them.

'Good night,' said Anne. 'We'll try to go to sleep again! Blow that storm!'

Soon they were both asleep – but Timmy wasn't. Timmy was uneasy. Very uneasy! And quite suddenly he broke into a volley of such loud barks that both girls woke up in a panic.

'Timmy! What's the matter? Oh Tim, what is it?' cried George. She clutched his leather collar and held on to him.

'Don't leave us! Timmy, what's scared you?'

[7]

Strange happenings

Timmy stopped barking and tried to get away from George's hand on his collar. But she would not let him. George was not easily frightened, but what with the thunderstorm, the strange old cottage and now Timmy's sudden excitement, she wanted him near her.

'What is it?' asked Anne, in a scared whisper.

'I don't know. I can't even imagine,' said George, also in a low voice. 'Perhaps it's nothing – just the thunderstorm that has upset him and made him nervous. We'll keep awake a bit, and see if we hear anything peculiar.'

They lay quietly in their corner, and George kept a firm hand on Timmy. He growled once or twice, but did not bark any more. George began to think it really must have been the storm that had upset him.

A rumble of thunder came again – the storm was returning, or else another one was blowing up!

George felt relieved. 'It's all right, Anne. It must have been the thunder and lightning in the distance that upset Timmy. You're silly, Timmy – scaring us like that!'

Crash – rumble – crash! Yes, certainly the storm was gathering force again! Timmy barked angrily.

'Be quiet! You make more noise than the thunder!' said George, crossly. 'No you can't go out into the rain, Timmy. It's begun again, as bad as before. You'd only get dripping wet – and then you'd want to come and sit as close to me as possible and make me wet too. I know you!'

'No – don't let him go, George,' said Anne. 'I like him here with us. My word – what a storm! I hope it won't strike this cottage.'

'Well, considering that it must have stood here for three or four hundred years, and have seen thousands of storms, I expect it will come safely through one more!' said George. 'Where are you going, Anne?'

'Just to look out of the window,' said Anne. 'Or out of the place where the window used to be! I like to see the countryside suddenly lit up for just one moment in a lightning flash – and then go back to darkness again.'

She went to stand at the window. There came the crash of thunder, not far away, and a brilliant flash of lightning. Anne stared over the countryside, which had suddenly become visible in the flash – and then disappeared like magic in a second!

Anne gave a sudden cry and stumbled back to George. 'George – George . . .'

'Whatever's the matter?' asked George, alarmed.

'There's someone out there – people!' said Anne, clutching George and making her jump.

'I saw them just for an instant, when the lightning flashed.'

'People? What sort of people?' said George, astonished. 'How many?'

'I don't know. It was all so quick. I think there were two – or maybe three. They were standing some way off – quite still, out there in the storm.'

'Anne, those are *trees*!' said George, scornfully. 'There are two or three small trees standing against the sky out there – I noticed them the other day.'

'These weren't trees,' said Anne. 'I know they weren't. What are people doing out there in this storm? I'm frightened.'

George was absolutely certain that Anne had seen the group of little trees that she knew were there – they would look just like people, in a quick flash of lightning. No sooner did you see something in a storm than it was gone!

She comforted Anne. 'Don't worry, Anne! it's the easiest thing in the world to imagine seeing things in a lightning flash. Timmy would bark if there were people around. He would—'

'Well, he *did* bark, didn't he?' said Anne. 'He woke us both up with his barking.'

'Ah yes – but that was just because he heard the storm coming up again,' said George. 'And you know he gets angry when he hears the thunder growling.'

Just at that moment the thunder crashed again – then the lightning flashed its weird and brilliant light.

This time *both* the girls screamed, and Timmy gave an enormous bark, trying his hardest to get away from George.

'There! Did you see *that*?' said Anne, in a shaky voice.

'Yes. Yes, I did. Oh, Anne, you're right! Someone was looking in at the window! And if we saw him, he must have seen *us*! Whatever is he doing here in the middle of the night?'

'Well, I told you I saw two or three people,' said Anne, still shakily. 'I expect it was one of them. Maybe they saw the cottage in one of the lightning flashes, and thought they might shelter here – and sent one of their number to see.'

'Maybe. But what in the world is anyone *doing*, wandering about here at night?' said George. 'They can't possibly be up to any good. Let's go home tomorrow, Anne. I wish the boys were here! They'd know what to do, they would have some good plan!'

'The storm's going off again,' said Anne. 'Timmy has stopped barking too, thank goodness. Don't let him go, George. You never know – those people, whoever they are, might do him harm. Anyway, I feel safer when he's with us!'

'I wouldn't dream of letting him go,' said George. 'You're trembling, Anne! You needn't be as scared as that! Timmy won't let you come to any harm.'

'I know! But it wasn't very nice suddenly seeing somebody looking in at the window like that, outlined in a lightning flash!' said Anne. 'I can't possibly go to sleep again. Let's play some silly game to take our minds off it.'

So they played the Alphabet game with animals. Each had to think in turn of an animal beginning with A, and a mark went to the one who could keep it up longest! Then they went on to B and to C and to D.

They were doing the Es when they heard a loud and very comforting sound.

'Timmy's snoring,' said George. 'He's fast asleep. What an elephantine snore, Tim!'

'E for elephant,' said Anne, quickly.

'Cheat! That should have been *my* E!' said George. 'All right. E for Eland.'

'E for Egg-Eater,' said Anne, after a pause.

'Not allowed – you made that up!' said George. 'My mark!'

By the time they got to M, Anne was two marks ahead, and the dawn was breaking. It was a great relief to the two girls to see the silvering of the sky in the east and to know that soon the sun would be up. They immediately felt much better. George even stood up and went bravely to the window, where there was nothing to be seen but the quiet countryside outside, with its stretches of heather, gorse bushes and silver birches.

'We were silly to be so scared,' said George. 'I don't think we'll go back home today after all, Anne. I hate running away from anything. The boys would laugh at us.'

'I don't care if they do,' said Anne. 'I'm going back. If the boys were here, I'd stay – but goodness knows when they'll come – it might not be till next week! I'm just NOT staying here another night.'

'All right, all right,' said George. 'Do as you like – but for goodness' sake tell the boys it was *you* who wanted to run away, not me!'

'I will,' said Anne. 'Oh dear – now I feel sleepy all over again. I suppose it's because daylight is here and everything seems safe, so I know I can fall asleep.'

George felt the same! They cuddled down

together on the rug again and immediately fell asleep. They did not wake till quite late – and even then something woke them, or they might have slept on for hours, tired out with their broken night and the fright they had had.

They were awakened by something scuttling round them, making a very loud noise indeed. Then Timmy barked.

The girls awoke and sat up, rather dazed. 'Oh, it's *Jet*!' said Anne. 'Jet, have you come to see if we're all right, you dear, funny little one-eyed thing!'

'Wuff-wuff!' said Jet and rolled over on his back to be tickled, his long thin tail wagging all the time. Timmy leaped on him and pretended to eat him. Then a loud voice called to them.

They looked up. The boy was standing at the door, grinning widely.

'Hallo, sleepy-heads! I came to see if you were all right after that awful storm. I know I promised I wouldn't come here, but I felt a bit worried about you.'

'Oh. Well, that's nice of you,' said Anne, getting up and brushing the dust from her skirt. 'We're quite all right – but we had rather a peculiar night. We—'

She got a hard nudge from George and stopped suddenly. George was warning her not to say anything about the people they had seen – or the person at the window. Did she think they might have anything to do with this boy? Anne said no more and George spoke instead.

'Wasn't it a dreadful storm? How did you get on?'

'All right. I sleep down in a trench, and the rain can't get at me. Well – so long! Come on, Jet!'

The boy and the dog disappeared. 'That was nice of him,' said Anne. He doesn't seem crazy this morning, does he – quite normal! He didn't even contradict us. I think I quite like him after all.'

They went to their soaked tent and got a tin

of sardines out to eat with bread and butter. Just as they were opening it, they heard someone whistling and looked up.

'Here comes that boy again!' said Anne.

'Good morning. I don't want to butt in – but I just wondered if you were all right after the storm,' said the boy, without even a smile. The girls stared at him in amazement.

'Look – don't start being crazy all over again!' said George. 'You know jolly well we're all right. We've already told you.'

'You haven't. And I *didn't* know!' said the boy. 'Well, I only came out of politeness. Sorry to see you are still barmy!'

And off he went. 'There!' said Anne, vexed. 'Just as we thought he was nice again, and not crazy, he starts all over again. I suppose he thinks it's funny. Silly ass!'

They set their things out to dry in the sun, and it was half past twelve before they were ready to pack and go back to Kirrin Cottage. George was rather cross about going, but Anne was quite firm. She was NOT going to spend another night on the common.

George was just strapping a package on her bicycle, when the two girls heard the sound of voices – and then Timmy went quite mad! He barked wildly, and set off down a path at top speed, his tail wagging nineteen to the dozen!

'Oh! It can't be – surely it can't be Julian and Dick!' shouted George, in sudden delight, and she shot off after Timmy.

It was! It *was* Julian and Dick! There they came, packs on their backs, grinning all over their faces! Hurrah! The Famous Five were all together once more!

[8]

All together again!

There was such excitement at the arrival of the boys that at first nobody could make themselves heard. Timmy barked at the top of his very loud voice and simply would *not* stop! George shouted, and Dick and Julian laughed. Anne hugged them, and felt proud of two such brown, good-looking brothers.

'Ju! We never guessed you'd come so soon!' said the delighted George. 'Gosh, I'm pleased to see you!'

'We got fed up with French food,' said Dick. 'I came out in spots and Julian was sick, and it was SO hot. Phew! Next time I go there I'll go when it's cooler.'

'And we kept on thinking of Kirrin and the bay, and you two girls and Timmy,' said Julian, giving George a friendly punch. 'I think we *really* got a bit homesick. So we packed up before we should, and flew home.'

'Flew?' said George. 'You lucky things! And then did you come straight down here?'

'We spent the night with Mother and Dad at home,' said Julian, 'and then caught the first train here that we possibly could this morning – only to find that you weren't at Kirrin!'

'So we packed camping-out things in smaller bags and came straight along to you!' said Dick. 'I say, George, old thing, do you think you could possibly make Timmy stop barking? I'm going a bit deaf!'

'Shut up, Tim,' ordered George. 'Let other people bark a bit. Do you notice his collar, Julian?'

'Can't help seeing it!' said Julian. 'He looks a scream in it, doesn't he? Ha ha! You're an Elizabethan dog with a ruff, Timmy – that's what Uncle Quentin told us – and that's what you look like, old fellow!'

'He looks most comical, I must say,' said Dick. 'Enough to make a cat laugh, hey, Timmy!'

Anne looked at George. Goodness, what would she say to hear *Julian and Dick* laughing at Timmy and making fun of him! Would she lose her temper at once?

But George only grinned. In fact she gave a little laugh herself. 'Yes – he does look funny, doesn't he? But he doesn't mind a bit!'

'You know, we came here to camp because George couldn't bear people laughing at—' began Anne, thinking that she wouldn't let George get away with this! But George gave her such a beseeching look, that she stopped at once. George could never bear to look small in front of Julian and Dick. She prided herself on being just like a boy – and she was suddenly certain that her two cousins would think she was 'just like a *girl*' if they heard the fuss she had made about people laughing at Timmy's collar.

'I say – you two seem to be packing up,' said Julian, looking at the package strapped to the back of George's bicycle. 'What's happened?'

'Well – it got a bit lonely and Anne was . . .' and then in her turn George caught a beseeching look from Anne! She knew what it meant. I didn't tell tales on *you* – so don't tell tales on *me* – *don't* say I was scared!

'Er – Anne was certain that there was something funny going on here,' went on George, who had quite meant to say that Anne was scared and insisted on going home. 'And we didn't feel that we could tackle it ourselves – though if you had been here we wouldn't have *dreamed* of going home, of course.'

'What do you mean – something funny?' asked Dick.

'Well – you see – it began like this,' said George, but Julian interrupted.

'If there's a tale to tell, let's have it over a meal, shall we? We've had nothing to eat since six o'clock this morning, Dick and I – and we're ravenous!'

'Yes. Good idea,' said Dick, and began to undo a big package which he took out of his bag. 'I've a picnic lunch here from your mother, George – a jolly good one, I can tell you. I think she was so relieved to think that she was going to get rid of us that she really surpassed herself! We've got a marvellous piece of boiled ham – look! It'll last us for ages – if we don't give bits to Timmy. Get away, Tim. This is *not* for you! Grrrrrr!'

George suddenly felt so happy that she could hardly speak. It had been fun camping with Anne – but what a difference the boys made! So confident of themselves, so merry, full of jokes, so idiotic, and yet so dependable. She felt that she wanted to sing at the top of her voice!

The sun had been hot again that morning and had dried the common beautifully. It wasn't long before the Five were sitting down in the heather with a very fine feast before them.

'I wouldn't sell anyone my hunger for a hundred pounds,' said Dick. 'Now then – who's going to carve this magnificent piece of gammon?'

There were no plates, so they had to make sandwiches of the ham. Dick had actually brought some mustard, and dabbed it generously over the slices of ham before George put them between pieces of bread. 'Aha, Tim – this is one way of making sure you won't get even a *bite* of these wonderful ham sandwiches!' said Dick. 'You can't bear mustard, can you? Ju, where's the meat we brought for Tim?'

'Here. Pooh – it smells a bit strong,' said Julian. 'Do you mind taking it to a nice secluded corner, Tim?'

Timmy immediately sat down close to Julian. 'Now – don't be so disobedient!' said Julian, and gave Timmy a friendly push.

'He doesn't understand the word "secluded",'

said George, with a grin. 'Tim – buzz off a bit!'

Timmy understood that and took his meat a little way away. Everyone took a ripe red tomato, and a little lettuce heart from a damp cloth brought by Julian, and settled down happily to munch sandwiches.

'Lovely!' said Anne, contentedly. 'Goodness gracious – I can hardly believe we had such a peculiar time last night!'

'Ah – tell us all about it!' said Dick.

So first Anne, then George related all that had happened. Anne told of the night she had seen a light in the old cottage and had heard whispers and footfalls inside.

'We did think I might have been dreaming,' she said, 'but now we don't think I was. We think I really did see and hear those things.'

'What next?' asked Julian, taking his third sandwich. 'This all sounds most interesting. Quite Famous Five-ish, in fact!'

George told of the storm in the night, and

how they had had to leave their heather bed and go to shelter in the old cottage – and how, in the flashes of lightning, Anne had seen two or three people standing outside – and then how they had *both* seen someone standing silently, looking in at the window.

'Strange,' said Julian, puzzled. 'Yes – something is up. I wonder what? I mean – there's absolutely nothing on this lonely bit of common that's at all interesting.'

'Well – there are the remains of an old Roman camp,' said Anne. 'And a boy there who is examining them to see if he can find anything old and interesting.'

'A completely *mad* boy,' said George. 'He doesn't seem to know what he says or doesn't say. Contradicts himself all the time – or to put it another way, tells the most idiotic fibs.'

'And he apparently thinks it's awfully funny to meet us somewhere, and then double round on his tracks and appear suddenly somewhere else,' said Anne. 'Sometimes I can't help liking him – other times he's too idiotic for words.'

'He's got a little one-eyed dog called Jet,' said George, and Timmy gave a sudden bark as he heard the name. 'You like Jet, don't you, Tim?'

'This all sounds most interesting,' said Dick. 'Pass me the tomato bag, Ju, before you eat the lot. Thanks. As I said, *most* interesting – a one-eyed dog, a mad boy, Roman remains – and people who come to an old ruined cottage in the dead of night and look into windows!'

'I wonder you two girls didn't pack up and go home,' said Julian. 'You must be braver without us than I thought possible!'

George caught Anne's eye and grinned mischievously, but said nothing. Anne owned up, red in the face.

'Well – I did tell George I was going home this very morning, I was so scared last night. George didn't want to, of course, but she was coming, all the same. But now you've turned up, things are different.'

'Ah – well, do we stay on, or don't we, Ju?' said Dick. 'Are we scared or are we not?'

Everyone laughed. 'Well – if you go back *I* shall stay on alone!' said Anne. 'Just to show you!'

'Good old Anne!' said Dick. 'We all stay, of course. It may be nothing – it may be something – we can't tell. But we'll certainly find out. And the first thing to do is to have a look at the Roman remains and the mad boy. I'm looking forward to meeting him, I must say! After that we'll tackle the ruined cottage!'

Timmy came up to see if he could get any tit-bits. Julian waved him away. 'You smell of too-strong meat, Timmy,' he said. 'Go and get a drink. By the way, *is* there anything to drink here, George?'

'Oh yes,' said George. 'A lovely spring. Not far off, either. Let's take the remains of our meal there, and the mug. We've only got one unfortunately, so it's no good getting water unless we all sit by the spring and take turns at the mug. Come on!'

The boys thought that the spring was a really splendid one. They grouped themselves around it and took turns at filling the mug and drinking from it. They were now eating slabs of Joanna's fruit cake and it was very good.

'Now, you girls unpack again,' said Dick, when they had finished their meal. 'Goodness, I did enjoy that! We'd better unpack too, Julian.'

'Right. Where shall we put our things?' asked Julian, looking around. 'I don't somehow like to leave everything under that little tent, with a mad boy about, and a one-eyed dog. I feel that both of them might like the rest of that ham.'

'Oh, it's too hot to leave ham out in this sun,' said George. 'We'll have to put it into the old cottage, on a shelf. We'll put *everything* there, shall we? Move in properly, in case it rains again at night. It's so tiresome to have to bundle everything indoors in the dark and the rain.'

'I agree,' said Dick. 'Right. We'll move into

the ruined cottage. What fun! Come on, everyone!'

They spent the next half-hour taking their
things into the cottage and putting them in
corners or on shelves. George found a dark
corner behind the fireplace where she put the
food, for she was half-afraid that Jet, nice little
dog though he seemed, might perhaps smell the
ham and gobble up most of their food.

'Now!' said Julian. 'Are we ready to go and
see the Roman remains and the Mad Boy? Here
we go, then – the Famous Five are off again,
and who knows what will happen!'

[9]

A little exploration

The Five walked off together, Timmy at the back, delighted to have all his friends with him again. He kept nudging first one person's heels and then another, just to remind them that he was there.

As they came near the old camp, they saw a boy sitting beside a bush, reading.

'There's that boy we told you of!' said George. 'See?'

'He looks fairly ordinary,' said Dick. 'Very absorbed in his book, I must say. Determined to take no notice of us!'

'I'll speak to him,' said George. So, as they drew near, she called to the boy.

'Hallo! Where's Jet?'

The boy looked up, annoyed. 'How do I know?'

'Well, he was with you this morning,' said George.

'He was not,' said the boy. 'He's never with me! Please don't disturb me, I'm reading.'

'There you are!' said George to the others. 'He came to see us this morning with Jet – and now he says the little dog is never with him. Quite, quite mad!'

'Or plain rude,' said Dick. 'Not worth bothering about, anyway. Well, if he's not doing any excavating in his Roman camp, perhaps we can explore it without being ordered off!'

They walked on slowly and came to the camp, and at once heard a cheerful whistling going on, and the sound of someone digging. George looked over the top of the dug-out trench in surprise. She almost toppled in, she was so amazed at what she saw!

The boy was there, digging carefully, whistling as he did so! He brushed his tousled hair from his hot forehead and caught sight of

George and the others. He looked rather astonished.

'How on earth did you get down here so quickly?' said George. 'Do you have wings or something?'

'I've been down here all the afternoon,' said the boy. 'For at least an hour, I should think.'

'Fibber!' said George. The boy looked very angry, and shouted back at once.

'I'm tired of you two girls – and now you've brought your friends too, I suppose you think you can come and aggravate me even more!'

'Don't be an idiot,' said Dick, feeling as puzzled about this boy as George and Anne had been. How in the world had he run around them and got down in the trench so quickly? Did he enjoy playing tricks like that? He really didn't *look* mad!

'Is this your property, this old camp?' asked Julian.

'No. Of course not. Don't be daft!' said the boy. 'As if I could own a whole camp like this!

It was discovered by my father some time ago, and he gave me permission to work here for the hols. It's pretty exciting, I can tell you. See my finds?'

He pointed to a rough shelf where stood a broken pot, something that looked like an old brooch, a long pinlike thing, and part of a stone head. Julian was at once interested. He leapt down into the trench.

'I say – you've certainly got something there!' he said. 'Any coins too?'

'Yes – three,' said the boy and put his hand in his pocket. 'I found this one first – then these two close together yesterday. They must be hundreds and hundreds of years old.'

By this time all the others were down in the trench too. They looked about with much interest. Evidently the place had been well excavated by experts, and now the boy was working here and there on his own, hoping to find something that had been overlooked.

Dick went out of the trench and began to

clamber about over the great stones and rocks. A small animal suddenly caught his eye – a young rabbit.

It stared at him in fright and then disappeared behind a slab of stone. It peeped out at Dick again, and he was amused. He went cautiously over to the slab, and the little rabbit disappeared – but soon two or three whiskers poked out. Dick got down on hands and knees and looked behind the slab. A dark hole was there.

Dick pulled out his torch and flashed it into the hole, wondering if the small rabbit was hiding there, or whether it was the entrance to a burrow.

To his surprise there was a very big hole indeed – a hole that seemed to go down and down and down – his torch could make out no bottom to it.

'It's far too wide for a rabbit hole,' thought Dick. 'I wonder where it leads to. I'll ask that boy.'

He went back to where the boy was still showing his things to Julian, talking eagerly. 'I say,' began Dick, 'there's a most interesting hole behind one of the stone slabs over there – what is it?'

'Oh that – my father says it was explored and that it was only a place for storage – meat in hot weather, or loot, or something like that. Actually nothing whatever was found there – most uninteresting. As a matter of fact it may be nothing to do with the camp at all.'

'I say, look – here's another shelf with things on it,' said George, suddenly spying a little collection of things on a rough shelf in another part of the trench. 'Are these yours too?'

'Those? No,' said the boy. 'Nothing to do with me at all. Don't touch them, please.'

'Whose are they then?' asked George, curiously. The boy took no notice whatever of her question and went on talking to Julian. George took down a beautiful little round pot.

'Hey! I told you NOT to touch those!' yelled the boy, so suddenly and angrily that George almost dropped the pot. 'Put it back – and clear out if you can't do what you're told.'

'Easy, old man, easy!' said Julian. 'No need to yell at her like that. You scared that little dog of yours and made him jump almost out of his skin! We'd better go, I think.'

'Well – I don't like being disturbed too much,' said the boy. 'People always seem to be wandering around. I've turned off quite a lot.'

'People?' said Julian, remembering Anne's story of two or three figures standing outside the cottage the night before, and of someone looking in. 'What kind of people?'

'Oh – nosey ones – wanting to get down and explore – disturbing me – it's surprising how many idiots there are wandering about this lonely place,' said the boy, picking up a tool again and setting to work. He grinned suddenly. 'I don't mean you. You really *know* something about this kind of thing.'

'Was anyone about last night?' asked Julian.

'Well – I rather think so,' said the boy. 'Because Jet here barked like mad. But it might have been the storm that frightened him – not that he's *usually* frightened of storms.'

'What's your name?' asked Dick.

'Guy Lawdler,' said the boy, and Dick whistled.

'My word – is your father the famous explorer, Sir John Lawdler?' he asked. The boy nodded.

'Well, no wonder you're so keen on archaeology!' said Dick. 'Your father's done pretty well in that line, hasn't he?'

'Come on, Dick!' said George. 'Let's go now. We might have time for a swim in the pool. We forgot to tell you about that.'

'Right,' said Dick. 'Come on, Julian. Goodbye, Guy!'

They left the rather desolate old camp and went back to the cottage to get their swimsuits and change. It wasn't long before they were running over the heather to the pool.

'Hallo – Guy's having a swim!' said Dick, in surprise. Sure enough, a boy was there, his hair falling over his forehead as usual.

'Hey, Guy!' shouted George. 'Have a swim with us!'

But the boy was already getting out of the water. Dick shouted. 'Wait a minute – don't go. We'd like to have a swim with you, Guy!'

But the boy turned defiantly. 'Don't be an ass!' he said. 'My name's not Guy!'

And, leaving four astonished people behind him, he ran lightly over the heather and disappeared.

'There you are – he's mad after all!' said Anne. 'Don't bother about him. Come on in – the water's lovely and warm.'

They lazed about afterwards and began to feel hungry. 'Though how *any* of us could feel hungry after eating about fifty sandwiches between us at lunch-time, I don't know!' said

Dick. 'Race you back to the cottage, Ju!'

They changed back into ordinary clothes and then had tea – fruit cake, shortbread biscuits and tinned pineapple on bread. They kept the juice and diluted it with cold spring water – it was simply delicious.

'Now let's explore the cottage,' said Dick.

'We already have, Anne and I,' said George. 'So I don't expect you'll find anything much.'

They went methodically through the old house, and even up the old stone stairway to the two rooms upstairs – though they could hardly be called rooms, for they had very little roof and not much wall!

'Nothing much here, that's certain,' said Dick, clattering down the stone stairway. 'Now let's go to the outbuildings – not that there's much left of them either!'

They examined everything, and came last of all to the old stables. It was dark inside, for the windows were very small, and it was some seconds before anyone could see properly.

'Old mangers,' said Dick, touching them. 'I wonder how long ago it is since they were used – and—'

'I say!' said George, suddenly. 'There's something funny here. Anne, look – this bit of floor was undisturbed yesterday, wasn't it?'

Anne looked down at the big white flagstone on which George was standing. It was quite obvious that it had been lifted, for the edges were not as green with moss as the others were, and the stone had been put back a little crookedly.

'Yes – someone's been interested in this stone – or in what is beneath it!' said Dick. 'I bet something is buried underneath!'

'Those men last night – that's what they came about!' said George. 'They went into these stables and lifted this stone. Why?'

'We'll soon find out!' said Julian. 'Come on, everyone, loosen it with your fingers – then we'll heave it up!'

[10]

What can be happening?

Forty fingers and thumbs were very hard at work trying to loosen the heavy stone. At last Julian got hold of a corner which could be held more easily than any other part of the stone. He tried to lift it and it came away a little.

'Help me this side, Dick,' said Julian, and Dick put his strong fingers there too. 'Heave-ho!' he said – and up came the stone.

It went over with a crash and Timmy barked loudly, jumping aside. Everyone peered down – and then looked exceedingly disappointed!

There was nothing there at all. Not even a hole! The black earth, hard as iron, lay underneath, and nothing else.

They all stared down at the dry, hard earth, puzzled. George looked up at Julian.

'Well – that's strange, isn't it? Why should anyone lift up this heavy stone if there is nothing hidden underneath?'

'Well, it's clear that whoever was here didn't find anything – nor did he *hide* anything either,' said Julian. 'Dear me – why should anyone lift up a heavy store and put it back – just for nothing?

'He was obviously looking for something that wasn't here,' said Anne. 'The wrong stone, probably!'

'Yes. I think Anne's right,' said Dick. 'It's the wrong stone! Probably there is something very interesting under the *right* stone! But which one is it?'

They all sat and looked at one another, and Timmy sat too, wondering why all this fuss was made about a flat white stone. Julian thought hard.

'From what you've told me, Anne – about seeing a light in the cottage that first night you were here – and hearing voices – and then seeing those figures outside last night in the storm – it looks as if someone is urgently hunting for something round about here.'

'Yes – something under a stone. Treasure of some sort, do you think?' said George.

Julian shook his head. 'No. I hardly think that much treasure would be hidden anywhere about this old cottage – all the people who lived here must have been fairly poor. The most they would have hidden would have been a few pieces of gold, and that would have been found long ago.'

'Well – someone modern might have hidden something valuable here – even something stolen,' said Anne.

'Yes. We can't tell. It's obviously important and urgent to somebody,' said Dick. 'I wonder if the people that Guy said came bothering him were anything to do with this?'

'They may have been,' said Julian. 'But they have clearly decided that what they are looking for is here now, whatever it is. And they must have been most annoyed to find you and Anne here last night, George. That's why someone came and looked in at the window, I expect – to make sure you were asleep! And you weren't.'

'I don't know whether I want to stay on here or not now,' said Anne, alarmed. 'If they haven't found what they want, they'll probably come again – in the night too.'

'Who cares?' said Dick. 'We've got Timmy, haven't we? I'm not turning out of here because somebody's got a habit of turning up big stones!'

Julian laughed. 'Nor am I. Let's stay on! And I don't see why we shouldn't do a bit of pulling up of stones ourselves! We might come across something very interesting!'

'Right. It's decided that we stay on then, is it?' said Dick. 'What about you, Anne?'

'Oh yes – of course I'll stay,' said Anne, not wanting to in the least, but knowing that she simply could not bear not to be with the others.

The Five walked round and about the cottage for a while, trying to make out where the people that the girls had seen the night before had come from – from what direction did they come and where did they go?

'The figures I saw first in the lightning stood about there,' said Anne, pointing. 'Let's go and see if there are any footprints. It was pouring with rain and the ground must have been very muddy.'

'Good idea,' said Dick, and off they went to where Anne had pointed. But it was a heathery piece of ground, and difficult to tell even if anyone *had* trodden there, for the heather was thick and springy.

'Let's look just outside the window now – the one where Anne saw someone looking in,' said Dick. And there they had a find! Just in front of the window were two quite deeply printed footmarks. One was slightly blurred as if the maker of them had turned his foot sideways as he waited. The other was very clear indeed.

Dick got out a piece of paper. 'I rather think I'll measure these,' he said, 'and make a note of the pattern on the soles. They had rubber soles and heels – look at the markings – crêpe rubber I should think.'

He measured the prints. 'Size eight shoes,' he said. 'Same as yours, Ju.' Then he carefully drew an exact picture of the sole and heel markings.

'You're quite a detective, Dick,' said Anne, admiringly, and he laughed.

'Oh, anyone can copy footprints!' he said. 'The thing is to match them up with the owner!'

'I have a feeling it's getting on for suppertime – if anyone *wants* any supper,' said George. 'It's half past eight! Would you believe that the time could fly so fast?'

'I don't *really* feel very hungry,' said Dick. 'We've done pretty well today.'

'Well, don't waste our precious food if you don't feel hungry,' said George. 'We shall have to keep going home for more if we eat everything too quickly.'

Nobody felt terribly hungry. They made a cosy corner in the cottage and had a slice of cake and a biscuit each, with a drink of pineapple juice and spring-water. George had had the bright idea of filling the big empty pineapple tin, and they each filled a mug from it in turn, and drank.

'It's getting dark,' said Julian. 'Are we going to sleep inside the cottage or out?'

'In,' said Dick, promptly. 'We'll make things just as difficult for any night prowlers as possible!'

'Right,' said Julian. 'I bet they won't be pleased to find old Timmy here too. Shall we go out and get some heather for beds? I don't fancy sharing a thin rug between the four of us.'

Soon they were all dragging in armfuls of the springy heather. They laid it in the front room, in two corners, for the boys thought they would rather be in the same room as the girls, in case of danger.

'You need an awful lot of heather to make a *soft* bed,' said Dick, trying his. 'My bones seem to go right through the clumps and rub against the floor!'

'We can put our jackets over our heather,' said Julian. 'That will help. The girls can have the rug. We shan't need any covering, it's so hot.'

By the time they had finished, it was dark. George lay on her heather and yawned. 'I'm going to sleep,' she announced. 'We don't need to keep guard or anything like that, do we? Timmy will bark if anyone comes near.'

'You're right. I really don't think we need take turns at keeping awake,' said Julian. 'Move up, Dick – you've left me no room.'

Julian was the last to go to sleep. He lay awake puzzling over the lifted stone slab. It was clear that someone had expected to find something under it. How did they know it was that particular slab? Had they a map? If so, it must have shown the wrong stone – or perhaps the searchers read the map wrong?

Before he could work it out any further, he was asleep. Timmy was asleep too, happy because all the others were under his care. He had one ear open as usual, but not *very* much open!

It was enough to let him hear a small mouse of some kind run across the floor. It was even enough for him to hear a beetle scraping its way up the wall. After a while his ear dropped down and he didn't even hear a hedgehog outside.

But something caused his ear to listen again and it pricked up. A noise crept inside the cottage – a noise that got louder and louder – a weird and puzzling noise!

Timmy woke up and listened. He pawed at George, not knowing whether to bark or not. He knew he should not bark at owls, but this was not an owl. Perhaps George would know.

'Don't, Timmy,' said George sleepily, but Timmy went on pawing her. Then she too heard the noise and sat up in a hurry.

What a truly horrible sound! It was a whining and a wailing, rising and falling through the night. A sound of misery and woe, that went on and on.

'Julian! Dick! Wake up!' called George, her heart beating wildly. 'Something's happening.'

The boys awoke at once and so did Anne. They sat and listened to the weird noise. What in the world could it be? There it went again – wailing high in the air, and then dying away with a moan, only to begin again a few seconds later.

Dick felt the roots of his hair pricking. He leapt off the heather bed and ran to the window. 'Quick! Come and look at this!' he cried. 'What is it?'

They all crowded to the window, Timmy barking now as loudly as he could. In silence the others gazed at a very strange sight.

Blue and green lights were shining here and there, sometimes dimly, sometimes brightly. A curious round white light was travelling slowly in the air, and Anne clutched George, breathing fast.

'It won't come here,' she said. 'It won't, will it? I don't like it. What is happening, Julian?'

'I wish that awful wailing, whining noise would stop,' said Dick. 'It gets right inside my head. Do you make anything of all this, Julian?'

'Something very strange is going on,' said Julian. 'I'll go out with Timmy and see what I can find.' And before anyone could stop him, out he went, Timmy barking beside him.

'Oh Julian – come back!' called Anne, listening as his footsteps became distant. They all waited tensely at the window – and then suddenly the wailing noise stopped and the strange lights gradually began to fade.

Then they heard Julian's footsteps coming back firmly in the darkness.

'Ju! What was it?' called Dick, as his brother came in at the doorway.

'I don't know, Dick,' said Julian, sounding very puzzled. 'I simply – don't – know! Perhaps we can find out in the morning.'

[11]

Interesting discoveries –
and a plan

The four sat in the dark and talked over the
horrible noises and the weird blue and green
and white lights. Anne sat close to Julian. She
really was frightened.

'I want to go back to Kirrin,' she said. 'Let's
go tomorrow. I don't like this.'

'I didn't see a thing just now,' said Julian,
puzzled, his arm close round Anne. 'I seemed to
go quite close to those wailing sounds – and
then they stopped as soon as I got fairly near.
But although Timmy barked and ran around,
there didn't seem to be anyone there.'

'Did you get near the lights?' asked Dick.

'Yes, fairly near. But the odd thing was that
they seemed high up when I got near them – not

near the ground as I expected. And *again* Timmy couldn't find anyone. You would have thought if there was anyone about, playing the fool, that Timmy would have found them. But he didn't.'

'Woof,' said Timmy, dolefully. He didn't like this funny business at all!

'Well, if *nobody's* making the noises and lights, it makes it even worse,' said Anne. 'Do let's go home, Julian. Tomorrow.'

'All right,' said Julian. 'I don't feel particularly thrilled about all this myself. But there is *one* idea I've got in my mind which I'd like to sort out tomorrow.'

'What's that?' said Dick.

'Well – it may quite well be that somebody very badly wants us out of here for some reason,' said Julian. 'And that somebody may want to come and lift other stones and have a thorough search all over the place – which he can't do with us around. So he's trying to frighten us out!'

'Yes, I believe you are right, Julian,' said Dick. 'Those noises – and lights – they would be enough to scare anyone out of a place. Too eerie for words! Well, let's have a good snoop round in the daylight, to see if we can find any trace of a trickster!'

'We will – but it's extremely odd that *Timmy* didn't find him,' said Julian. 'Timmy can smell anyone out of any hiding place! Yes – we'll have a very very good hunt round tomorrow.'

'And if you find nothing and nobody, we'll go home?' asked Anne.

'Yes, we will. I promise you,' said Julian, hugging Anne. 'Don't worry. You shan't have to stay here one night longer, unless you want to! Now, let's try and go to sleep again!'

It took the four a long time to go to sleep after all this excitement in the middle of the night. Anne kept listening for the wailing noises again, but none came. She kept her eyes shut tightly in case she should happen to see any more of the strange lights outside the window.

George and the boys lay awake too, puzzling out the problems of lights and noises which were not apparently caused by anyone! Julian especially was puzzled.

Only Timmy was unconcerned. He went to sleep before anyone else, though he kept one ear *wide* open – and up went the other one when George moved, or Dick whispered to Julian.

The excitement of the night made them all sleep late. Julian awoke first, and stared at the low ceiling in surprise. Now – where was he? In France? No. Ah, of course he was in the old ruined cottage!

He woke Dick, who yawned and stretched. 'Remember those strange lights and noises last night?' asked Dick. 'What a fright they gave us! It seems silly to think we were all so puzzled and scared, now that the sun is shining in at the window, and we can see the countryside around for miles!'

'I'm pretty certain someone is trying to scare

us away,' said Julian. 'We are in their way here – they want to do some thorough explorations and they can't, because of us! I've a good mind to take the girls home, Dick, and come back here with you.'

'Anne might go, but George wouldn't,' said Dick. 'You know what old George is like – she doesn't like to miss out. Let's not decide anything till we have had a look round this morning. I don't really believe there's anything spooky about this at all – I agree with you that it's just a few tricks to frighten us away.'

'Right,' said Julian. 'Let's wake the girls. Hey, George! Anne! Sleepyheads! Get up and get us breakfast!'

George sat up, looking furious, as Julian intended. 'You jolly well get your own b—' she began, and then laughed as she saw Julian's amused face.

'I was only just striking a little match to set you alight!' said Julian. 'Come on – let's all go for a swim in the pool!'

They set off together happily in the warm sunshine, Timmy padding along, his tail waving vigorously. As soon as they got to the pool, they saw the boy there, floating lazily on his back.

'There's Guy!' said Anne.

'I wonder if he will admit to his name or not this morning!' said George. 'Remember how he told us his name was Guy – and then said it wasn't a little while after? Silly ass! I can't make out if he's quite mad, or just thinks it's funny to keep playing the fool!'

They came to the pool. The boy waved to them, grinning. 'Come on in – it's fine!'

'Is your name Guy this morning or not?' called George.

The boy looked surprised. 'Of course it's Guy!' he said. 'Don't be idiotic! Come on in and have a game.'

They had a fine swim and a mad one. Guy was like an eel, swimming under the water, catching their legs, splashing, swimming away fast, doubling round and going underwater just as they got up to him!

At last they all sat panting on the edge of the pond, the sun shining down warmly on them.

'I say, Guy – did you hear anything strange last night?' asked Dick. 'Or see anything?'

'I didn't *see* anything strange – but I thought I heard somebody wailing and crying in the distance,' said Guy. 'Just now and again when the wind brought the sound this way. Jet didn't like it at all – did you, Jet? He went and hid under my legs!'

'We heard it too – quite near us,' said Julian. 'And saw strange lights.'

They discussed the matter for some time, but Guy could not really help them, because he had not been near enough to the noises to hear them as clearly as the others had.

'I'm getting hungry,' said George, at last. 'I keep thinking of ham and tomatoes and cheese. Let's go back to the cottage.'

'Right,' said Julian. 'Good-bye, Guy – see

you sometime soon. Good-bye, Jet, you mad little thing.'

They went off together, their swimsuits almost dry already in the sun.

'Well, Guy was perfectly sensible this morning,' said Anne. 'Funny! I wonder why he's so silly sometimes.'

'See – isn't that him – running down the path there – to the right, look!' said George, suddenly. 'Now how did he get there so quickly? We left him by the pool!'

It certainly looked like Guy! They called to him, but he didn't even look round or wave, though he must have heard them. They went on, puzzled. How could one person be so different each time – and why? What was the point?

They had a good breakfast and then went out to look round and see if they could find anything to explain the strange happenings of the night before.

'The noises seemed to come from about here,

when I came out last night,' said Julian, stopping near the little group of trees. 'And the lights seemed to start about here too – but not near the ground – they were high up, above my head.'

'Above your head?' said Dick, puzzled. 'That seems odd.'

'It doesn't!' said Anne. 'Not a *bit* odd! What about those trees there? Couldn't somebody climb up them and do the wailing and whining there, with some strange instrument – and set off the weird lights?'

Julian stared up at the trees and then round at Anne. He grinned suddenly.

'Anne's got it! Clever girl! Of course someone was up there – or maybe two people – one doing the noises with some weird instrument and the other playing about with fireworks of some kind. Not the noisy kind – just coloured fire or balloons lit up from inside.'

'Yes! *That's* why the lights seemed to be so high up, when you came out!' said Dick. 'They were sent out by someone up in a tree!'

'And floated away to scare us,' said Anne. 'Golly – I *do* feel glad that it was silly tricks like that that frightened us so. They wouldn't frighten me *again*!'

'It explains something else too,' said George. 'It explains why Timmy didn't find anyone! They were safely up trees! I bet they hardly breathed when they knew Tim was down below.'

'Yes. Of course! That puzzled me too,' said Julian. 'It was too spooky for words when even old Tim couldn't find anyone real about – just noises and lights!'

'Here's something, look – a wrinkled little rubber-skin – pale green!' said Dick, picking something up from the ground. 'That's what those lights were – balloons lit up from inside in some way and sent floating away in the air.'

'Most ingenious,' said Julian. 'I expect they had quite a lot of funny tricks at their disposal last night. Yes – they certainly mean to scare us away!'

'Well, they won't,' said Anne, unexpectedly. '*I'm* not going, for one. I won't be scared away by stupid tricks!'

'Good old Anne!' said Julian, and clapped her on the back. 'Right – we'll all stay – but I've got an idea.'

'What?' asked everyone.

'We'll *pretend* to go!' said Julian. 'We'll pack up everything – remove our things from here – and go and camp somewhere else. But Dick and I will *hide* somewhere here tonight – and watch to see if anyone comes, and where they look for whatever it is they're hunting for, and why!'

'That's a fantastic plan,' said Dick, pleased. 'We'll do it! Roll on, tonight! Adventure is about – and we'll be ready for it!'

[12]

A good hiding place

The Five spent quite a pleasant day, but when late afternoon came, they decided that it was time to carry out their plan and pack as if they were leaving.

'I imagine someone is spying on our doings,' said Dick. 'And won't he be pleased to see us apparently on the point of leaving!'

'How can anyone be spying?' asked Anne, looking all round as if she expected to see someone behind a bush. 'Timmy would be sure to sniff out anyone in hiding.'

'Oh, he won't be near enough for Timmy to smell out,' said Dick. 'He'll be a long way off.'

'Then how can he possibly see us – or know that we're leaving?' asked Anne.

'Anne – I don't know if you've heard of field-glasses,' began Dick, solemnly. 'Well, they're things that can spot anything half a mile away . . .'

Anne went red and gave Dick a punch. 'Don't be an ass! Of course – that's it! Field-glasses used by someone on a hillside some-where – trained on the old cottage.'

'Actually I think I know where the someone is,' said Dick. 'I've caught sight of a little flash every now and again on the hill over there – the kind of flash that is made by the sun on glass – and I somehow think that our spy is sitting near the top of the hill, watching us carefully.'

Anne turned to look at the hill, but Julian at once spoke sharply. 'No – don't stand and stare up there, anyone. We don't want the watcher to know that *we* know we are being watched.'

They went on with their packing, and soon began to stagger out with their bundles. George was told to strap her things on her bicycle, and stand well out in the open as she did so, so that the watcher on the hill would be able to observe all her doings.

Julian was in the midst of carefully folding up his things to go into his knapsack, when Anne gave a sudden exclamation.

'Someone's coming!'

Everyone looked round, imagining that they would see a sinister-looking foreigner, or someone peculiar in some way.

But all they saw was a countrywoman hurrying along, a shawl over her head, and a basket under her arm. She wore glasses, had no make-up on, and her hair was pulled straight back under the shawl. She stopped when she saw the Five.

'Good afternoon,' said Julian, politely. 'Isn't it glorious weather!'

'Beautiful,' said the woman. 'Are you camping out – you've certainly chosen a very good time!'

'No – actually we're packing,' said Julian. 'We've been sleeping in the old cottage, but we've decided to move out. Is it very, very old?'

'Oh yes – and it's supposed to have strange things happening in it at nights,' said the woman.

'We know that!' said Julian. 'My word – we were pretty scared last night, I can tell you – weird noises and horrible, ghostly lights. We decided not to stay there any longer.'

'That's right,' said the woman. 'Don't you stay! You get as far from this place as you can! I can tell you, *I* wouldn't come by it at night. Where are you going?'

'Well, our home is at Kirrin,' said Julian, evading the question. 'You know – on Kirrin Bay.'

'Ah yes – a fine place,' said the woman. 'Well, don't you stay another night! Good-bye!'

She hurried off, and was soon lost to sight.

'Go on packing,' said Julian to the others. 'The watcher is still up in the hills. I caught sight of a flash again just then.'

'Julian, why did you tell all that to the woman?' asked Anne. 'You don't usually say

so much when we are in the middle of something funny!'

'My dear, unsuspecting Anne – do you mean
to say that you thought that woman was really
what she pretended to be – a woman from a
nearby farm?' said Julian.

'Well – wasn't she?' said Anne, surprised.
'She looked like one – no make-up – and that
old shawl – and she knew all about the old
cottage!'

'Anne – farm women don't have gold fillings
in their teeth,' said Julian. 'Didn't you notice
them when she smiled?'

'And her hair was dyed,' said George. 'I
noticed it was blonde at the roots and black
above.'

'*And* what about her hands?' said Dick. 'A
farmer's wife does a great deal of hard, rough
work, and her hands are never white and
smooth – they are rough and brown. This
woman's hands were as white as a princess's!'

'Well yes, I did notice them,' said Anne. 'And

I did notice too that she sometimes spoke with an accent and sometimes without.'

'Well, there you are!' said Julian. 'She's one of the unpleasant gang that tried to scare us last night – and when the watcher on the hill reported that we appeared to be packing up and going, she was told to go and make sure. So she pretended to be a countrywoman and came by – but unfortunately we weren't quite so stupid as she thought we would be!'

'You certainly fooled her!' said Dick, with a grin. 'The gang will be down here tonight, digging up all the big stones they can find. You and I will have a marvellous time, snooping round them.'

'You'll be careful they don't see you, won't you?' said Anne. 'Where will you hide?'

'We haven't planned that yet,' said Dick. 'Now come on and we'll make a new camp somewhere that won't be easily seen. You and George and Timmy can sleep there tonight, and Ju and I will come and watch here.'

'I want to come too,' said George at once. 'Anne will be all right with Timmy.'

'You aren't joining us this time, George,' said Ju. 'The fewer people watching the better. Sorry, old thing – but you'll have to stay with Anne.'

George scowled and looked sulky at once. Julian laughed and slapped her on the shoulder. 'What a *lovely* scowl! One of your best! I haven't seen it for quite a long time. Keep it up, George – go on, scowl a bit harder, it suits you!'

George grinned unwillingly, and pulled herself together. She hated being left out of anything, but she did see that it was no use having a crowd of people watching that night. All right, she would stay with Anne and keep her company.

It seemed as if the watcher on the hills must have gone, because there were no more sudden flashes such as came when he lifted his field-glasses to watch the Five.

'That disguised countrywoman has convinced the watcher that we're going! Any ideas, anyone, where we can go? Not too far away – but somewhere where the watcher can't follow us with his glasses, if he's still up there.'

'I know a place,' said George. 'There's a simply colossal gorse bush on the other side of the spring. And underneath it is all hollow and dry. It's almost like a kind of gorse cave.'

'Sounds all right,' said Julian. 'Let's go and find it.'

George led the way, trying to remember exactly where it was. Timmy followed, still in his enormous cardboard collar, which was now rather the worse for wear. George stopped when they had gone a little way past the spring.

'It was somewhere here,' she said. 'I know I could still hear the sound of the spring when I found the hollow under the bush. Ah – there it is!'

It certainly was a great bush, green and spiky outside, with a few yellow blooms on it still.

Under it was a big hollow place, where the ground was soft and fine, scattered with dry old prickles.

The main trunk – for it was almost a trunk that supported the big bush – was not quite in the middle, so there was a good bit of room. Julian caught hold of the branches that hid the hollow, using a folded sheet of paper to hold them by, for the bush was very prickly.

'This is fine,' he said. 'Plenty of room for you two girls – and Timmy. My word, he'll have difficulty with his collar though, won't he – squeezing in and out!'

'Take it off!' said Dick. 'His ear really is practically healed now. Even if he scratches it, he can't do much damage. Dear old Timmy, we simply shan't *know* you without your collar.'

'Right,' said George. She took a quick look at the ear. It was still covered by a piece of elastoplast, but it was quite obvious that the ear was healthy. She cut the thread that bound the two ends of the circular collar and then bent it so that it came off.

They all stared at Timmy, who looked most surprised. He wagged his tail gently as if to say 'Well – so you've taken that thing off – I wonder why?'

'Oh Tim – you look sort of *undressed* without that collar now!' said Anne. 'It *is* nice to see you without it, though. Good old Tim! You'll guard me and George tonight, won't you? *You* know that we're in the Middle of Something again, don't you?'

'Woof,' said Timmy, wagging his tail violently. 'Woof!' Yes – he knew all right!

[13]

On watch in the cottage

It was getting dark – and under the gorse bush it was very dark indeed! All the Five had managed to squeeze in there, and Timmy too. One torch only was allowed to be used at a time, to save the batteries of the others.

The Five were having supper. The ham was now practically finished, but there were still a few tomatoes and plenty of cake.

Julian opened the last tin of sardines, and made some sandwiches for himself and Dick to take with them. He also wrapped up two enormous chunks of cake and pocketed two slabs of chocolate each.

'We shall need something to while away the time when we're on the watch tonight!' he said, with a grin. 'I don't know if the Weepies and

Wailies and Floating Lights will be along to give us a show – but I fear not. They would be wasted on an empty cottage!'

'I do hope you'll be careful,' said Anne.

'Anne – that's the seventh time you've said that,' said Dick. 'Don't be an ass. Don't you understand that Ju and I are going to *enjoy* ourselves? You'll be the one that has to be careful.'

'How?' asked Anne, surprised.

'Well – you'll have to be careful of that big black beetle squatting over there,' said Dick. 'And mind that a hedgehog doesn't sit down on your bare legs. And be careful in case a snake wants to share this nice safe warm place with you . . .'

'Now *you're* being an ass!' said Anne, giving him a punch. 'When will you be back?'

'We shall be back at exactly the moment you hear us squeezing under here,' said Julian. 'Now Dick – what about it? I think we might be going, don't you?'

'Right,' said Dick, and began to squeeze out carefully so as not to be pricked more than he could help. 'Oh – why are gorse bushes so horribly spiteful! Jab jab – anyone would think the bush was *trying* to prick me!'

The two girls sat quite still when the boys had gone from the bush. They tried to hear their footsteps, but they couldn't. Dick and Julian trod too softly on the wiry grass.

'I do so hope they'll be—' began Anne, and George groaned.

'If you say that again I shall slap you, Anne! Honestly I shall.'

'I *wasn't* saying it,' said Anne, 'I was only going to say that I hope they'll be *successful* tonight. I'd like to get back to Kirrin and have some fun swimming and boating, wouldn't you?'

'Yes. And some of Joanna's marvellous cooking,' said George. 'Sausages and mash – and tomatoes with it.'

'Yes. And fried plaice fresh from the sea with

Joanna's best chipped potatoes,' said Anne. 'I can almost smell it.'

'Woof,' said Timmy, sniffing hard.

'There! He thought I meant it!' said Anne. 'Isn't Timmy clever?'

They had a pleasant talk about how very very clever Timmy was, and Timmy listened and wagged his tail so hard that he made it quite dusty in the gorse hollow.

'Let's go to sleep,' said Anne. 'We can't talk all night – and keeping awake won't help the boys!'

They curled up on the rug they had brought and cuddled together – not so much for warmth, because it was a hot night, but because there was so little room! Anne put out her torch, and the little place immediately became black and dark. Timmy put his head on George's tummy. She groaned.

'Oh Tim – be careful, please! I had rather a lot of supper!'

Anne giggled and pulled Timmy's head close

to her. It was comforting to have old Timmy there. She agreed with George that he was the best dog in the whole world.

'I wonder what the boys are doing now,' she said, after a while. 'Do you suppose they are in the middle of something exciting? Perhaps they are!'

But they weren't! Julian and Dick were feeling extremely bored at that minute. They had gone cautiously to the cottage when they had left the girls, not using their torches at all, for fear of giving anyone warning that they were about. They had debated beforehand where would be the best place to hide, and had decided that it would be a good idea to climb up the little stone stair and hide in the roofless rooms above.

'There's no roof there – and hardly any walls,' said Dick. 'We can peep over any side to watch – and no one would guess that anyone was above them, spying down! It's a good thing it's such a starry night – once we get used to the dim light, we shall be able to see fairly well. Pity there's no moon.'

They had approached the cottage very cautiously indeed, stopping at every step and listening with bated breath for any sound. But there was none.

'Not even the light of somebody's torch, either,' said Dick in Julian's ear. 'I don't think anyone is here yet. Let's get into the cottage and up those stairs as soon as we can.'

They tiptoed into the cottage, not daring to put on their torches. They fumbled across to the little stone stairway, and climbed it with as little sound as they could. Holding their breath made their hearts thump loudly.

'Can you hear my heart thumping?' Dick whispered to Julian, as they at last stood on the floor of the roofless rooms above.

'No. Mine's just the same, thumping away! Well, we're safely here. Let's just shuffle to and fro and see if there are any loose stones we might fall over, and so give ourselves away!'

They cleared away a few loose stones, and then sat down silently on the low broken wall of the two ruined rooms. The wind blew gently but warmly. Everything was still except the rose-rambler climbing over the old house. It moved a little in the wind and made a faint scraping noise. Dick caught his hand on a thorn, and sucked his finger. The rambler was everywhere, across the floor, and over the walls and even up what was left of the little chimney.

The boys had been there for about three-quarters of an hour when Julian gave Dick a slight nudge.

'Here they come!' he whispered. 'See – over there!'

Dick looked round and about and then caught sight of a small, moving light, just a prick in the darkness. It cast a faint glow before it.

'A torch!' he whispered. 'And another – and another! Quite a procession! A slow one, too.'

The procession made very little noise. It made its way to the cottage, and then split up.

'Having a look to see if we really *are* gone,' whispered Julian. 'Hope they won't think of coming up here.'

'Let's get behind the chimney, in case,' whispered back Dick. So very quietly they rose and made their way to where the remains of the chimney stood, a dark shadow in the starry night. The chimney was quite big, though rather crumbly. The two boys crouched close to it, on the side farthest from where the stone stairway came up in the corner.

'Someone *is* coming up!' whispered Dick, his sharp ears catching the sound of someone's feet on the stone stairs. 'I hope he gets caught by the rambler – there's a big spray near the top!'

'Sh!' said Julian.

Someone came right up the stairway, and gave a sharp exclamation of annoyance near the top. 'Good!' thought Dick. 'He *has* got caught by the rambler!'

A torch shone out over the ruined rooms, the crumbling walls and the remains of the chimney. The boys held their breath, and stood like statues. The light of the torch played over the place for one second and then a voice called down the stairs.

'No one here. The kids have gone. We can get on with the job!'

The boys let out a long breath. Good – they were safe – for the time being at any rate! The visitors down below were no longer cautious – they spoke in ordinary voices and torches flashed all over the place. Then someone lit two lanterns, and the little cottage shone quite brightly.

'Where do we start?' said a voice. 'Here, Jess – where's that plan?'

'I've got it. I'll spread it on the floor,' said a voice that the boys recognised at once. It was the voice of the 'countrywoman' who had spoken to them that day! 'Not that it's much use. Paul's no good at drawing!'

Evidently the searchers were now leaning over the plan. Voices came up the stone stairway.

'All we know for certain is that we have to find that white stone slab – and we know the size. But we don't know the place, except that we think it *must* be here. After all – we've searched the old Roman camp, and there are no slabs there that size!'

Julian nudged Dick. So some of the visitors that Guy had complained of must have been these searchers! Whatever was it they were looking for, hidden behind a slab of stone?

He knew a minute later! A drawling voice said: 'If we have to get up every great slab in this neighbourhood, we will. I'm going to find that secret way if it's the last thing I do! If we don't find that, we don't find those blueprints – and if we don't find *them*, we might as well go into the poorhouse for the rest of our lives.'

'Or prison!' said someone.

'Not prison,' said the drawling voice. 'It'll be

Paul who goes to prison. *He* managed to steal them, we didn't!'

'Can't you get Paul to draw a better plan than this?' said the voice of the 'country-woman'. 'I can't understand half that's written here.'

'He's ill – almost off his head, too,' said someone. 'No good asking him. He had such a time escaping with those prints, he nearly died. No good asking him, I say.'

'I can't make out this word here,' said the woman.

' "W-A-D-E-R" – whatever does it mean?'

'I don't know – wait, though, I do! It might be W-A-T-E-R – water. T not D in the middle. Where's the well? Anywhere in this kitchen? That's it, that's it. *Water*! I bet there's a slab over the well. That's the way to the secret hiding place!'

Julian clutched Dick. He was as excited as the man down below. They listened eagerly, straining their ears.

'Here's the old sink – and this must be the remains of the pump. The well's underneath this slab – and see the stone is just about the right size. Get busy! Buck up, get busy!'

[14]

An exciting night –
and a surprising morning

Soon there came the sound of loud breathing and grunts, as the searchers tried to prise up the stone by the pump. It was obviously very heavy, and very difficult to move, for it had become almost part of the floor itself, through the centuries!

'Drat the thing! It's tearing my hands to pieces!' said a voice. 'Lend me that jemmy, Tom – yōu don't seem to be doing much good with it!'

After a lot more struggling and panting the stone was loosened. 'Up she comes!' said a voice, and up came the stone so suddenly that it sounded as if most of those pulling at it had sat down very hard on the floor!

The two hidden boys were beside themselves with interest and excitement. How they wished they could go and watch! But it was impossible. They must just listen and try to make out what was happening from what the men said below them.

'Is it a well down there? Yes, it is! My, the water's pretty far down – and black as pitch too.'

There was a silence as the well was examined in the light of torches. Then an exasperated voice, the one with the drawl, said: '*This* is no secret way! Who's going to get through that water! It's just an ordinary small well, and nothing else. That word *can't* have meant Water.'

'All right, boss. What *does* it mean then?' said the woman. '*I* don't know. This isn't a plan, it's a riddle! Why couldn't Paul have made it clear where the stone slab is – he just goes and does a lot of scribble round it – and all we can make out is that it's on this common, somewhere near here – and the secret way is behind the slab!'

'And all we have to do is to go and look behind dozens of heavy slabs!' said someone else. 'I'm fed up. We've lifted slabs in that wretched camp – we've lifted some here – and we still don't know if we're anywhere near the right one.'

'Shut up,' said the voice of the drawler but now the voice was sharp and angry. 'If we have to pull this cottage down, if we have to lift every slab there is, if we have to take over that camp, I'll do it! I tell you, this makes all the difference between wealth and poverty! Anyone who wants to back out can do so – but he'd better be careful!'

'Now boss, now boss, don't you fly off the handle!' said the woman. 'We're all in this! We'll do all you say. Look, let's start by lifting a few more slabs. There are not so very many that are the size that Paul figured on this plan.'

Then began a boring time for the two hidden

boys, as slab after slab was lifted and put back. Nothing was found under any of them, apparently.

The men went to the outbuildings too, leaving the woman in the cottage. The boys thought she had gone as well, and Julian moved a little, feeling rather cramped after being still for so long. The woman's ears must have been sharp for she called out at once.

'Who's there? Is it you, Tom?'

The boys stiffened and stood like statues. The woman said no more. It was not long before the men came back, talking among themselves. It sounded as if there were three of them.

'No go,' said the drawler. 'I think we'll have to search that camp really well again.'

'That's going to be difficult with someone already there,' said the woman.

'We'll deal with him,' said a voice, grimly. Julian frowned. Did that mean that Guy was in danger? He had better warn him!

'I'm fed up with this place,' said the woman.

'Let's go. I don't think the slab is anywhere here! We're wasting our time!'

To the boys' great relief, the four searchers left the cottage and went off together. Julian and Dick leaned over the crumbling wall of the room they stood in, and watched the lights of the torches and lanterns getting dimmer and dimmer over the common. Good! Now they could go back to the girls!

'I'm stiff!' said Dick, stretching himself.

'Well, Ju – we know a lot more now, don't we? It's clear that someone called Paul had stolen some valuable blueprints of something – maybe a new plane, or battleship perhaps – and has hidden them in some secret place he knew of about here – and to get to it you have to lift a slab of stone of a certain size.'

'Yes. And we know the size because we've already seen the one they lifted in the old stables,' said Julian. 'I vote we go there and measure it – or measure the one by the sink. I should think that the right slab will be somewhere in the old camp. We'd better tell Guy and let him into the secret. He'll help us to search!'

'What a peculiar business this is to find ourselves mixed up in,' said Dick. 'All because George didn't like people laughing at old Timmy with a cardboard collar round his neck! Timmy's the cause of this!'

The boys went down the stone stairs, and, of course, Dick quite forgot about the rambler, which caught him neatly round the ankle and almost tripped him headlong down the stairs!

'Blow!' he said, clutching Julian and nearly making him topple too. 'Sorry. It was that rambler again. It's ripped my ankle all round. Put on the torch for goodness' sake.'

They carefully measured the stone slab by the sink and then made their way out of the cottage and up towards the spring, hoping that they would find the great gorse bush in the dark. They tried to get under the wrong one at first, but at last found the right one. They heard a small welcome bark from Timmy.

'Oh! Julian! Dick! Is it you?' said Anne's voice, as the boys squeezed through into the hollow middle. 'Oh, what AGES you've been! We haven't slept a wink. Keep still, Timmy, do – this place is too small for you to rampage about in!'

The boys settled down and torches were put on. Julian related the curious happenings to the two interested girls. George was thrilled.

'Oh I *say*! Fancy all this springing up out of the blue so suddenly! What are you going to do?'

'Warn Guy first thing in the morning – and then get in touch with the police, I think,' said Julian. 'We ourselves can't stop the men searching the camp, and as soon as they *do* find the slab they're looking for, they can easily get what they want and go off with it!'

'Well, it's really thrilling,' said George. 'I wish I'd been with you. I'll never go to sleep tonight!'

But they did manage to drop off to sleep, for

they were all very tired. After a few hours, just as dawn was breaking, Timmy lifted his head and growled. George awoke at once.

'What is it, Tim? I can't hear anything.'

But Timmy could, that was certain. George woke Julian, and made him listen to Timmy's continuous growling.

'What do you think he's growling at?' she asked. 'He keeps on and on. I can't hear a thing, can you?'

'No,' said Julian, listening. 'Well, it's no use my creeping out and going searching in the dark for whatever Timmy's growling at. It might be something silly like a weasel or a hedgehog or a stoat. Shut up, Tim. That's enough.'

Although it was as dark as night under the thick old gorse bush, outside it was just getting light. What *was* Timmy growling at? Were there people about again? Or was it just one of the hedgehogs he so heartily disliked?

He stopped growling at last and put his head

down on his paws, closing his eyes. George patted him.

'Well, whatever it was, it's gone. Are you comfy, Julian? It's very cramped in here – and hot too, isn't it?'

'Yes. We'll get up fairly early and go to warn Guy – then we'll have a swim,' said Julian, yawning. He switched off his torch and went to sleep again.

It was late when they awoke. Dick was the first, and he looked at his watch. He gave an exclamation.

'Gosh! It's half past eight! Hey, Ju – Anne – George wake up, it's almost afternoon!'

Everyone felt stiff and cramped, and they went off to have a swim and to warn Guy. As they came near the camp, they stopped in amazement.

Someone was howling down in the trench, howling so miserably and so broken-heartedly that the Five felt quite panic-stricken. Whatever in the world could have happened? They ran to the edge of the excavations and looked down into the trench.

The boy was there, lying on his face, sobbing. He kept lifting his head and howling, then putting it down again.

'Guy! GUY! Whatever's happened?' shouted Julian. He leapt down beside the boy. 'Are you hurt? Is Jet hurt? What's the matter?'

'It's Guy! He's gone! They've taken him,' howled the boy. 'And I was so awful to him. Now he's gone. He'll never come back, I know he won't!'

'Guy's gone? But – but *you're* Guy!' said Julian in astonishment. 'What do you mean?'

He felt sure that the boy really *was* mad now – quite mad – talking about himself like that. He patted him on the shoulder. 'Look, you're ill. You come along with us. You need a doctor.'

The boy sprang to his feet, his face swollen and stained. 'I'm not ill! I tell you Guy's gone. I'm *not* Guy. He's my twin. There are two of us.'

Everyone gasped. It took half a minute to think about this and get everything straight – and then, of course many things were clear! There was not one mad boy, there were two ordinary boys – but they were twins! There wasn't, as they had thought, just *one* boy who contradicted himself all the time, who seemed continually to appear suddenly and unexpectedly, and who was sometimes nice and sometimes not.

'Twins! Why on earth didn't we think of that before?' said Julian. 'We thought there was only one of you. You were never together.'

'No. We quarrelled – quarrelled bitterly,' said the boy, tears in his eyes again. 'And when twins quarrel, *really* quarrel, it's worse than any quarrel there is! We hated one another then – we really did! We wouldn't be with one another, we wouldn't eat together, or dig together, or sleep together. We've often quarrelled before, but not like this – not like this! I just pretended that he didn't exist – and he did the same with me!'

'What a to-do!' said Julian, astonished and worried. 'Well now, what's happened to make you so upset? Tell me!'

'Guy wanted to be friends with me again last night,' said the boy. 'And I wouldn't. I hit him and walked away. Then this morning I was sorry and went to find him and be friends – and – and . . .'

He stopped and howled again. Everyone felt very sad and uncomfortable. 'Go on, tell us,' said Julian, gently.

'I was just in time to see him fighting two men, and screaming at them, and kicking – then they hustled him away somewhere!' said the boy. 'I fell down in the trench and hurt my leg – and by the time I dragged myself up, Guy had gone – and so had everyone else!'

He turned away and wept again. 'I'll never forgive myself, never! If I'd made friends last night I could have helped him – and I didn't!'

[15]

Well done, George!

It was Anne who comforted the boy. She went to him and pulled him down on a stone beside her. 'Let me look at your leg,' she said. 'It's pretty bad, isn't it? Look, I'll bind it up for you. Don't be so upset – we'll help you. I think we know what's happened, don't we Julian?'

The boy looked at Anne gratefully, and sniffed hard. When she offered him her handkerchief, he took it and wiped his face. Dick gave Anne his big hanky to bind up the boy's cut and bruised leg. He must have fallen right into the trench in his fright at seeing his brother fighting and being taken away.

'How do *you* know what's happened?' he said to Julian. 'Can you get Guy back? Do say you can! I'll never forgive myself for this. My twin brother – and I wasn't there to fight by his side when he needed me!'

'Now don't soak my hanky all over again!' said Anne. He gave her a forlorn little smile and turned to Julian again.

'My name's Harry Lawdler, and Guy and I are mad on old camps and buildings and things. We spend almost all our holidays together, digging and finding all kinds of things, like these.' He nodded his head towards the little shelf of relics that the four had seen before.

'Yes, Guy told us,' said Dick. 'But he never said a word about you. We were often very puzzled – we thought you and he were one boy – not two, you see – and we couldn't understand a lot of things you both said. You're so very, very alike.'

'Well, I tell you, we each pretended that the other didn't even exist,' said Harry. 'We're like that. We love each other best in the world, and we hate each other worst – when we quarrel. We're simply *horrible* then!'

'Can you tell us a bit about the people that Guy was fighting?' asked Dick.

'Yes. They were some that came before, wanting Guy to clear out while they had a look round,' said Harry, wiping his face again. 'Guy was pretty rude to them. In fact I heard him say that if they messed about his camp he would throw stones at them – he's like that, you know, very fierce, when he's roused.'

'And you think these were the same people?' said Dick. 'Which way did they go with Guy?'

'That way,' said Harry, pointing. 'I've hunted the whole camp round, but they're gone – disappeared into thin air! It's extraordinary!'

'Let's have a hunt round,' said Julian. 'We might find something. But I imagine that the searchers have taken Guy off with them because he knew too much – perhaps they found here what they were looking for, and saw Guy watching.'

'Oh! Then we're too late!' said George, in deep disappointment. 'They've got what they want – and they'll disappear now and never be caught. I expect by now they are speeding away in a fast car – and have taken Guy with them to make sure he doesn't talk before they're safely in another country!'

'Oh no!' cried Harry. 'He's not kidnapped, is he? Don't say that!'

'Come on – let's have a hunt,' said Julian, and they all made their way among the various trenches and pits, looking for they hardly knew what.

They gave it up after a while. There were too many slabs and stones of all sizes! Besides, what good would it be even if they found the right one? The birds had flown – presumably with what they had come for! In fact, if Guy hadn't come along and seen the searchers, nobody would even have known that they had been in the camp and made a successful search!

'It's no good,' said Julian, at last. 'This is too big a place to know where to look for anything that might help us. Let's go back to the gorse bush and collect our things, return to Kirrin and go to the police. It's the only sensible thing left to do!'

'Come along, Harry,' said Anne, to the miserable twin. He was so full of remorse that her handkerchief was now soaked for the third time! 'You'd better come with us and tell all you know.'

'I'll come,' said Harry. 'I'll do anything to get Guy back. I'll never quarrel with him again. Never. To think that—'

'Now don't go all through that again,' said Anne. 'Look, you're upsetting Timmy so much that his tail is down all the time!'

Harry gave another forlorn little smile. They all left the camp and made their way back to the gorse bush. It was only when they got there, and began pulling out the tins of food, as well as the rug and other things, that they realised how extremely hungry they were!

'We've had no breakfast. We've been up for

ages, and it's very late. I'm simply starving!' said George.

'Well, if we finish up all the food, we shan't have to carry the tins!' said Dick. 'Let's have a meal. Ten minutes more here can't make much difference.'

They were thankful not to have to sit under the gorse bush again. They sat outside in the sun, and discussed everything.

'I believe when Timmy began to growl and growl about six o'clock this morning, it was because he could hear those people coming quietly by to go to search the camp,' said George.

'I think you're right,' said Julian. 'I bet they searched the camp well – till Guy woke and came on the scene and fought like fury. It's a pity I didn't squeeze out from under the bush and follow them, when Timmy growled.'

'Anyone want a drink?' said George. 'I'll go and fetch some water from the spring. Where's the pineapple tin?'

Anne passed it to her. George got up and took the little rabbit path that led to the spring. She could hear it gurgling and bubbling as she came near – a very pleasant noise.

'Water always sounds nice,' said George to herself. 'I love the sound of water.'

Water! Now why did that ring a bell in her mind just then? Who had been talking about water? Oh – Dick and Julian, of course, when they had come back from the old cottage last night. They had told Anne and herself about the word on the plan – the word that might have been WATER, not WADER.

'I wonder which it was,' said George to herself as she idly held the pineapple tin to the gurgling water. She gazed at the beautiful little spring, jutting up from the stony slabs – and then another bell rang loudly in the mind.

'Stone slabs! Water! Why – I wonder – I just wonder – if one of *these* slabs is the one! This one just here is about the right size!'

She stared at it. It was set firmly in a high

little bank at the back of the place where the spring gurgled up and then ran into the clean stony channel. *Did* it hide anything behind it?

George suddenly dropped the tin and ran back to the others at full speed. 'Julian! Julian! I believe I've found the slab! It's been staring us in the face the whole time!'

Julian was very startled. So were the others. They stared up at George in astonishment.

'What do you mean, George?' said Julian, jumping to his feet. 'Show me!'

Followed by everyone, George ran back to the spring. She pointed to the white slab behind the water. 'There!' she said. 'That's the right size, isn't it? And it's beside WATER – just as it said in the plan you told us about – only the people thought it was WADER.'

'Gosh, I wonder if you're right, George,' said Julian, excited. 'You might be – you never know. Sometimes springs come from underground passages – secret hidden ways into the earth.'

'Let's try and move it,' said Dick, his face red with sudden excitement. 'It looks pretty hefty to me.'

They began to struggle with the stone, getting extremely wet as they splashed about in the spring. But nobody minded that. This was too exciting for words. Harry helped too, heaving and tugging. He was very strong indeed.

The stone slab moved a little. It slid to one side and stuck. More tugging. More pulling. More panting and puffing!

'I believe we'll have to get help,' said Julian at last. 'It really is too heavy and well-embedded.'

'I'll go and get some of my tools,' said Harry. 'I'm used to heaving stones about with them. We can easily move it if we have the right tools.'

He flew off at top speed. The others sat down and mopped their streaming foreheads.

'Phew!' said Julian. 'What a job this is for a hot day! I'm glad Harry remembered his tools. Just what we want!'

'How funny that he and Guy are twins!' said George. 'I never even thought of such a thing!'

'Well, they behaved so idiotically,' said Julian. 'Always pretending there was just one of them, and neither of them even mentioning the other. I wonder where Guy has been taken to. I don't think he'll come to much harm – but it will be worrying for his family.'

'Here comes Harry,' said Anne, after a pause. 'One of us ought to have gone with him to help him. He's brought dozens of tools!'

The things he had fetched proved very useful indeed, especially a big jemmy-like tool. The stone soon began to move when this was applied by Julian and Harry!

'It's slipping – it's coming away – look out, it will fall right down into the spring!' cried Dick. 'Look out, you girls!'

The stone was prised right out, and fell into the stony channel where the water ran. The five children stared at the opening it left.

Julian leaned forward and looked into it.

'Yes – there's a big hole behind,' he said. 'Let me shine my torch in.'

In great excitement he flashed his torch into the opening. He turned round, his face glowing.

'Yes! I think we've got it! There's a tunnel behind, going down and down. It widens out behind this hole!'

Everyone was too thrilled for words. George gave Dick a punch, and Anne patted Timmy so hard that he whined. Harry beamed round, all his woes forgotten.

'Do we go down now?' asked Dick. 'We'll have to make the opening a bit wider. Earth and roots have narrowed it very much. Let's make it bigger.'

'Then we'll explore it!' said George, her eyes shining. 'A secret tunnel only known to us! Quick – let's explore it!'

[16]

The secret way

All the children were so excited that they got into each other's way. Julian pushed them back.

'Let's be sensible! We can't *all* make the opening wider – let Harry and me get at it with the tools – and we'll soon make it bigger!'

It took only a minute to hack away at the sides of the hole to make it big enough for even Julian to climb through. He stood there panting, smiling broadly.

'There – it's done! I'll get in first. Everyone got torches? We shall need them! It's going to be dark in there!'

He clambered up and into the hole. He had to crawl on hands and knees for a little way, and then the hole suddenly went downwards and became considerably bigger. Julian could walk in it, if he bent down, for at that point the tunnel was about three feet high.

He called back to the others. 'Follow me! Take hold of each other's shirts or jerseys and hang on. It's pitch black in here!'

George followed after Julian, then Anne, then Dick, then Harry. Timmy went with George, of course, pushing and shoving like all the rest. Everyone was excited, and nobody could talk in a normal voice. They all shouted!

'I'll give you a hand! One good shove and you're in!'

'I say – isn't it dark!'

'What a crawl! I feel like a fox going into its den!'

'Timmy, don't butt me from behind like that! I can't crawl any faster!'

'Ah – thank goodness I can stand up now! What size of rabbit do you think made *this* burrow!'

'It was made by water at some time perhaps. Don't *shove*, Timmy!'

'Water doesn't run uphill, ass! Hang on to my jersey, Harry. Don't get left behind.'

Julian, bent almost double at times, walked carefully along the narrow tunnel, which went steadily downwards. Soon it widened and became higher, and then it was easier to walk in comfort.

'Do you suppose this is the right secret way?' called George, after a time. 'We don't seem to be getting anywhere.'

'I can't tell. In fact we shan't know till we find something hidden somewhere – if we ever do!'

A sudden scuttering noise in front of him made Julian stop suddenly. Immediately everyone bumped into the one in front, and there were shouts at once.

'What's up, Ju?'

Julian's torch shone on to two pairs of bright, frightened eyes. He gave a laugh.

'It's all right – just a couple of rabbits using our burrow! There are small holes running out

of the tunnel which, I imagine, are rabbit burrows. I bet we're giving the bunnies a shock!'

The tunnel wound about a good deal, and
then suddenly the rather soft ground they were
treading on turned to rock. The passage was
now not so high, and the children had to bend
down again. It was most uncomfortable.

Julian stopped once more. He had heard
another sound. What was it?

'Water!' he said. 'There must be an underground stream here! How thrilling! Everyone
all right?'

'Yes!' shouted those behind him. 'Get on,
Julian – let's see the water!'

The tunnel suddenly ended, and Julian found
himself in a big cave with a fairly high roof.
Almost in the middle of it ran a stream – not a
very big one, and not a very fast one. It gurgled
along in a small channel of rock, which it had
carved out for itself through hundreds of years.

Julian shone his torch on it. The water
looked very black and glittered in the light of

the torch. The others came one by one out of the tunnel and stared at the underground stream. It looked rather mysterious, slipping through the cave, gurgling quietly as it disappeared through a hole at one end.

'Strange,' said Dick.

'It's not unusual, this,' began Harry. 'In some parts of the country round about here, the ground below our feet is honeycombed with many little streams. Some come up as springs, of course, some join other streams when they come out into the open, others just run away goodness knows where!'

Julian was looking up round the cave. 'Does our tunnel end here?' he wondered. 'Is this where we have to look for whatever is hidden?'

'We'll have a look round the cave and see if there are any exits,' said Dick. Using their torches the five separated, Timmy keeping close to George, not seeming in the least surprised at this underground adventure.

'I've found another tunnel over here, leading

out of the cave!' called Dick. No sooner had he said that than Anne called out too.

'There's one here as well!'

'Now – which do we take?' said Julian. 'How annoying that there should be two!'

'Would the fellow – what's his name – Paul – have marked the correct underground way on his plan?' said George. 'I mean – I don't see how he could possibly expect either himself or anyone else to find what he had hidden, if there are numbers of passages to choose from down here!'

'You're right!' said Julian. 'Let's look about and see if we can find anything to help us.'

It wasn't long before Dick gave another shout. 'It's all right! This is the passage to take, over here – the one I found just now. There's an arrow drawn in white chalk on the wall.'

Everyone crowded over to Dick, stepping across the little stream as they did so. Dick held his torch up and they all saw the white arrow, drawn roughly on the wall.

Julian was pleased. 'Good. That helps a lot! It shows we're going the right way – and that this *is* the secret way that Paul chose. Come on!'

They entered the tunnel, left the little stream behind, and went on again. 'Anyone got any idea in which direction we're going?' called Dick. 'East, west, north, south?'

Harry had a compass. He looked at it. 'I think we're going rather in the direction of the old Roman camp,' he said.

'Ah – that's interesting,' said Julian. 'This tunnel was probably used in olden times.'

'Guy and I have seen the plan of the camp as it probably used to be,' said Harry. 'And there are plenty of tunnels and caves and holes shown on it – just roughed in, not a proper plan of them. Gosh, I never thought I'd be exploring one! My father warned me not to, in case of roof-falls and things like that.'

The tunnel suddenly forked into two. One passage was nice and wide, the other narrow. Julian took the wide one, thinking that the other was really too narrow to get through. But after a minute or two, he stopped, puzzled.

'There's a blank wall of rock here – the tunnel's ended! We'll have to turn back! I suppose we should have taken that very narrow opening.'

They went back, Harry leading the way now. Timmy suddenly took it into his head that *he* would like to lead, too, and made himself a real nuisance, pushing his way between everyone's legs!

They came back to the fork. Harry shone his torch in at the second opening, the very narrow one. There, clearly marked on the right hand wall, was a white arrow in chalk!

'We're idiots,' said Dick. 'We don't even look for the signposts! Lead the way, Julian!'

This tunnel was very narrow indeed, and had rough, jutting rocky sides. There were loud 'aahs!' and 'oohs!' as elbows and ankles were knocked against hard rock.

And then again there came a blank wall of

rock in front of Julian, and again he had to stop!

'Can't go this way either!' he said. 'There's a blank wall again – this is a blind alley too!'

There were cries of dismay at once.

'Blow! It can't be!'

'What's gone wrong? Look all round, Ju – flash your torch down at your feet and above your head!'

Julian shone his torch over his head, and gave an exclamation.

'There's a hole above my head!'

'Is there a white arrow anywhere?' called Harry.

'Yes! And it's pointing up, instead of forwards!' called back Julian. 'We're still all right – we've got to go upwards now – but how?'

George, who was just behind him, shone her torch on the side walls. 'Look!' she said. 'We can easily get up to the hole. There are rough, natural steps up – made by ledges of rock. Look, Julian!'

'Yes,' said Julian. 'We can manage to get up quite easily, I think. George, you go first – I'll give you a boost up.'

George was delighted to go first. She put her torch between her teeth, and began to climb up the ledges, Julian pushing her as best he could. She came to the hole and immediately saw that it would be quite easy to hoist herself through.

'One more boost and I'll be through!' she called to Julian. And with one last heave George was up, rolling on the floor of a small cave above! She called down in excitement to the others.

'I believe this is the place where those things are hidden! I can see something on a ledge. Oh, do buck up!'

The others followed eagerly. Dick slipped off the rocky ledges in his excitement and almost squashed poor Harry as he fell on him. However, everyone was up at last, even Timmy, who was the most difficult of all to heave through! He seemed to have far too many vigorous legs!

Harry found no difficulty at all. 'I'm used to this kind of thing,' he said. 'Guy and I have explored a whole lot of tunnels and caves in hills and other places.'

George was pointing her torch at a broad ledge of rock. On it was a brown leather bag, and beside it, marked on the rock, was a very large arrow indeed.

Julian was overjoyed. He picked up the bag at once. 'My word – I hope there's something in it!' he said. 'It feels jolly light – as if it's empty!'

'Open it!' cried everyone – but Julian couldn't. It was locked – and alas, there wasn't a key!

[17]

Full of surprises

It's locked – we can't open the bag,' said Julian, and shook it vigorously as if that might make it fly open and spill whatever contents it had!

'We don't know if it's got anything of value in it or not,' said Dick, in deep disappointment. 'I mean – it might be some trick on that fellow Paul's part – he might have taken the blue-prints, or whatever they were he hid, for himself, and left the bag just to trick the others.'

'Can we cut it open?' asked George.

'No. I don't think so. It's made of really strong leather. We would need a special knife to cut through it – an ordinary penknife wouldn't be any use,' said Julian. 'I think we'll just have to assume that we've got the goods, and hope for the best. If they're not in here, it's just bad luck. Someone else has got them, if so.'

They all looked at the tantalising bag.

Now they would have to wait for ages before they found out whether their efforts had been successful or not!

'Well – what do we do now?' said George, feeling suddenly flat. 'Go back all through that long tunnel once more? I'll be glad to be in the open air again, won't you?'

'You bet!' said Julian. 'Well – I suppose we'd better get down through that hole again.'

'Wait!' said Anne, her sharp eyes catching sight of something. 'Look – what does all this mean?'

She shone her torch on to various signs on the wall. Again there were arrows drawn in white chalk – but very oddly, a line of them ran downwards across the wall of the little rocky room, right to the edge of the hole – and another line of arrows pointing the *other* way, ran horizontally across the wall!

'Well, do you suppose that's just meant to muddle people?' said Dick, puzzled. 'We know jolly well that the way out of this room is down that hole, because that's the way we came into it.'

'Perhaps the other line of arrows means that there's a second way out,' suggested George. They all looked round the little rocky room. There didn't seem any way out at all.

'Where's Timmy?' said Anne, suddenly, flashing her torch round. 'He's not here! Has he fallen down the hole? I never heard him yelp!'

At once there was a great to-do. 'Timmy, Timmy, Timmy! TIMMY! Where are you?'

George whistled shrilly, and the noise echoed round and round the little room. Then, from somewhere, there was a bark. How relieved everyone was.

'Where is he? Where did that bark come from?' said Dick. 'It didn't sound as if it came from below, down that hole!'

There came another welcome bark, and the sound of Timmy's feet. Then to everyone's amazement, he appeared in the little rocky room as if by magic – appearing straight out of the wall, it seemed!

'Timmy! Where were you? Where have you come from?' cried George, and ran to see. She came to a standstill and exclaimed loudly.

'Oh! What idiots we are! Why, just behind this big jutting-out piece of rock, there's another passage!'

So there was! A very, very narrow one, it is true – and completely hidden from the children because of the enormous slab of rock that jutted out from the wall that hid it! They stood and stared at it, shining their torches on the narrow way. The arrows ran round the wall to it.

'We never even looked properly!' said Dick. 'Still – it's a passage that would be extremely difficult to spot – hidden round the corner of that rock – and very narrow at that. Well, I do know one thing for certain about that man called Paul!'

'What?' asked Anne.

'He's thin – thin as a rake!' said Dick. 'No one but a skinny fellow could squeeze through *this* opening! I doubt if *you* can, Julian – you're the biggest of us.'

'Well, what about trying?' said George. 'What does everyone say? This might be an easier, shorter way out – or it might be a harder, longer one.'

'It won't be longer,' said Harry. 'By my reckoning we must be pretty well near the camp now. It's likely that the way leads straight there – though where it comes out I can't imagine. Guy and I have explored the camp pretty thoroughly.'

Dick suddenly thought of something he had noticed at the camp – the big hole behind the slab of stone, where he had seen the baby rabbit a day or two before! What had Guy said about that? He had said there was a great hole underground, which had been explored – but that it was probably just an ancient storage place for food or for loot! He turned eagerly to Harry.

'Harry, would this lead to that enormous hole underground – the one that Guy once told me had been explored, but was of no interest – probably just an old store place?'

'Let me see,' said Harry. 'Yes – yes, it *might* lead to that. Most of these underground ways are throughways – ways that led from one place to another. They don't as a rule stop suddenly, but have usually been of use as secret escape routes or something of that kind. I think you may be right, Dick – we're fairly near the camp, I'm sure, and we may quite well find that if we go on, instead of going back, we shall come into the camp itself – probably through that great hole!'

'Then come on,' said Julian. 'It will certainly be a shorter way!'

They tried to squeeze through the narrow opening that led out of the little rocky room.

Dick got through all right, and so did the others – but poor Julian found it very very difficult and almost gave up.

'You shouldn't eat so much,' said Dick, unkindly. 'Go on – one more try, Ju – I'll haul on your arm at the same time!'

Julian got through, groaning. 'I'm squashed flat!' he said. 'Now, if anyone makes any more jokes about too much breakfast, I'll pull his nose!'

The passage grew wider immediately, and everyone was thankful. It ran fairly straight, and then went steeply downwards, so that the five slithered about, and Timmy found himself suddenly running. Then it came to a stop – a complete stop! This time it was not a blank wall of rock that faced them – it was something else.

'A roof-fall!' groaned Dick. 'Look at that! Now we're done!'

It certainly looked most formidable. Earth, rocks and stones had fallen from the roof and blocked up the whole passageway. There was no use in going on – they would just have to turn and go back!

'Blow it!' said Dick, and kicked at the mass of earth. 'Well, there's no use staying here – we'd better turn back. My torch isn't too good now, and neither is yours, George. We don't want to lose any time – if our torches give out, we shall find things very difficult.'

They turned to go back, feeling very despondent. 'Come on, Timmy!' said George. But Timmy didn't come. He stood beside the roof-fall, looking very puzzled, his ears cocked and his head on one side. Then he suddenly gave a sharp bark.

It made everyone jump almost out of their skins, for the sound echoed round and about in a very strange way.

'Don't, Timmy!' said George, almost angrily. 'Whatever's the matter? Come along!'

But Timmy didn't come. He began to paw at the pile of earth and rocks in front of him, and barked without stopping. Wuff-wuff-wuff-wuff-wuff-WUFF!

'What's up?' said Julian, startled. 'Timmy, what on *earth's* the matter?'

Timmy took absolutely no notice, but went on feverishly scraping at the roof-fall, sending earth and stones flying all over the others.

'There's something he wants to get at – something behind this roof-fall,' said Dick. 'Or perhaps *somebody* – make him stop barking, George, and we'll listen ourselves and see if we can hear anything.'

George silenced Timmy with difficulty, and made him stand quiet and still. Then they all listened intently – and a sound came at once to their ears.

'Yap-yap-wuff-wuff-wuff!'

'It's Jet!' yelled Harry, making everyone jump violently again. 'Jet! Then Guy must be with him. He never leaves Guy! What's Guy doing here? He may be hurt. GUY! GUY! JET!'

Timmy began to bark wildly again and to scrape more furiously than ever. Julian shouted to the others above the barking.

'If we can hear Jet barking, this roof-fall can't be very big. We'd better try and get through it. Two of us can work in turn with Timmy. We can't all work at once, the passage is too narrow.'

Then began some very hard work – but it didn't last as long as Julian feared, because, quite suddenly, the mass of rubble and rock shifted as they worked, and a gap appeared at the top of the heap, between it and the roof.

Dick began to scramble up, but Julian called to him at once. 'Be careful, ass! The roof can't be too good here – it may come down again, and you'll be buried. Go carefully!'

But before Dick could go any further, a little figure appeared on the top of the rubble over their heads, and slid down to them yapping loudly, and waving a long wiry tail!

'Jet! Oh, Jet! Where's Guy?' cried Harry, as the little dog leapt into his arms and licked his face lavishly, barking joyfully in between the licks.

'GUY!' yelled Julian. 'Are you there?'

A weak voice came back. 'Yes! Who's that?' An absolute volley of voices answered him.

'It's us! And Harry! We're coming to you, we shan't be long!'

And it wasn't long, either, before the roof-fall was slowly and carefully climbed by each one – though Timmy, of course, scrambled up, over and down at top speed!

On the other side of the roof-fall was a passage, of course, the continuation of the one the children had come along. Guy was there, sitting down, looking very pale. Jet flung himself on him and licked him as if he hadn't seen him for a month, instead of just a minute or two before!

'Hallo!' said Guy, in a small voice. 'I'm all right. It's just my ankle, that's all. I'm jolly glad to—'

But before he could say a word more, Harry was beside him, his arms round him, his voice choking.

'Guy! Oh, Guy! I've been a beast. I wouldn't be friends! What happened to you? Are you really all right? Oh Guy, we *are* friends again, aren't we?'

'Look out Harry, old son,' said Julian gently. 'He's fainted. Now just let's be sensible and everything will come all right. Flap your hanky at him, Dick, and give him a little air. It's only the excitement!'

In half a minute Guy opened his eyes and smiled weakly. 'Sorry!' he said. 'I'm all right now. I only hope this isn't a dream, and that you really *are* here!'

'You bet we are!' said Dick. 'Have a bit of chocolate, then you'll know we're real!'

'Good idea!' said Julian. 'We'll all have some – and I've some biscuits in my pocket too. We'll eat and talk – and we'll make plans at the same time. Catch, Guy – here's a biscuit!'

[18]

The way out

Guy soon told his story. It was much as the others had imagined.

'I was fast asleep this morning, with Jet curled up to me,' he said. 'He began to bark and I wondered why, so I got up to see – and I saw four people in the camp.'

'The four we know!' said Dick, and Julian nodded. 'Go on, Guy.'

'They were looking all over the place,' said Guy, 'prising up rocks, messing about – so I yelled at them. But they only laughed. Then one of the men, who was trying to prise up a slab – the slab that covers that great hole underground, Harry – you remember it? – well, this man gave a yell and said "I've got it! This is the way in – down here, behind this slab!"'

Guy stopped, looking very angry. Jet licked him comfortingly. 'Well,' he went on. 'I set Jet on them, and they kicked him cruelly – so I went for them.'

'You're a plucky one, aren't you!' said Dick, admiringly. 'Did you knock them all out, by any chance?'

'No. Of course not,' said Guy. 'One of the men pretty well knocked *me* out though. He hit me on the head and I went down, dazed. I heard him say "Drat this kid – he'll be fetching help, and we shan't be able to get down and hunt for the goods." And then another man said "We'll take him with us then", and they got hold of me and dragged me through the opening.'

'But how did they get down into that great hole?' said Harry in wonder. 'There is such a steep drop into it. You need a rope.'

'Oh, they had a rope all right,' said Guy, munching his biscuit and chocolate and looking decidedly better. 'One of the men had one tied round and round his waist. They knotted it fast round a rock – that big one we can't move, Harry – and then they swung down on it. All except the woman. She said she'd stay at the top and keep watch. She hid behind a bush some way off.'

'I never saw her when I came along!' said Harry. 'I never thought of looking there! What about you? Did you get down too?'

'Yes. I screamed and shouted and kicked and howled, but it wasn't a bit of good. They made me swing down the rope – and I fell off halfway down and hurt my ankle. I howled at the top of my voice for help, and they hurried me along with them, shaking me like a rat.'

'The beasts!' said Harry, fervently. 'Oh, the beasts!'

'I heard one of them say that there should be a tunnel out of the hole somewhere, it was marked on Paul's plan – whatever that may be – and then I think I must have fainted – the pain of my ankle, you know. And when I came to myself again, we were all here, the three men and I – beside this roof-fall – though I really don't know how we got here. They must have dragged me along with them!'

'And that's all, is it?' asked Julian.

'Not quite. They were furious when they saw the roof-fall, but as soon as they began to scrabble in it a rock rolled down and hit one of the men quite a crack – and after that they were afraid to do anything. They stood and talked for a bit – and then they decided to go and get some tools, and come down again to see if they could remove all this stuff and get through it.'

'Good gracious!' said Julian, startled. 'Then they may be back at any moment!'

'I suppose so. They left me here because they couldn't think of anything else to do with me! They knew I couldn't walk, because of my ankle. I think it's broken. So of course I couldn't possibly find my way out myself! And here I've been waiting for those brutes to come back, and to hack through the rubble to go after whatever it is they want!'

Everyone began to feel rather uncomfortable at the thought that three violent men might be appearing at any moment. 'Is it very far to the opening you came down?' asked Julian. But Guy didn't know. He had fainted, as he had said, and he didn't even know what way they had come.

'It can't be far,' said Harry. 'I think it would be worth while trying to find the opening, see if the men have left the rope there, and get out that way. If Guy's ankle really is broken, he couldn't possibly manage to go back the long way we've come.'

'No. That's true,' said Julian, thoughtfully. 'Well, that's what we'll do then. But we'll go jolly cautiously, without a sound, because it might be just our luck to meet those fellows on their way back here!'

'Shall we start?' said George. 'What about Guy?'

Julian knelt down beside the boy, and gently examined his ankle. 'I've done my first aid training, like everybody else!' he said. 'And I *ought* to know if his ankle is broken or just sprained.'

He examined the swollen ankle carefully. 'It's not broken. I believe I could bandage it tightly with a couple of large hankies. Give me yours, Dick.'

The others watched admiringly as Julian deftly and confidently bandaged Guy's swollen ankle. 'There!' he said. 'You can perhaps hobble on it now, Guy. It may hurt, but I don't think it will damage it. Try. You'll have to go barefoot because your ankle is too swollen for your shoe to go on.'

Very gingerly Guy stood up, helped by Harry. He tried his hurt foot, and it certainly seemed all right to hobble on, though it was very painful. He grinned round at the others' anxious faces.

'It's fine!' he said. 'Come on, let's go! We don't want to bump into those fellows if we can help it. Thank goodness we've got Jet and Timmy.'

They set off down the passage, flashing their torches in front as usual, to show them the way. The tunnel was quite wide and high here, and in a very short time came out into an enormous pit underground.

'Ah – this is the hole I saw down behind the slab where the rabbit went,' said Dick. 'We weren't very far from the camp, as we thought. I'm surprised that when this pit was explored, the underground passages were not discovered, Guy.'

'I expect the men exploring it came to the roof-fall and thought there was nothing beyond,' said Guy. 'Or maybe they were afraid of going further in case of further falls. They can be very danger-ous, you know. Many a man has been buried under one and never heard of again.'

They looked round the enormous hole – it was really a huge round pit. Daylight showed in the roof at one place.

'That's the opening into it,' said Guy, ea-gerly. 'The one I came through, on the rope.'

He limped a few steps forward to look for the rope. Harry held him by the arm, thankful that the ankle was holding up so well. Guy pointed upwards.

'Yes. I can see the rope. The men have left it there, thank goodness. They must have been certain that I couldn't get to it!'

The rope hung down from the little opening high above their heads. Julian looked round at Anne.

'Can you manage to climb up the rope, Anne?' he said, doubtfully.

'Of course!' said Anne, scornfully. 'We do rope-climbing in the gym at school often enough. Don't we, George?'

'Yes, but our gym rope is a bit thicker!' said George.

'I'll go up first,' said Harry. 'We've got a much thicker rope, Guy and I, that we use when we want to haul on very heavy stones. I'll find it, and let it down.'

'Well, we can't afford to waste any time, in

case those fellows come back,' said Julian. 'I daresay the girls can manage all right. George, you go up first.'

George went up like a monkey, hand over hand, her legs twisted round the rope. She grinned down when she got to the top.

'Easy!' she said. 'Come on up next, Anne, and show the boys how to do it!'

Before the boys could leap to the rope, Anne was on it, pulling herself up lithely. Julian laughed. He called up to George.

'George! You might have a squint round and see if there's any sign of people about. If they were going to borrow *Guy's* tools, they would have been back long ago, so I think probably they've had to go to Kirrin or some farmhouse to borrow them.'

'They wouldn't get my tools,' said Guy, 'or Harry's. We had them stolen once, and now we always hide them where no one can possibly find them.'

'That settles it then,' said Julian. 'They've

had to go a good way, I expect, to get satisfactory tools to tackle that roof-fall. They probably imagine that it's a pretty *big* fall! All the same, keep a watch out, George, till we're all up.'

It was difficult to get Guy up, for he was feeling weak, but they managed it at last. The two dogs had to have the boys' shirts tied round them so that the rope would not cut them when they were hauled up. They didn't seem to mind at all. Timmy was very heavy to pull up because he appeared to think that he had to try and make his legs do a running action all the time – just to help! All that happened was that he began to spin round and round, as he went up!

Everyone was up in the open air at long last, hot and perspiring. Julian had the precious bag safely under his arm. Timmy sat down panting. Then he suddenly stopped panting, and pricked up his ears.

'Woof,' he said warningly, and stood up.

'Quiet, Tim, quiet, Jet,' said Julian, at once

aware that somebody must be about. 'Hide, everyone – quickly. It may be those fellows coming back!'

'Wuff,' began Jet, but Guy stopped him immediately. The six children separated and went into hiding at once, each choosing the best place he or she could see. There were plenty of hiding places in the old camp!

They heard voices coming near. Nobody dared to peep out and see who was coming – but Julian and Dick recognised the drawling voice of one of the men!

'What a time we've been!' said the man. 'Just chuck the spades and things down the hole – then we'll all climb down again. Buck up! We've wasted too much time already. Anyone might come on the scene at any moment!'

The spades and jemmies went hurtling down the hole. Then one by one the men went down the rope. The children could not hear the woman's voice. They thought she must have been left behind.

Julian gave a low whistle and all the others popped up their heads. 'We'll spring for it!' said Julian. 'Buck up!'

They all shot out of their hiding places at once and made off – except Julian. He stayed behind for a minute or two. What *could* he be doing?

Julian was doing something very simple indeed! He was hauling up the rope that dangled underground! He slipped it off the rock that held it and tied it round his waist, looking suddenly very bulky.

He grinned a very wide grin and went after the others. How very, very angry those men were going to be!

[19]

Back to Kirrin Cottage

Julian ran after the others. 'What were you doing?' said George. 'Calling rude names down to the men?'

'No. I hope they'll go and dig for hours if they want to!' said Julian. 'They'll soon find that when they've got through it, that roof-fall is nothing much, and they'll go on till they come to the little room – and what they'll say when they find that the bag is gone, I really don't know!'

'I wish I could be there!' said Dick.

'What are we going to do about Guy?' asked Harry. 'He really can't walk *very* far on that bad foot.'

'If he can walk as far as the gorse bush where we've left our things, I've got a bike there,' said

George. 'He could pedal with one foot, I should think.'

'Oh yes, I could easily do that,' said Guy, pleased. He had dreaded the thought of having to walk all the way to Kirrin – but neither did he want to be left behind!

He limped along, helped by Harry, who couldn't do enough for him. Jet ran along beside them, excited and happy at being with so many people. Timmy sometimes wuffed a little bark to him, which made Jet as proud as Punch. He thought the big Timmy was wonderful!

They came to the gorse bush, and found their things all safe. The bicycle was there, with its packages strapped to it. George unstrapped them, meaning to carry them herself, so that Guy would not have too heavy a weight to pedal with his one foot. They all started off together, Guy riding ahead on the bicycle.

'We will go to Kirrin, dump our things at the cottage, and get Aunt Fanny to ring the police and ask them if they'll come along and collect this bag from us,' said Julian. 'I don't want to leave it at the police station – I want to see it opened in front of us!'

'I do hope it won't be empty,' said Anne. 'It does feel terribly light!'

'Yes. It does,' said Julian, swinging it to and fro. 'I can't help fearing that Paul, who drew the plan that the men found so difficult to understand, may have double-crossed his friends – drawn a deliberately difficult plan – and then left the bag quite empty in the place he marked on the plan! It would be the kind of hoax that a trickster loves to play – and would give him time to get away in safety.'

'But they said he was ill,' said Dick. 'Still – perhaps he might have been pretending that too! It's a mystery!'

'How are you getting on, Guy?' called George, as they overtook the boy. He kept riding on by himself for a little way, and then resting, waiting for them to catch up with him before he pedalled on again with his one good foot.

'Very well indeed, thank you,' said Guy. 'This bike was a very good idea of yours. What a blessing you had it with you!'

'Your foot doesn't seem any more swollen,' said Anne. 'I expect you'll be able to walk on it properly in a day or two. Oh, dear – it does make me laugh when I think how puzzled we all were when we thought there was just one of you, not twins!'

'We met first one of you, then the other, and thought you were the same boy,' said George, with a chuckle. 'We were absolutely wild with you sometimes, you seemed so mad and contradictory!'

'Don't remind us of it,' said Harry. 'I can't bear thinking that if I'd only been with Guy, all this trouble of his would never have happened.'

'Oh well – it's an ill wind that blows nobody any good! said George. 'The bad and the good have fitted together very well this time, and made a most exciting adventure!'

'Here's Carters Lane at last,' said Anne.

'What a long walk it seemed over the common. It will be much easier for you to ride that bike when you're on a proper road, Guy. It won't go bumping over heather clumps now.'

They went down the long lane and came into Kirrin at last, realising that they were all very hungry indeed. 'It must be well past lunchtime,' said George, looking at her watch. 'Good gracious – it's a quarter to two! Would you believe it! I hope there's some lunch left over for us – Mother doesn't know we're coming.'

'We'll raid Joanna's larder!' said Dick. 'She never minds so long as she's there to grumble at us while we do it!'

They went in at the gate of Kirrin Cottage and up to the front door, which was open. George shouted.

'Mother! Where are you? We've come back!'

Nobody answered. George yelled again. 'Mother! We've come home!'

The door of the study opened and her father looked out, red in the face and frowning.

'George! How many times am I to tell you not to shout when I'm working? Oh, my goodness me, who are all these?'

'Hallo, Father!' said George, mildly. 'Surely you know Anne and Julian and Dick! *Don't* say you've forgotten them already!'

'Of course not! But who are these?' and George's father pointed to the startled twins. 'They're as like as peas. Where did *they* come from? I haven't seen them before, have I?'

'No, father. They're just friends of ours,' said George. 'Where's Mother? We've just had an adventure and we want to tell her. Oh, and we want to ring the police – and I think we ought to get a doctor to see to Guy's foot – and Father, look, Timmy's ear is healed!'

'Bless us all! There's never any peace when you are about, George,' said her father, groaning. 'Your mother's at the bottom of the garden, picking raspberries – or it might have been strawberries.'

'Oh no, Father – it's August, not June!' said George. 'You always—'

Julian thought he had better get his uncle safely back in his study before a row blew up between him and George. Uncle Quentin did *not* like being disturbed in his complicated work!

'Let's go and find Aunt Fanny,' he said, 'we can tell her everything out in the garden. Come on!'

'Wuff-wuff!' said Jet.

'Good gracious – that's not *another* dog, is it?' said George's father, scowling. 'How many times have I said that—'

'We won't disturb you any more, Uncle,' said Julian, hurriedly, seeing Guy's scared face. 'We'll go and find Aunt Fanny.'

They all went thankfully out in the garden, hearing the house echo to the slam of Uncle Quentin's study door. George shouted.

'Mother! Where are you?'

'Shut up, George – we don't want to make

your father leap out of the window after us!' said Dick. 'Ah – there's Aunt Fanny!'

His aunt was very surprised to see him and the others advancing on her. She went to greet them, a basket of raspberries on her arm.

'Well! I thought you wanted to stay away for longer than this!'

'We did – but an adventure descended on us!' said Dick. 'We'll tell you all about it in detail later on, Aunt Fanny.'

'But just now we want two things – can we ring the police – or will *you* – and ask them to come here?' said Julian, very grown-up all of a sudden. 'There's something that might be very important for them to know. And also do you think we should let a doctor see Guy's foot – he's sprained his ankle, I think?'

'Oh dear!' said Aunt Fanny, distressed to see the boy's swollen foot. 'Yes, he ought to have that seen to properly. Who is he? Dear me – there's another of them! Aren't they alike?'

'Twins,' said George. 'I don't know how I

shall be able to tell one from t'other when Guy's bad foot is better.'

'I'm going to ring the police,' said Julian, seeing that his aunt could now only think of Guy's swollen foot. He went off indoors, and they heard him speaking on the telephone. He put it down and came out again.

'The inspector himself is coming,' said Julian. 'Shall I ring the doctor now, Aunt Fanny?'

'Oh yes. His number is in the book,' said his aunt. 'How *did* you get such an ankle, Guy?'

'Mother, you don't seem at all interested in our adventure,' complained George.

'Oh, I am, dear,' said her mother. 'But you do have such a lot, you know. What have you been up to this time?'

But before George could do more than begin, a black police car drew up at the front gate, and the inspector of police got out and marched up to the front door. He knocked extremely loudly on the knocker.

Which, of course, had the immediate result of

bringing George's father hotfoot out of his study in another rage! He flung open the front door.

'Hammering at the door like that! What's the matter? I've a good mind to report you to the police! Oh – er – hm – good afternoon, Inspector. Do come in. Are we expecting you?'

Smiling broadly, the inspector came in. By this time Julian had come back in the house again and greeted him. His uncle went back into his study, rather red in the face, and actually closed the door quietly!

'You wanted me to come along at once, because of something important?' said the inspector. 'What is it?'

The others came into the room now, with Julian's aunt behind them. Julian nodded round at them. 'They're all in this – except my aunt, of course. We've brought something we think may be important. Quite a lot of people were looking for it – but we managed to get hold of it first!'

He put the brown bag on the table. The inspector's eyes went to it at once. 'What is it? What's inside? Stolen goods?'

'Yes – blueprints of some kind, I think. But I don't know what of, of course.'

'Open the bag, my boy! I'll examine them,' said the inspector.

'I can't open it,' said Julian. 'It's locked – and there's no key!'

'Well – we'll soon manage *that*!' said the inspector, and took out a small, strong-looking tool. He forced the lock, and the bag opened. Everyone leaned forward eagerly, even Timmy. What was in the bag?

There was nothing there! Absolutely nothing! Julian groaned in bitter disappointment.

'No wonder it felt so light. It's empty after all. Would you believe it!'

[20]

*The adventure ends –
as it began!*

It was a moment of great disappointment for all
the children. Although they had talked about
the possibility of the bag being empty, everyone
had secretly felt certain that something exciting
would be inside.

The inspector was astonished. He looked
round sharply. 'Where did you get this bag?
What made you think it had stolen goods
inside – and what kind of blueprints were
they?'

'Well – it's rather a long story,' said Julian.

'I'm afraid you'll have to tell it to me,' said
the inspector, taking out his notebook. 'Now –
how did this all begin?'

'Well – it really began with Timmy hurting

his ear and having to wear a cardboard collar,' said George.

The inspector looked most surprised. He turned to Julian. '*You'd* better tell it,' he said. 'I don't want to waste time on cardboard collars!'

George went red and put on a scowl. Julian grinned at her, and began the story, making it as clear and short as he could.

The inspector became more and more interested. He laughed when Julian came to the weird noises and lights.

'They certainly wanted to get rid of you,' he said. 'You were plucky to stay on. Go on – there's something behind all this, that's certain!'

He jotted down the names 'Paul', 'Tom' and 'Jess', the name of the woman. He noted that one man had a drawl. 'Any other clues to them?' he asked.

'Only this,' said Julian and handed his drawing of the crêpe-soled shoe to the inspector.

This was carefully folded and put into the notebook too. 'Might be of use. Might not,' said the inspector. 'You never know!'

He listened intently to the tale of the underground passages, and picked up the bag again.

'I can't understand why it's empty,' he said. 'It isn't really like a crook deliberately to mislead his friends when they know quite well where he is and can get at him whenever they like.' He shook the bag hard. Then he began to examine it very very carefully.

Finally he took out a sharp knife and gently slit the lining at the bottom of the bag. He turned it back.

Something was there – under the lining! Something blue, folded very carefully. Something covered with thousands of minute figures, thousands of lines, thousands of strange little designs!

'Wheeeeeew!' whistled the inspector. 'So the bag's *not* empty, after all! Now what is this? It's a blueprint of some project – but what?'

'My father would know!' said George, at once. 'He's a scientist, you know, Inspector – one of the cleverest in the world. Shall I get him?'

'Yes,' said the inspector, laying out the blue-print on the table. 'Get him at once.'

George flew off and returned with her father, who didn't look very pleased.

'Good afternoon, once more. Sorry to disturb you,' said the inspector. 'But do you happen to know whether this document is of any importance?'

George's father took it up. He ran his eyes over it, and then gave a loud exclamation.

'Why – why – no, it's IMPOSSIBLE! Good heavens, it's – no, no, it can't be! Am I dreaming?'

Everyone gazed at him, surprised and anxious. What did he mean? What could it be, this blueprint?

'Er – it's important then?' said the inspector.

'Important? IMPORTANT? My dear fellow, there are only two of these prints in existence –

and at the moment I have the second one, which I am checking very carefully indeed. Where did this come from? Why – I simply can't believe it! Sir James Lawton-Harrison has the other. There isn't a third!'

'But – but – there must be if you have one here and Sir James has the other!' said the inspector. 'It's obvious there is a third!'

'You're wrong. It isn't obvious!' shouted George's father. 'What *is* obvious is that Sir James hasn't got his! I'll ring him up – this very minute. Astounding! Most disturbing! Bless us all, what will happen next?'

The children did not dare say a word. They were full of astonishment. To think that the blueprint was so important – and that George's father actually had the pair to this one. What was its importance?

They heard George's father shouting into the telephone, evidently angry and disturbed. He slammed it down and came back.

'Yes. Sir James's copy has been stolen – but

it's been kept very hush-hush because of its importance. Good heavens – they never even let *me* know! And to think I spilt a bottle of ink over mine yesterday – gross carelessness. Stolen! A thing like that – stolen out of his safe under his very nose. Now there's only my one copy left!'

'Two,' said the inspector, tapping the copy on the table. 'You're so upset to hear that Sir James's copy has gone that you've forgotten we have it here!'

'Bless us all! Thank goodness! Yes, I *had* forgotten for the moment!' said Uncle Quentin. 'My word, I even forgot to tell Sir James it was here.' He leapt up to go to the telephone again, but the inspector caught his arm.

'No. Don't telephone again. I think we should keep this as quiet as possible.'

'Father – what *is* this a blueprint of?' said George, voicing the thoughts of everyone there, the inspector included.

'This blueprint? I'm certainly not going to tell

you!' said her father. 'It's too big a thing even to speak of to you children – or the inspector either for that matter. It's one of the biggest secrets we have. Here, give it to me.'

The inspector placed his big hand on it at once. 'No. I think I must take it with me, and send a secret messenger to Sir James with it. It wouldn't do to have the only two copies in one place. Why, your house might catch fire and both prints might go up in flames!'

'Take it, then, take it! We can't possibly risk such a thing!' said George's father. He glared round at the children. 'I still don't understand how *you* came to possess it!' he said, looking suddenly amazed.

'Sit down, won't you, and listen to their tale,' said the inspector. 'They've done very well. They haven't finished their story.'

Julian went on with it. The inspector sat up straight when he heard where the three men were – down in the great pit below the Roman camp.

'You saw them go down into that pit?' he said. 'Watched them swing down on the rope? They may be there now!' He glanced at his watch. 'No, they won't. They'll be gone.'

He groaned loudly. 'And to think we might easily have caught three clever rogues. They've slipped through our hands again!'

'They haven't!' said Julian, his voice rising exultantly. 'They're still there!'

'How do you know?' said the inspector.

'Because I pulled up their rope and took it away – look, I've got it round me!' said Julian. 'They can't get out without a rope – and they won't know how to escape any other way. They're still there – waiting for you, Inspector!'

The inspector slapped the table so hard that everyone jumped and the two dogs barked.

'Good work!' he boomed. 'Magnificent! I must go at once and send some men out there. I'll let you know what happens!'

And out he went at a run, the precious blueprint buttoned safely in his pocket. He leapt into the driving seat and the police car roared away at top speed down the lane.

'Whew!' said Julian, flopping back into his chair. 'It's too exciting for words!'

Everyone felt the same, and began to talk at the tops of their voices. Poor Aunt Fanny couldn't make herself heard. But when Joanna came in and asked if anyone wanted anything to eat, they heard her at once!

The doctor came to see Guy's foot, and rebandaged it. 'Rest it for a day or two,' he said. 'It will soon be all right.'

'Well, you'll have to stay here with George and the others, Guy,' said George's mother. 'You can't go excavating in that camp of yours again yet. Harry can stay too. So can Jet.'

The twins beamed. They liked this jolly family, and the adventurous life they seemed to lead. It would be fun to stay with them for a while. They thought it would be even *more* fun, when Joanna arrived with a truly wonderful meal!

'Home-made veal-and-ham-pie! Stuffed to-matoes! And what a salad – what's in it, Joanna? Radishes, cucumber, carrot, beetroot, hard-boiled eggs, tomatoes, peas – Joanna, you're a marvel! What is the pudding?' George asked.

Soon they were all sitting down enjoying themselves, and talking over their adventure. Just as they were finishing, the telephone bell rang. Julian went to answer it. He came back looking thrilled.

'That was the inspector. They've got all three men! When they got to the pit, one of the men called up for help – said some idiot of a boy or some hoaxer must have taken their rope away. So the police – all in plain-clothes, so that of course the three men suspected nothing – the police let down a rope, and up came the men one by one . . .'

'And were arrested as soon as they popped out of the hole, I suppose!' said George, delighted. 'Oh, I wish I'd been there! What a joke!'

'The inspector's awfully pleased with us,' said Julian. 'And so is Sir James Lawton-Harrison too, apparently. We're to get a reward – very hush-hush, though. We mustn't say anything about it. There's to be something for each of us.'

'And for Timmy too?' said George at once.

Julian looked round at Timmy. 'Well, I can see what old Timmy ought to ask for,' he said. 'A new cardboard collar. He's scratching his ear to bits!'

George screamed and rushed to bend over Timmy. She lifted a woebegone face. 'Yes! He's scratched so hard he's made his ear bad again. Oh Timmy! You really are a stupid dog! Mother! Mother! Timmy's messed up his ear again!'

Her mother looked into the room. 'Oh George, what a pity! I *told* you not to take off that collar till his ear was absolutely healed!'

'It's maddening!' said George. 'Now everyone will laugh at him again.'

'Oh no they won't,' said Julian, and he smiled at George's scowling face. 'Cheer up – it's a very peculiar thing, George – this adventure *began* with Timmy and a cardboard collar – and bless me if it hasn't *ended* with Timmy and a cardboard collar. Three cheers for old Timmy!'

Yes – three cheers for old Timmy! Get your ear well before the next adventure, Tim – you really *can't* wear a cardboard collar again!

A complete list of the FAMOUS FIVE
ADVENTURES *by Enid Blyton*

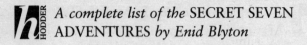

A complete list of the SECRET SEVEN
ADVENTURES *by Enid Blyton*

Ireland's
Seashore

Ireland's Seashore

Lucy Taylor
Emma Nickelsen

The Collins Press

First published in 2018 by
The Collins Press
West Link Park
Doughcloyne
Wilton
Cork
T12 N5EF
Ireland

A CIP record for this book is available from the British Library.

Paperback ISBN: 978-1-84889-341-2

Cover photos
Front: Common starfish
Spine: Beadlet anemone
Back: (above) Furbelows/sea hedgehog, (below) common whelk

Design and typesetting by Fairways Design
Typeset in Gill Sans
Printed in Poland by Białostockie Zakłady Graficzne SA

Contents

Introduction

Flowering Plants — 16

Lichens — 36

Worms | 175

Sponges and Sea Squirts | 186

Urchins and Starfish | 192

Roche's Point Lighthouse at the entrance to Cork Harbour.

Introduction

The Irish Coast

Including the many inlets and islands, Ireland has approximately 7,500km of shoreline. This ranges from exposed rocky shores that receive the full power of the Atlantic's wildest waves to enclosed sea loughs and sheltered sand flats. Ireland's northern latitude means that some Arctic species find a home here, but the warm currents that flow up from the Gulf of Mexico make Irish shores habitable for species also found in southern Europe, the Canaries and the Mediterranean. For a variety of reasons, more and more species from temperate coasts around the world are settling on our shores. We have no endemic species, but we do have a particular set of species, each of which is adapted to life on our shores in its own way.

Historically, our shores have provided food and income for many coastal communities who have fished and harvested shellfish and seaweed. They have also provided wonder for people mesmerised by phosphorescence on a still autumn night, or who find unusual and mystifying objects washed up from across the Atlantic. There are few people who fail to be captivated by the power of an Atlantic storm or by the beauty of the sun setting over a calm ocean.

The strong force of Atlantic waves.

Forces of Nature

Tides

Inhabitants of the intertidal zone on Irish coasts – the area between the high- and low-tide marks – live in an ever-changing environment. Twice in any day they are exposed to the air and at risk of drying out, overheating or being eaten by terrestrial predators. At other times they are covered by metres of salt water and are at the mercy of ocean forces and marine predators, but also immersed in a soup of nutrients and microscopic plankton. Plants and animals that live at the lowest or highest reaches of the tide may only be fully uncovered or covered by the water twice a month.

The difference between high and low tide becomes greater as you move towards the poles. Ireland's northerly position and its openness to the Atlantic Ocean mean that the difference between high and low tide can be up to 5 metres in depth. In gently sloping, shallow inlets, such as Dublin Bay or Tralee Bay, a large area of land is uncovered at low tide.

The height and time of the tide are controlled by the magnetic forces of the moon and the sun. The full daily cycle of the tide is a little more than 24 hours, so the times of high and low tide are different every day. The highest and lowest (spring) tides occur in the days following the new and full moon. In the days following the first and third quarter of the moon, the difference between high and low tide is less dramatic. In addition, because the Earth does not move around the sun in a perfect circle, it is closer at certain times of the year. At the times of the equinoxes, March and September, the combined pull of the moon and the sun create the largest tidal movement.

The movement of the tide is itself a force that can shape the coast and the community of plants and animals that can survive there. In Lough Hyne in west Cork, the tide enters and exits the lough through a narrow channel known as 'the rapids'. As the water is forced in and out, it can reach speeds of 10km per hour, which makes it very difficult for many species to live there. However, for those that can cling on, this rapid movement provides a regular supply of fresh, highly oxygenated water, and carries away sediment and excrement. For some species, such as mussels or kelp, this is the ideal environment.

Waves

Ireland's shoreline is famous for its rocky cliffs and its long, sandy beaches. On the west coast, where the full extent of the Atlantic meets the solid land, these cliffs are at their most spectacular, and the wide, flat beaches absorb the impact of the ocean. On the east coast, the beaches are narrower and carved by the back-and-forth of waves in the enclosed Irish Sea.

Waves originate in the open ocean, and the size and impact of them are affected by the distance that they can travel – the 'reach'. The vast Atlantic allows waves to move without any obstacles that might reduce their energy. They slam into the cliffs of Ireland or crash onto its beaches.

Waves do not just mould our shoreline; they also play a part in dictating the plants and animals that can live on any given shore. The exposure of a shore describes the level of wave energy that reaches it – think of the bare cliffs of Moher as totally exposed. Waves bring oxygen and assist in moving and refreshing water. They also create splash, which keeps some creatures damp enough to survive above the high-tide line. Sheltered shores, however, are more habitable for plants and animals that might be swept away by strong waves. Where there is less exposure, particles can settle to the ground. This is good for deposit-feeding animals, and it allows sand and sediment to build.

Ocean Currents

Looking at a globe, it is sometimes surprising to see just how far north Ireland is. Across the Atlantic, Newfoundland and the coast of Canada can experience extremes of weather that we are completely unfamiliar with. The currents that flow anticlockwise around the North Atlantic bring warm water up our coast. This gives us our temperate climate, and also brings with it species that are at home in the Canaries, Portugal and the Mediterranean. Many of these southern species reach their northern limit on Irish shores, where they overlap with northern species whose range extends up into the Arctic.

Coastal Habitats

Rocky Shores

Rocky shores are the most stable of shore types – they are unlikely to be eroded or changed in the lifetime of most seashore creatures. Because many rocky shores are rugged and craggy, there is a range of habitats and a large surface area for plants and animals to occupy. Crevices, the undersides of rocks and shady rock pools can be cool, damp places to shelter, hide and live. Flat rock surfaces and sunny rock pools are more appealing for species that like heat and are not at risk of being eaten during the day. Many rocky shores are a treasure trove of seaweeds, crabs, snails, barnacles, anemones, fish, sponges and starfish.

The craggy limestone of the west coast can provide shelter for hardy plants and animals.

Rocky Shores provide a stable surface for many plants and animals to live on.

In addition to the range of physical forms and types of habitat within a rocky shore, the exposure to air, light, temperature, fresh water, predators, competition and wave action all determine the distribution of living organisms along a rocky shore. Each species has developed its own way of coping with these challenges.

Very few animals can survive on the more exposed shores of the west coast.

Rocky shores can be divided into several zones. These extend from the land that receives only splashes of seawater from waves at high tide, to the extreme low-water mark below which the tide never falls. Each zone is dominated by a different group of plants or animals.

The rocky shore can be divided into three main zones: the high shore/splash zone/supralittoral zone, the mid shore/eulittoral/intertidal zone and the low shore/sublittoral fringe zone.

Exposed shore

Sheltered shore

High Shore
High Mid Shore
Low Mid Shore

Low Shore

Rocky shore zonation

The high shore, or the supralittoral zone, is usually only dampened by sea spray but becomes covered in seawater during storms and extremely high tides. Organisms here must endure hot, cold, salty and dry conditions. Therefore, only a few resilient species live here. The high shore zone is dominated by lichens. At the lower edge, you start to find periwinkles and the tough brown channel wrack.

The mid shore, or the eulittoral zone, is often broad. It is uncovered at low tide and immersed at high tide. Depending on the steepness of the shore, you might notice distinct bands of organisms creating sub-zones (high mid shore and low mid shore) caused by the amount of time spent in/out of the water. Generally, the mid-shore zone is dominated by wracks, barnacles, limpets and some mussels.

The low shore, or the sublittoral fringe, is only exposed to the air at low-water spring tides. This zone is dominated by kelps and red seaweed. While you cannot always access the sublittoral fringe without getting wet, it's worth it. This zone is rich in species not found in higher zones.

It is interesting to consider how the different dominant species have adapted to life at a particular shore height or zone. Species of the high shore have adapted to the possibility of drying out and to the possible stresses of heat, cold and fresh water so they can live in areas that are uninhabitable for others. Low-shore species prefer more stable conditions, adapting instead to deal with increased competition.

Pebble Beaches

Pebble or shingle beaches are a very difficult place to live. Even in fairly sheltered areas, the movement of waves and tides moves the pebbles or stones around so seaweeds cannot attach themselves and very few animals can survive between the stones.

In spite of this, some pebble shores can be a good place to go beachcombing. There is often a line of washed-up seaweeds, and you might find interesting shells, mermaid's purses and bits and

Constantly moving pebble beaches are a difficult place to live.

Only humans and burrowing animals are common on sandy shores.

bobs tangled in the weed. Even though these shores are less rich in living seashore creatures than other areas, washed-up seaweed is a food source for many insects, which can then attract birds.

Sandy Beaches

Even though sandy beaches are more appealing to people than other shore types, they are difficult for many plants and animals to live on. Unless they can burrow into the sand, they are in constant danger of being swept away. Some animals spend their entire life buried in the sand, while others are able to dig into the sand to hunt or hide.

Sandy beaches are often great places to search for shells. The empty shells will give you clues to the types of animal that live under the sand. You might also notice the entrances to the burrows of worms and other animals that live under the ground.

Mudflats and Estuaries

Muddy shores usually occur in estuaries where mud from the land is washed down a river. As the river reaches the sea, its flow is reduced, and the particles sink to the ground, forming mudflats. Grains on these shores are usually much finer than on sandy beaches, and water gets trapped in the tiny spaces between them, so these shores are often constantly waterlogged and difficult to walk on.

The combination of the tiny particles, the constantly shifting mud and the contrast between the salty ocean and the fresh river

Mudflats at low tide.

make this a challenging place for many species to live. For example, very few seaweeds can survive here, but you might find a high abundance of sea lettuce (see page 61), horned wrack (see page 83), and dwarf eelgrass (see page 22), which can grow happily without competition from the larger seaweeds. There is also a small number of shellfish that can occur in high densities on these shores as the mud is full of nutrients that are absent from sandy shores. These plants and animals often become food for the many migrating and resident birds that visit our mudflats.

Just under the surface of many mudflats, there is often a layer of heavy black sediment. This can be a bit smelly, but is not necessarily polluted. You might notice shells that are usually white becoming blackened on these shores. This black layer has no oxygen, so it is difficult for some species to live in.

Dunes

Dunes form a familiar backdrop to many of Ireland's most beautiful beaches. They are formed by plants that grow on the beach and allow sand to build up between their leaves and roots. Dunes are important for the plants and animals that live in them, and act as a buffer between the force of the ocean and the solid land. They are also a culturally important feature as so many people enjoy exploring dunes and appreciate them for their beauty.

Unlike muddy earth, dunes can constantly shift and rebuild. In fact, this constant movement is what makes them so special

Dunes are formed when plants trap sand between their leaves and roots.

and different from the land. If dunes are hemmed in by walls and solid structures, they can become waterlogged and muddy and will eventually cease to be dunes. Where there is a problem with erosion, many communities now prefer to plant dune-forming grasses that allow dunes to build and to slow erosion with their strong, tangled roots.

Caring for our coasts

Here are a few points to remember when you visit the coast:

- Be careful not to crush delicate animals.
- If you turn over rocks or stones, put them back as you found them, and be gentle.
- Don't take animals home – they won't survive.
- Don't leave any litter or food waste.
- Don't remove animals from rock pools and put them in fresh water. If you have a bucket of salt water, don't leave the animals in it for long. Return them to where they came from.
- We all love shells, but don't remove excessive amounts from the shore – remember that a hermit crab might be looking for one to move into!

The Plastic Problem

Bits and pieces washed up on shores following storms or high tides have long been a feature of our shorelines. Driftwood, seeds and seaweed are natural flotsam that are a part of the seashore ecosystem. Some items, such as the remains of dead marine animals, may be quite unpleasant, but are not necessarily unnatural. Other items, such as sea glass (glass weathered by the sea) and wooden or metal items are, technically, litter, but can be exciting to find, can provide habitats for marine creatures and can even add to beautiful beach scenes. Overall, however, marine litter is increasing in volume and the majority of this is plastic. As all of the plastic that we have ever produced still exists, plastic pollution on the shore and at sea is a rapidly growing problem.

Plastic is now found on even the remotest shores, in the deepest ocean and in the stomachs and organs of many marine creatures. Birds build nests with it, causing some chicks to become entangled and unable to leave the nest. Many animals mistakenly eat bits of plastic, which blocks their digestive systems so that they become malnourished.

It can be very depressing to visit a beautiful shore only to realise that it has been tainted by human waste. However, you can do your bit by picking up litter that you find on the shore and disposing of it safely, by reducing the amount of disposable plastic items that you buy and use, and by ensuring that you are careful when you picnic or visit the beach that none of your waste gets blown or washed away.

Marine litter, including discarded fishing gear, can damage and kill marine animals.

Other threats to the seashore

Even though our coastline appears to be wild and rugged, it is also a very delicate ecosystem. Threats to seashore plants and animals include:

- Trampling by beachgoers
- Pollution from sewage, agricultural run-off, industry, and chemicals such as antifouling paints and fuels
- Damage to the seabed from moorings and boat anchors
- Irresponsible fishing and harvesting

- Litter and pollution, both from the land and washing in from the sea
- Rising sea levels and more powerful storms.

One other problem for plants and animals that inhabit the mid and high shore is a reduction in the space available for them in areas where the shoreline is modified by us. While this is necessary to protect certain towns and villages, it can cause problems for some coastal species. For example, the dwarf eelgrass (see page 22) only survives in very shallow water. This means that eelgrass beds move and change in response to changes in the seabed, the sea level and water clarity or salinity.

If the coast is modified with walls, drainage pipes, walkways or other artificial structures, the seagrass may run out of space to move to, or the environment might change in such a way that it becomes uninhabitable for the eelgrass. This can have a knock-on effect on birds that graze on the grass, on the animals that live among the blades and roots, and on the water as the seagrass bed may be unable to trap particles and keep the water clear or use up nutrients present in the water.

For this reason, it is important that we strike a compromise between developing infrastructure and allowing natural systems to evolve or remain in their own way.

How to use this book

When exploring our seashore, you will encounter a huge variety of creatures. Seashore species belong to a long list of *Phyla* or biologically distinct groupings. Many of these you won't find on land. Each group has some unique features, which make it stand out from the rest. In this book, species are in ten broad groups. For simplicity, some of these groups comprise several *Phyla*, which may be more difficult to decipher.

Now, have a look around the shore and pick out a creature that you would like to know a little more about. Once you have found something, the following list of questions will help guide you to the right chapter.

1. It has a shell and...

It has legs → Go to Crabs, Barnacles and their Relatives

It looks like this and has no legs → Go to Snails, Mussels and their Relatives

It is snail-like → Go to Snails and Relatives

It is tube-like → Go to Worms

It is rounded with bristles or spikes → Go to Urchins and Starfish

If it has two opposite shells – is it attached to a hard surface?

Yes, by threads → Go to Snails and Relatives

Yes, by a foot → Go to Crabs and Relatives

No, it lives in sand or mud → Go to Snails and Relatives

It has a pyramidal shell, which is...

Comprised of one piece → Go to Snails and Relatives

Comprised of several pieces → Go to Crabs and Relatives

2. It is jelly-like and...

It is free-floating ➤ Go to Jellyfish and Other Stingers

It moves like a slug ➤ Go to Snails and Relatives

It is round, attached to the substrate and...

It has tentacles ➤ Go to Jellyfish and Relatives

It has two openings ➤ Go to Sponges and Sea Squirts

3. It is worm-like and...

It is wriggly ➤ Go to Worms and Relatives

It is made of sand ➤ Go to Worms and Relatives

It has small fins and a distinctive face ➤ Go to Fish

4. It is star-shaped

 ➤ Go to Starfish and Relatives

5. It is fast-swimming and fleshy

 → Go to Fish

6. It is spread across rocks and...

It is soft and has pores → Go to Sponges and Similar

It is above high tide and is flaky → Go to Lichens

It is pink and stone-like in pools → Go to Seaweeds

7. It is plant-like and...

It grows in sand or soil above the high tide → Go to Flowering Plants

It is slippery and translucent → Go to Seaweeds

It is pink and crispy → Go to Seaweeds

8. It has been washed up and does not resemble any of the above

 → Go to Flotsam & Jetsam

Flowering Plants

Coastal plants need to be tough. They get a much harder time than inland varieties. One reason for this is salt. At the coast, there is salt in the air, in the soil and in the water. Coastal plants need to be well adapted to live in salty conditions. Another challenge facing coastal plants is dryness. It may seem strange to call the coast a dry environment, but soil on beaches and cliffs does not retain water like inland clay soils. Therefore, coastal plants need to ensure that they do not dry out. Finally, another factor for which some coastal plants must be adapted is the constant movement of the sand that they live on.

To survive in this harsh environment, many of the plants that grow on our shores have similar features. To withstand the salty conditions, many coastal plants have thick, fleshy leaves with a waxy texture. These are also designed to store water, which helps them to survive the dry conditions. Other adaptations to prevent drying out include having curled leaves or a hairy texture. Finally, many coastal plants have complex, web-like root systems, which bind the sand and prevent it from blowing away in the wind.

Many plants have been foraged for food and medicine for centuries. While the number of plants that are eaten nowadays has decreased dramatically, most of the plants in this book have a historic culinary or medicinal use.

Coastal plants not only brighten up our shores, many are important for creating habitats and maintaining the structure of our coastlines. In particular, dune-forming plants protect the coast from erosion.

Overall, they are beautiful, tough, sometimes tasty, full of stories and vital in protecting our coasts! Pretty fantastic little things.

Lyme grass leaves are flat.

Flower heads are rounded and spiky.

Lyme Grass

Irish Taithneán   **Latin** *Leymus arenarius*

Size 60–120cm tall
Distribution Sand and shingle in newly forming dunes
Similar species Sand couch, marram grass

Lyme grass grows above the high-tide line at the edge of sand dunes. It has broad blue-green leaves with pointy tips. These leaves do not curl inwards like the marram grass (see page 20). Lyme grass produces tall, spiked flower heads between July and August. These flower heads are not flattened like sand couch flowers (see page 19).

Lyme grass is important in developing dune systems (embryo dunes), along with sand couch. It gathers sand in its root system and catches sand being carried in the wind, helping to form dunes. However, the faster-growing marram grass usually takes over as the sand builds up and the dune increases in size.

Sand couch leaves are flat and curl inwards at the edges.

Flower heads are flattened.

Sand Couch

Irish Broimfhéar gainimh   **Latin** *Elytrigia juncea*
Size Up to 50cm
Distribution Sand and shingle in newly forming dunes
Similar species Marram grass, Lyme grass

Sand couch grows just above the high-tide line in loose sand and shingle. It has waxy blue-green leaves which are slightly inward-curling along the edges. It produces flowering stems with flattened flower heads. This distinguishes it from Lyme grass and marram grass, which both have more three-dimensional flower heads.

Similar to Lyme grass, sand couch is important in the formation of new dunes by capturing and retaining sand in its root system. It is quickly outcompeted by marram grass and smothered by the increased sand deposition once the dunes become larger, so you'll find it along the edge of the dune closest to the sea.

Marram Grass

Irish Muiríneach **Latin** *Ammophila arenaria*

Size Up to 120cm tall
Distribution Large sand dunes all over Ireland
Similar species Lyme grass

Marram grass is one of the most common sand dune plants. Its leaves are grey-green, with a waxy surface. The underside is slightly hairy and curls inwards to prevent water loss – an adaptation to survive in windy, dry conditions. In July and August, marram grass produces upright, thick, spiked flower heads which are greyish green or yellow. These flower heads are not flattened like those of sand couch (see page 19).

You might associate marram grass with being scratched and poked when climbing sand dunes. Even though this makes it seem like a nuisance, marram grass is a vital dune species. The roots can grow many metres long as they reach downwards in search of water, and widthways, allowing the plant to spread. These roots hold the dune system together while the tall leaves catch sand from the wind, helping the dunes to grow. Planting marram grass is an increasingly popular way to prevent erosion along storm-beaten coastlines.

Spiky marram grass leaves curl inwards.

Marram grass often covers the sea edge of dunes.

Cord grass colonises mudflats and estuaries.

Cord Grass

Irish Spairtíneach ghallda **Latin** *Spartina anglica*

Size Up to 1m tall
Distribution Mudflats and estuaries
Similar species Marram grass

Cord grass shoots are very tough and spiky to touch. The shoots can be as wide as a drinking straw. From this base, blades of about 0.5cm wide grow. They narrow to a sharp point at the tip. Each blade has a fold line running down the centre as if it has been ironed and unfolded. Cord grass grows in mudflat areas, just below the high-tide mark.

Cord grass is an invasive species. It grows in very dense stands and can form small islands as it gathers sediment and raises the level of the mudflat that it grows in. Originally, people thought this was very useful as it could reclaim land and stabilise dunes. However, cord grass grows quite aggressively and reduces the area available for eelgrass (see page 22) and for bivalves that burrow in the mud, such as edible cockles (see page 163). This, in turn, limits the amount of food available for many grazing and wading birds.

Dwarf Eelgrass

Irish Miléarach **Latin** *Zostera noltii*
Size < 20cm
Distribution Sheltered sandy bays

Dwarf eelgrass grows between the tide marks in sheltered sandy bays and estuaries. The grass blades float upright when the tide is in and then flop over when the tide goes out. Dense 'beds' of eelgrass appear in the summer months, but are grazed by migrating seabirds in the autumn. The tangled roots remain underground all year.

Eelgrasses are thought to be important in reducing coastal erosion. They grow better where the water is unpolluted. The roots and leaves of dwarf eelgrass provide shelter and structure for other animals to inhabit.

If you find much longer blades of eelgrass washed up on the shore following stormy weather, these belong to the larger subtidal eelgrass, *Zostera marina*.

The larger eelgrass (Zostera marina) grows underwater, but can get washed up on beaches.

Dwarf eelgrass beds become dense in the summer.

Spiky sea holly grows on sand dunes. The tiny flowers are bright blue.

Sea Holly

Irish Cuileann trá **Latin** *Eryngium maritimum*

Size < 50cm tall

Distribution Dunes and sandy shores

Sea holly stands apart from many of the other seashore plants with its tough, spiky leaves, powder-blue colour and blue flowers that appear in little pom-poms throughout the summer. Sea holly leaves are not glossy. They have white veins and a white border. Despite its name and the shape of the leaves, it is not related to the holly bush found in woodlands and hedgerows. In fact, sea holly belongs to the same family as carrots and cow parsley.

Its roots are long, which helps this intrepid plant to stay anchored on sandy or shale shores where the ground is always moving. The fleshy roots were traditionally boiled with sugar to make sweets that are reported to be good for giving energy. The young shoots are also edible.

Orache can grow abundantly above the high-tide line on sandy beaches.

Frosted orache has a distinctive sandy texture.

Orache

Irish Eilifleog **Latin** *Atriplex* spp.

Size Spreads to 30cm
Distribution Sand and shingle high shore

Orache (pronounced 'orak') grows above the high-tide line on sandy and shingle shores. The leaves are diamond-shaped and silvery green in colour, with a wavy edge. There are a few different species of orache, many of which sprawl across beaches with tough red or yellow stems.

One of the easiest to distinguish is frosted orache, which has a powdery coating that gives the leaves their characteristic frosty-morning appearance. Frosted orache flowers between July and September, producing tiny green or yellow clustered flowers at points where leaves and the stem meet. Populations are often small and sporadically distributed and are less commonly found on the west coast of Ireland.

Other common varieties of orache have similar dagger-shaped leaves, but do not have the frosty coating.

Sea Beet

Irish Laíon na trá **Latin** *Beta vulgaris maritima*

Size < 100cm
Distribution Widespread on shingle shores

Sea beet grows on shingle beaches, coastal rocks and cliffs, and along sea walls and salt marshes. It can be either upright or sprawling. The leaves are dark green, triangular, fleshy and glossy. Between July and September, sea beet plants produce green, leafy spire-shaped flowers. These flowers then give way to corky fruits, which can float and are dispersed by the tide.

The familiar cultivated sugar beet and beetroot are variants of sea beet. They all have a sugary, rounded taproot. Sea beet is sometimes referred to as wild spinach, and is popular among foragers for its tasty leaves and roots.

Leaves are glossy and smooth.

Sea beet is hardy enough to grow on sand and shingle shores.

Sea rocket grows on sand and helps to form dunes.

Flowers are delicate and pale.

Sea Rocket

Irish Cearrbhacán mara   **Latin** *Cakile maritima*

Size 15–45cm tall
Distribution Sand or shingle shores

Sea rocket grows high up on sand or shingle shores. The leaves are irregularly shaped, like salad rocket leaves, but they are fleshy and glossy. Sea rocket can grow quite upright, or it can sprawl along the ground. There is usually quite a lot of bare stem. The flowers appear between June and August. They are 2cm across and have four very pale lilac petals.

Sea rocket has disappeared from many beaches where it gets trampled by visitors. However, it can reappear after many years because the seeds sometimes remain dormant in the ground.

Rock Samphire

Irish Craobhraic **Latin** *Crithmum maritimum*
Size < 50cm
Distribution Rocky coasts

Rock samphire, not to be confused with the similarly named marsh samphire, grows on rocky shores, cliffs and shingle beaches. It has fleshy stems and leaves. Each leaf is divided twice into narrow segments. Between June and August, flat-topped yellow flowers appear.

Up until the 19th century, the collection of rock samphire for food from shores and cliffs was a very common, and sometimes dangerous, practice. It was even referred to by William Shakespeare in *King Lear*: 'Half-way down hangs one that gathers samphire; dreadful trade!' Whilst it is less commonly used in cooking these days, rock samphire is known for its aromatic flavour.

Rock samphire can grow in very exposed places.
Leaves and stems are fleshy.

Flowers are pale and
appear in summer.

Rock sea-spurrey has fleshy, tubular leaves and delicate pink flowers.

Rock Sea-spurrey

Irish Cabróis na gcloch   **Latin** *Spergularia rupicola*
Size 5–15cm tall
Distribution Coastal rocks and cliffs

Rock sea-spurrey often lives high up on rocks and cliffs above the shoreline. It is a small plant – no more than 15cm tall. Its flowers are small with five petals and are a uniform pink colour. There are ten bright yellow stamens inside each flower. The fleshy, pointed leaves grow in rings (whorls) around the stem and are hairy with a slightly sticky texture.

While this species is common on Irish coasts, the Irish population of rock sea-spurrey is important in a European context as over 25 per cent of the European population occurs in Ireland alone.

Bird's-foot Trefoil

Irish Crobh éin **Latin** *Lotus corniculatus*

Size < 60cm
Distribution Widespread
Similar species Kidney vetch

The hardy bird's-foot trefoil is widespread throughout Ireland on the coast and in grasslands and hedgerows. Between June and September, it produces bright yellow flowers similar to those of a pea plant, often with little streaks of red on the petals. The plant tends to creep or sprawl along the ground. It is an important plant for pollinating insects, such as bees and butterflies.

Bird's-foot trefoil is one of about 70 common names for *Lotus corniculatus*. Others include 'bacon and eggs', 'crow toes' and 'God-Almighty's thumb and finger', all referring to the shape or colour of the flower or seed pods. The plant was often associated with evil in folklore because its black seed pods were thought to resemble the devil's claws.

Flowers are bright yellow (above left) and Bird's-foot trefoil can grow on rocky shores (top right).

Seed pods look like a bird's claws.

Kidney vetch flowers appear in woolly flower heads.

Kidney vetch leaves.

Kidney Vetch

Irish Méara Muire   **Latin** *Anthyllis vulneraria*
Size 10–40cm tall
Distribution Coastal rocks and cliffs
Similar species Bird's-foot trefoil

Kidney vetch can be distinguished from other plants by its overall hairiness. The leaves and stems are silky and silvery green. Flowering occurs between June and September. Each flower head bears many small, yellow, kidney-shaped flowers which are bedded in a woolly cushion. If you look closely at the flower heads you will notice that while one part is in flower, the other part will either only be coming into bloom or will have ripening seeds. This prolongs the flowering season of each plant.

The flowers are an important food source for many insects, especially the rare small blue butterfly, Ireland's smallest butterfly, which relies entirely on kidney vetch for food.

The Latin name, *vulneraria*, means 'healer of wounds', which refers to the traditional belief that kidney vetch had healing properties.

Thrift/Sea Pink

Irish Rabhán **Latin** *Armeria maritima*

Size 15–40cm
Distribution Widespread on coastal rocks and salt marshes

Thrift grows on rocks, cliffs and salt marshes. It forms cushiony mounds of narrow, fleshy leaves. The flowers grow on long, straight stems. The flowers are pink, small, scented and rounded, with papery scales at the base.

Between May and August, thrift flowers profusely, creating beautiful drifts of pink along our coastlines. It can be very abundant, sometimes covering small islands in bouncy mats of foliage. Thrift is perennial, meaning that each plant can live for many years.

Top left: Sea pinks create blooms of papery pink flowers. Top right: Sea pink flower clusters.
Bottom: Sea pinks form cushiony mounds.

Sea campion forms leafy cushions.

An entire island covered with Sea Campion

Sea Campion

Irish Coireán mara   **Latin** *Silene uniflora*

Size < 30cm
Distribution Cliffs and shingle beaches

Sea campion grows on cliffs, sand dunes, rocks and shingle beaches. The plants are low-growing and form cushions of broad, hairless, waxy leaves. Between May and August, sea campion produces pure white or slightly pink blooms. Petals emerge from an inflated 'bladder' which may be either green, yellow or purple, and lined with red veins. Male and female flowers are produced on separate plants.

Sea campion was once called 'Dead man's bells' and was never picked or brought into the home, for fear of tempting death. Perhaps it was more the act of picking the plant from dangerous cliff ledges that was tempting death, than the plant itself.

Sea Mayweed

Irish Lus Bhealtaine **Latin** *Tripleurospermum maritimum*
Size 60cm tall; flowers < 4cm across
Distribution Sand or shingle shores

The daisy-like flowers of the sea mayweed appear between April and October. They have many long white petals and a yellow centre. The leaves are delicate and feathered and are a smooth, glossy green. The plant creeps along, low to the ground in some areas but more upright in others. It looks like other daisy plants, but can be told apart by the leaves. The ox-eye daisy, which has a similar flower, grows more inland and has short, spear-shaped leaves that grow close to the stem.

Sea mayweed is also called 'Sea chamomile' due to its chamomile-like scent when crushed. It is used in traditional medicine in similar ways to chamomile, by apparently soothing skin and reducing inflammation.

Sea mayweed has daisy-like flowers and delicate leaves.

Sea aster has ragged lilac flowers, which appear in late summer.

Leaves are elongated.

Sea Aster

Irish Luibh bhléine **Latin** *Aster tripolium*

Size < 80cm
Distribution Widespread on saltmarshes

Sea aster is a common inhabitant of salt marshes. It is a tall, fleshy plant with oblong leaves. Lilac or mauve daisy-like flowers with yellow centres usually appear between July and October. However, sea aster varies in appearance and flowering time depending on local geography and habitat. Sometimes the lilac petals are absent or sparse, leaving only the central yellow button-shape. It grows abundantly from the lower marsh to the high-tide mark. It also grows on sea cliffs, coastal rocks and along tidal rivers. Sea aster can be annual, biennial (two years) or a short-lived perennial.

Sea Sandwort

Irish Gaineamhlus mara **Latin** *Honckenya peploides*
Size 5–15cm tall
Distribution Sandy, stony and gravel high shore

Sea sandwort is a fleshy, creeping plant that is adapted to living on unstable ground, such as sand and gravel. It creates distinctive mats and is easily recognisable by its symmetrically arranged triangular leaves which appear in neat, opposite pairs up the stems.

As a halophyte, meaning it is salt-loving, sea sandwort has waxy, fleshy leaves that prevent it from becoming dehydrated and that can withstand the harsh effects of salty air and water.

Sea sandwort is important in maintaining and creating sand dunes. It grows at the very edges of dunes, stabilising and fertilising the ground. By doing so, it creates habitats for other dune plants, which have higher nutritional needs. As these other plants grow, sea sandwort is forced to move ever closer to the water as it is outcompeted by other plants. In this manner, it allows dunes to grow.

Sea sandwort creeps along sandy shores. It has tiny, fleshy, triangular leaves.

Lichens

Lichens are characteristic of Irish seashores. From a distance, they are a diagram of where the tide reaches on a certain shore, as they often appear in very distinct bands depending on whether they can tolerate only the spray from the sea, or can survive being covered by the tide completely.

Each species of lichen is actually a pairing of algae and fungi. The tiny algae live internally and create food by photosynthesis (using carbon dioxide, water and sunlight to make sugars and release oxygen). The fungi live externally and provide structure and shelter for the algae. This is called a symbiotic relationship – each benefits from the other. It is possible for the algae to live independently, but the fungi have no way of making their own food. Each separate lichen has its own species of fungus, but the algae can be the same in many types of lichen. To reproduce, the fungus releases spores into the air. These spores must combine with suitable algae to form a new lichen. Some species can also re-form if part of an existing lichen breaks off.

The main body of a lichen is called the thallus. This can grow in one of three ways: completely encrusted onto the rock and impossible to remove; leafy but still encrusted tightly to the rock; horizontally upright, or hanging from a central point that is attached to the rock (more like a typical plant).

Lichens grow on all rocky shores of Ireland except where the rock breaks up easily. They grow very slowly, so they need a stable surface that is unlikely to move. Lichens can live for 50 years or more. In the intertidal zone, below the high-tide mark, they must compete with other seaweeds and barnacles for space on the rock. This is one reason why lichens are less common in the intertidal zone. Higher up in the splash zone, you might come across large areas inhabited exclusively by lichens.

Generally, they are very sensitive to pollutants, which they absorb from the air. This means that they are a useful indicator of pollution locally. The abundance of delicate lichens on our coasts may be a sign of good air quality. Lichens are also a food source for some grazing animals.

Sea ivory grows alongside other lichens.

Sea Ivory

Irish Eabhar mara   **Latin** *Ramalina cuspidata/siliquosa*
Size < 5cm tall
Distribution Splash zone of rocky shores

There are two species of sea ivory, which are not easy to tell apart. They are both a pale grey-green colour and grow in tufts high up on rocky shores. They can occur together or in slightly separate bands. They are brittle or spiky to touch and have a dried-out, twiggy appearance.

Both species occur all over Ireland. In some areas, they are common enough to form part of the diet of sheep or goats. They are sensitive to air pollution, so Ireland's clean Atlantic air provides a good habitat. They look similar to species that grow on trees and rocks in woodland areas.

Yellow Leafy Lichen

Irish Léicean duilleach flannbhuí **Latin** *Xanthoria* spp.

Size < 1mm high
Distribution Splash zone of rocky shores

This yellow leafy lichen grows in large, bumpy, bright yellow or orange patches just above the high-tide mark on rocky shores. It clings tightly to the rock surface, but grows in a branching pattern like a miniature lava flow. Each branch is only about 1mm wide. The tips of these branches are rounded and often overlap each other. Yellow leafy lichen often overgrows black tar lichen (see page 44), forming strikingly contrasting patches of colour.

Notice the fruiting bodies, like discs.

Yellow leafy lichen growing over other lichens.

The deeply furrowed surface of orange sea lichen.

Orange Sea Lichen

Irish Léicean flannbhuí **Latin** *Caloplaca* spp.

Size < 1mm high
Distribution Splash zone of rocky shores

There are two species of orange sea lichen, which are easy to confuse. Both are a striking colour and occur close to the high-tide mark on rocky shores. The first, *Caloplaca marina*, grows in fragmented patches of bright orange granules, each of which grows to about 1mm across. The second, *Caloplaca thallincola,* grows in a circular pattern that looks as if it has exploded onto the rock. This disc is deeply furrowed into many rounded ridges. Both species grow high on rocky shores, but *C. thallincola* prefers more sheltered locations where it is protected from direct waves.

Orange sea lichen is grazed by periwinkles and limpets.
Another species, *Caloplaca verruculifera,* grows in a similar circular pattern, but is a pale green or yellow colour.

Black Shields

Irish Scála dubh **Latin** *Tephromela atra*
Distribution Splash zone of rocky shores
Similar species *Ochrolechia parella*

Black shields lichen is actually a grey-green or creamy-white lichen that appears on rocks around the high-tide mark as a cracked crust. It is called black shields because of the black fruits that appear within the pale patches. Patches of black shields appear like a dried, cracked desert landscape in miniature.

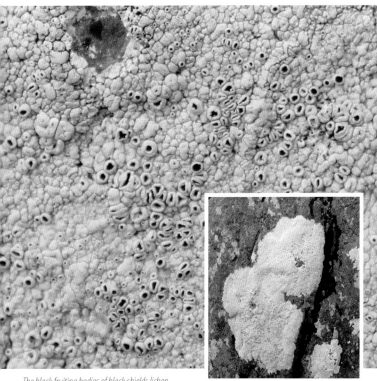

The black fruiting bodies of black shields lichen.

This lichen forms a thick white coating on rocks.

Ochrolechia parella

Distribution Splash zone of rocky shores
Similar species Black shields lichen

Ochrolechia parella creates a thick coating on rocks (and sometimes trees). It is white or light grey and forms large oval or oblong patches wherever it has the chance. There is often a bright white edge around these patches. Little fruiting bodies grow up out of the lichen. These are slightly funnel-shaped and are usually a similar colour to the rest of the lichen. They give the lichen a warty appearance.

This is one of the most common Irish coastal lichens. It forms the 'white zone' above the high-tide line on all suitable coasts. It thrives in bright sunlight on sandstone rocks.

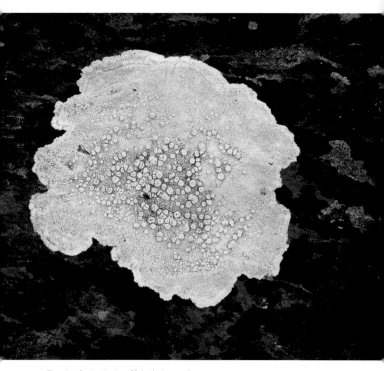

The white fruiting bodies of Ochrolechia parella.

A rough periwinkle grazing on black tufted lichen.

Black tufted lichen forms moss-like patches.

Black Tufted Lichen

Irish Léicean dosach dubh **Latin** *Lichina pygmaea/confinis*
Size < 1cm high
Distribution Mid to high on rocky shores

Black tufted lichen looks just like it sounds – it grows in patches of short tufts that are dark brown or black. You might find it growing amongst seaweeds or together with black tar lichen (see page 44). It is widespread around Irish coasts, especially on sheltered shores where there is good light. There are actually two species of black tufted lichen, but they are very difficult to tell apart.

Black tar lichen can coat entire shorelines.

Black Tar Lichen

Irish Léicean dubh tarra   **Latin** *Verrucaria maura*

Distribution Below the highest tide marks on rocky shores
Similar species Green tar lichen

Black tar lichen creates the distinctive black band between the tide marks on many of Ireland's rocky shores and cliffs. It is extremely common and widespread, especially on the more exposed Atlantic shores. It forms a coating on the rock face as if someone had spilled a tin of paint or tar and let it dry. It is surprising to think of it as a living thing.

Black tar lichen grows relatively quickly, so it can tolerate being grazed by periwinkles and limpets. Higher up the shore, it is sometimes overgrown by the yellow leafy lichen (see page 39).

Green Tar Lichen

Irish Léicean glas tarra **Latin** *Verrucaria mucosa*

Size Patches < 30cm
Distribution Mid to low rocky shores
Similar species Black tar lichen

Green tar lichen can be a striking bottle green or a paler olive colour. It has a smooth texture and is almost oily looking. Patches can be quite large. There may be a whitish border. Green tar lichen is particularly common on exposed shores. This could be because other species cannot survive, so there is more space for it to grow. Green tar lichen is also absent from silty shores where the water is murky, and from shaded areas.

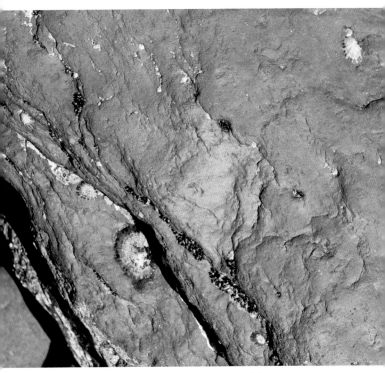

Green tar lichen is sometimes the only thing that can survive on exposed shores.

Flotsam and Jetsam

There's something irresistible about the treasures that are left behind as the tide goes out. Not only children find joy in collecting shells. The wonder of searching a shoreline for items that have travelled across the sea, or the remains of unseen creatures, lasts through adulthood. Often, amongst the seaweed and empty shells, there are some surprising and delightful finds.

Seeds, sea glass and driftwood are common in the flotsam and jetsam that the waves deposit. These items may have travelled thousands of miles across the ocean. These can act as rafts for travelling creatures. They often become more beautiful as the ocean smooths, bleaches and moulds them. There is a story that Columbus found sea beans on the coast of Galway and guessed that there must be land across the Atlantic. He noted in his diary that people of 'strange appearance' had washed up in Galway on floating logs; these could possibly have been Inuit washed across the Atlantic. The possibilities of what you might find stranded on the Irish coast are endless!

Items such as children's toys, known by some as 'beach heroes', occasionally fall off shipping containers in large quantities and become quirky collector's items. They can also give us insights into ocean currents and movements. Sea glass — pieces of ordinary glass that have been moulded and frosted by the force of the ocean — are sometimes called 'mermaid's tears' and are collected by many for their beauty, and as a material for crafts. Some people might even remember the illegal shipment of cocaine that was lost

Beach hero

overboard near west Cork in 2007. While nobody made their fortune from that contraband, there's always the possibility of finding a lump of ambergris. Also known as whale vomit, this is a very valuable substance in the perfume industry that sometimes washes up on our shores. We can't show you what it looks like, because we've never found any!

Many of the bits and bobs that you find on the seashore are bryozoans. These tiny animals come in many shapes and sizes and usually live in colonies. Some of these colonies are made up of identical individuals, but in other colonies, the individuals have different roles or functions within the colony. In this case, some individuals are a different shape or form, depending on their role (such as feeding or attaching to a surface). The individuals (zooids) are often too small to see without a microscope, but sometimes you can make out the shape of each zooid, and even the hairy tentacles that they use to trap microscopic food. There are many different species of bryozoans, but they are almost all marine.

Some of the most exciting treasures to uncover from entangled weed are mermaid's purses. These little packages are the egg cases laid by members of the shark family (skates, rays, catfish, etc.). Sharks have an amazing range of parenting techniques – some give birth to live young in a similar way to mammals; some have eggs that hatch internally, so that the juveniles live unattached inside their mother for a time (in these species it isn't uncommon for juveniles to eat each other); and others deposit tough mermaid's purses among kelp, deep-sea coral or other protective structures. These mermaid's purses contain a nutrient-rich yolk that sustains the juvenile until it is ready to hatch out into the open ocean and fend for itself. Many species of skate and ray are threatened or endangered around Ireland's shores, because they are very vulnerable to being caught as bycatch in fisheries. Therefore, it is always a joy to find fresh mermaid's purses and to know that there must be a population living nearby. (NB: Some mermaid's purses are unhatched. Don't collect these unless the juvenile has obviously hatched out.)

Some very intriguing and exciting items can turn up on Irish shores. If you find something unusual, take some photos and let us know!

Seaglass.

Bone from the elegant cuttlefish Sepia elegans.

Cuttlefish bones are usually white but can have a pinkish tinge.

Common Cuttlefish

Irish Cudal **Latin** *Sepia* spp.
Size < 18cm
Distribution All coasts

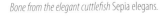

If you have ever kept a pet bird, you might recognise the skeleton of the cuttlefish as a dietary supplement often hung in bird cages for the birds to peck at. It is oval and white and has a light, brittle texture. When the cuttlefish is alive, this internal structure contains many tiny gas bubbles, which help the cuttlefish to float in the water column. When the cuttlefish dies, the skeleton floats and often washes ashore. Even though their shell is internal, these animals are actually part of the mollusc family (see page 124). Declines in cuttlefish populations have been observed, but not scientifically recorded, in recent years.

Traditionally, cuttlefish skeletons have been used as additives in toothpaste, antacids, and in crafts and jewellery making.

Like their relatives the squid and octopus, cuttlefish have eight arms. They have patterned skin that can change colour rapidly. Two frilly fins run the length of the body, and the eyes are large and have a characteristic H-shaped pupil.

Maerl can form 'coral beaches'.

Maerl is the washed-up remains of undersea reefs.

Maerl

Irish Méarla
Latin *Phymatolithon calcareum/Lithothamnion corallioides*
Distribution Rare, but can form entire beaches

Some beaches on the Irish coast, known as 'coral beaches', are formed almost entirely of maerl (it rhymes with 'curl'). This maerl is the washed-up remains of underwater reefs formed by calcium carbonate and algae, a little bit like the hard corals on tropical reefs. Living maerl reefs are a very important protected habitat because they provide shelter for many other species. Underwater, the branched arms are pink, but when they wash up on the shore they often dry out and become white.

Maerl reefs can be completely destroyed by certain fishing methods and can be damaged by heavy anchors dragging on the sea floor.

Sea Chervil

Latin *Alcyonidium diaphanum*

⚠ **Caution:** Can cause skin irritation
Size Usually < 15cm
Distribution Widespread

Sea chervil looks a bit like a twig or piece of a plant when it is washed up, but it is gelatinous and soft to touch. It is usually brown, but the colour can vary widely.

Contrary to its appearance and name, sea chervil is not a plant; it is not even one single organism. Like all bryozoans, sea chervil is a colony of tiny animals. This species forms an upright colony that attaches itself to rocks. Each tiny individual (called a zooid) has a separate function – anchoring the colony, brooding developing embryos or keeping the colony clean.

Bryozoans are eaten by sea slugs, urchins and fish. Be careful, because handling sea chervil can cause an itchy skin condition known as 'Dogger Bank Itch'.

Sea chervil is actually a colony of many tiny animals.

A large sea chervil colony.

Sea mat can coat seaweed.

The rectangular-shaped individuals are visible.

Sea Mat

Irish Milseán mara   **Latin** *Membranipora membranacea*
Size Colonies of microscopic organisms each 0.42 x 0.13mm
Distribution On stones and seaweeds

Notice the spiny hairs coming out of the sea mat.

If you look closely at a piece of kelp, you may spot a thin, white lacy layer covering its surface. This is a sea-mat colony. It is not a single animal, but a colony of clones. Now if you look even closer you may see the individual animals and notice that they are rectangular in shape with spines in the corners.

Colonies vary in size, often growing very quickly if conditions allow. They prefer fast-flowing water that provides food and oxygen. Sea slugs eat sea mat, and this sometimes causes the sea mat colony to grow more quickly.

Small-spotted Catshark

Irish Fíogach Beag **Latin** *Scyliorhinus canicula*

Size 5–7cm
Distribution All Irish coasts, especially where the seabed is muddy or sandy
Similar species Nursehound catshark

Confusingly, the small-spotted catshark is also known as the lesser spotted dogfish. Technically though, they are catfish, because dogfish give birth to live young. The egg case varies from pale yellow to dark brown. It has curly tendrils at both ends and is no more than 7cm long. The edges are delicate, unlike the rugged case of the nursehound catshark (see page 54), which has thick walls along either side.

The shark itself grows to less than 1m long and is one of the most common sharks in the north-east Atlantic. It does not migrate or move very far. It lives on the sea floor and eats fish and other small animals. The largest females can deposit up to 100 eggs per year. When the sharks emerge from the egg cases, they are about 7cm long.

Catsharks and dogfish of all sizes are caught as bycatch in bottom trawl and net fisheries. They are fished commercially in some Mediterranean countries. Their meat is sold as rock salmon or huss in Ireland.

Eggcases can vary in colour.

The delicate small-spotted catshark case.

Nursehound Catshark

Irish Fíogach mór **Latin** *Scyliorhinus stellaris*

⚠ **Caution:** Near-threatened in Ireland and the north-east Atlantic

Size < 10cm
Distribution Atlantic coasts, especially where the seabed is rocky
Similar species Small-spotted catshark

The egg case of the nursehound catshark is usually dark brown and around 10cm long. Unless they have become detached, there are long curly tendrils like wires from each of the four corners. The outer edges of the case are thick and flattened. The overall shape is very similar to that of the small-spotted catshark, but the nursehound case is larger and stronger looking.

Nursehounds are not widely studied: we don't know how many there are in the north-east Atlantic. It's possible that the population is in decline. They grow to a maximum of 1.5m long and live in fairly shallow water. They eat crabs, fish, and other animals.

The eggs are laid among seaweeds just under the low-tide mark. They take nine months to hatch. The young emerge from the egg case when they are about 10cm long.

The thickened sides of a nursehound eggcase.

Catshark eggcases have curly tendrils.

The horns at either end of a spotted ray eggcase are all of similar lengths.

Spotted ray eggcases are small and smooth-edged.

Spotted Ray

Irish Roc mín **Latin** *Raja montagui*

Size 6cm long (excluding horns)
Distribution All coasts, especially sandy seabeds
Similar species Undulate ray

The egg case of the spotted ray is dark brown or black. It feels smooth and is often shiny. The horns at either end are all similar lengths. The long edges are smooth, without the extra frilly keels (flattened flaps along the side) that some egg cases have.

Spotted rays are small, only about 6cm long. They are relatively common in the north-east Atlantic and the Mediterranean. They are not commercially fished as they are so small, but they are vulnerable to being caught accidentally. They prefer sandy areas and have a varied diet.

Spotted rays mature at around four years old. Females lay up to 60 eggs per year between April and July. The embryo takes about six months to develop inside the egg case.

Undulate Ray

Irish Roc dústríoctha **Latin** *Raja undulata*

⚠ **Caution:** Endangered in Ireland and worldwide

Size 8cm long (excluding horns)
Distribution A few sandy sites on the west coast
Similar species Spotted ray

This undulate ray case is unhatched, so we didn't collect it.

The egg case of the undulate ray is dark green or black. It is very similar to the shape of the spotted ray egg case (see page 55), but it is larger. It is worth soaking this egg case in water for a few hours so that it expands to its full size. The horns at each corner are roughly equal in length. There are no keels (flattened flaps along the side), but sometimes there is a mat of fibrous material at the side. Between the horns, one end of the purse is curved and the other is flattened, as if it has been pinched shut.

Undulate rays have highly decorated and beautiful bodies when they are alive. They grow to a full length of less than a metre. They are rarely found in Ireland any more. It is thought that they mature at around 14 years of age and live to about 23 years.

Undulate ray's eggcases are larger than the spotted ray's.

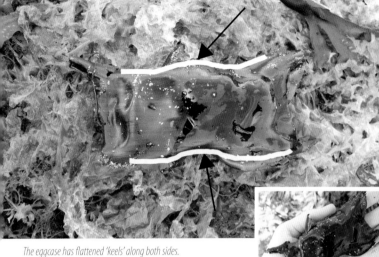

The eggcase has flattened 'keels' along both sides.

Blonde ray eggcases are one of the larger species found.

Blonde Ray

Irish Roc fionn **Latin** *Raja brachyura*
⚠ **Caution:** Near threatened in Ireland and worldwide

Size 10–14cm long (excluding horns)
Distribution A few sandy sites around the coast
Similar species Undulate ray

The egg case of the blonde ray is larger than most others you are likely to find. It is worth soaking this egg case if you find it dried out to ensure that it is at its maximum size. The horns are longer at one end than the other, but are often missing. There are flattened 'keels' along the edges and thin, skin-like pieces of material between the horns at both ends.

Blonde rays grow to over a metre long and are a commercially fished species despite their status as 'near threatened' (this means nearly endangered). They live all over the north-east Atlantic and the Mediterranean. Females can produce up to 30 egg cases per year, but very little is known about the lifestyle of this species.

Seaweeds

Seaweeds are integral to the seashore ecosystem. They support other organisms by providing food and shelter, and maintain healthy coastal environments by producing oxygen and recycling nutrients. Believe it or not, we also rely on seaweed in our daily lives.

Seaweeds are algae and, similar to plants, they photosynthesise. This means that they absorb sunlight and CO_2 to produce the oxygen and nutrients upon which all other creatures on the shores and in the oceans rely. In rock pools and further out to sea, seaweeds provide shade, shelter, food and solid structures for many animals and other algae. Large kelp forests around our coasts support highly biodiverse communities of creatures and are essential 'nurseries' in which young fish mature. Although Ireland has no coastal coral reefs, we have a rich variety of seaweeds that support life and provide colour all around our coasts. Without them, our underwater world would be relatively monotonous and a large proportion of our marine animals would disappear.

Seaweeds are a vital constituent of many foods and cosmetics, and are even a raw material in industry. Seaweed is in many everyday products: toothpaste, face creams, air fresheners, cheese, yoghurt, confectionery and processed meat products. In Ireland, seaweed has also long been used as a fertiliser for land.

Large stands of tough brown seaweeds, called kelp, can survive on all except the most wave-battered shores. They exist in the shallow waters around much of Ireland, sheltering our coastline and reducing erosion by dissipating the strong force of waves and storms before they hit land.

Seaweeds are divided into three main groups: green, red and brown. Their different colours are created by the pigments within the cells of the seaweed. Different pigments absorb different wavelengths of light used for photosynthesis. While all wavelengths of light can penetrate the very shallow water of small rock pools, only a few wavelengths can reach deeper waters. This allows seaweeds of different colours to grow at different depths of water. Green seaweeds get their colour from green chlorophyll pigments. They require the full spectrum of light and can grow only in shallow waters. Brown seaweeds contain chlorophyll and additional pigments which give the brown colour and allow for growth in deeper waters, although they are present in very shallow water also. Brown seaweeds are the largest, with kelps sometimes growing to several metres in length. Finally, the pigments in red seaweeds allow them to grow at far greater depths than the others. However, you will see them in rock pools too. They come in a wide variety of forms, from encrusting to feathery, and thin sheets to some with a calcium skeleton.

Seaweed is often seen as a problem where it washes up and rots. It can become smelly, and the sandhoppers and flies that feed on it are disliked by picnicking visitors. It also becomes entangled with human litter, such as plastic packaging and fishing nets. However, washed-up weed becomes the base of a food chain as the insects that feed on it are eaten by birds and the nutrients are fed back into the ground.

Beaches that are mechanically cleaned of seaweed may appear tidier, but it is likely that they can support little wildlife because the base of the food web and essential nutrients have been removed. For beachcombers, piles of washed-up seaweed can be rich picking grounds for interesting bits and bobs that become entangled in the weed and pulled ashore.

Important Features

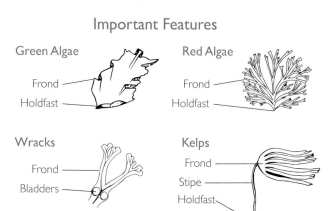

Green Algae
Frond
Holdfast

Red Algae
Frond
Holdfast

Wracks
Frond
Bladders

Kelps
Frond
Stipe
Holdfast

Gutweed can cover the surface of rock pools (left).
Gutweed fronds become inflated and tangled (right).

The fronds of Ulva compressa *are more flattened.*

Gutweed

Irish Líneal ghorm **Latin** *Enteromorpha intestinalis*

Size < 30cm
Distribution Widespread

This long, stringy alga is aptly named. The fronds are tubes that can look inflated, twisted and entangled, like bright green intestines. Gutweed attaches itself to hard surfaces using a holdfast, but the delicate fronds often become detached and float on the surface. Gutweed is particularly common where there is some fresh water, for example in estuaries or high-shore pools that become less salty when rain falls into them. It can cover the entire surface of these pools, especially in early summer as it grows quickest in late winter and early spring. You might see air bubbles in dense patches. These are caused by the process of photosynthesis, which produces oxygen. Another species, *Ulva compressa*, is very similar, but the fronds are slightly more flattened. Gutweed can be dried and used in cooking.

Sea lettuce is bright green and shiny.

Sea lettuce often has frilly edges.

Sea Lettuce

Irish Glasán **Latin** *Ulva lactuca*
Size < 25cm long
Distribution Widespread

Sea lettuce is common on sheltered shores. It is particularly common in July and August and where there is some fresh water. The fronds are bright green and translucent, and the thallus (stalk) is short. As its name suggests, sea lettuce is traditionally used as a salad. However, it often grows in water that has high nutrient content, possibly due to sewage or agricultural run-off, so be careful when harvesting and washing it. Sea lettuce is also eaten by brent geese when the tide is low enough for them to graze on it from the water surface.

There is some scientific debate about identifying different species of sea lettuce. Unless you are particularly interested in taxonomy, this isn't important.

Velvet Horn

Irish Beanna veilbhite **Latin** *Codium tomentosum*
Size < 30cm
Distribution Rock pools and the mid to low rocky shore

The fronds have a velvety texture.

Velvet horn is less common than many of the other green seaweeds. Its elongated, tubular fronds are quite solid and feel velvety, as the name suggests. Each frond branches into two as it grows. There are a few similar species and there is some debate about which are native and which may have been introduced. It also appears that velvet horn might be decreasing around Britain and Ireland. Pollution and invasive species could be to blame.

Velvet horn is present on the shore all year, but it reproduces in winter, and this is when it is most abundant. You will find it in rock pools and among other red and green seaweeds on rocky shores. It can tolerate quite a lot of wave and wind action.

Velvet horn has long, tubular fronds.

Velvet horn can become discoloured from sediment or microscopic algae.

Rock weed forms clumps that retain moisture.

Rock Weed

Irish Slobán **Latin** *Cladophora rupestris*

Size < 12cm
Distribution Rock pools and the mid to low rocky shore

Rock weed grows on all suitable rocky coasts, in rock pools, and under larger seaweeds, where it is sheltered from drying out. On some shores it forms a coarse, tufty mat. Rock weed is a very dark green. The fronds look feathery but feel quite rough, like clumps of coarse hair.

There are some very similar species which are difficult to separate. You will see it at all times of the year. Depending on where it grows, and whether or not it is grazed upon, it can have a slightly stunted appearance. At low tide, the clumps can hold quite a lot of moisture and you may find small animals sheltering under them. Mud, sediment or shells may also become trapped in the tufts.

Green Spaghetti Algae

Latin *Chaetomorpha* spp.

Size < 30cm

Distribution Sheltered shores

There are a few different species of green spaghetti algae, all grouped together as *Chaetomorpha*. These bright, pale green algae can be attached to rocks or other algae, or can form large free-floating mats. You might find these mats on the surface of the water or on the shore at low tide. Each filament is extremely fine, usually just one cell thick.

Green spaghetti algae can clog rock pools and inlets. It is often common in areas where there is a lot of fresh water, for example at the mouth of a river or in sea loughs. You might find it together with other green seaweeds, such as rock weed (see page 63) or velvet horn (see page 62), or with dwarf eelgrass (see page 22).

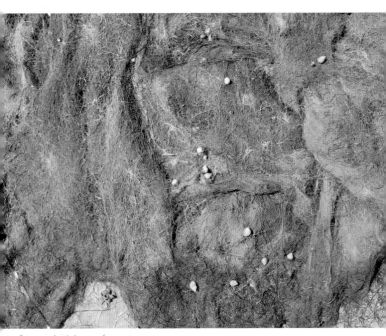

Green spaghetti algae can form mats.

Coral weed grows rigid and upright.

The bleached, skeletal remains of coral weed.

Coral Weed

Irish Feamainn choiréalach **Latin** *Corallina officinalis*

Size < 12cm tall

Distribution Rock pools and rocky shores

Although it is a red seaweed, the calcium that forms a skeletal crust in coral weed makes it appear dusty pink or mauve. Coral weed is common in rock pools and sheltered crevices of the mid to low shore. The feathery fronds have many branches and grow in clumps. When coral weed gets washed up onto the shore, the colour bleaches, leaving a jointed chain of chalky white segments.

The stiff structure of coral weed creates a protective habitat for many small animals, such as juvenile mussels and a variety of worms. There is even a species of prawn that has developed a pink camouflage for hiding in coral weed. These animals feed on the many microscopic organisms that become caught in the dense tufts. The crusty texture makes it inedible to most algae eaters.

Encrusting algae coating the shell of a limpet.

The pink and orange patch in this photo is formed by encrusting algae.

Encrusting Algae

Irish Gruánach **Latin** *Lithophyllum incrustans*
Size < 0.5cm thick
Distribution Rock pools and rocky shores

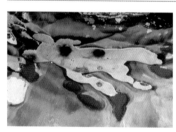

Encrusting algae can become bleached by the sun.

Encrusting algae can form very beautiful coloured coatings on rocks around the coast. These coatings are often pink, but can be yellow and can cover large expanses of rock. You could easily think that encrusting algae are part of the rock, but they are actually a plant. The algae excrete calcium carbonate to create the hard crust that you see. As they die, the red algae disappear, leaving only a white crust. In places, encrusting algae can form a smooth, thin layer on the rock; in other areas, they form thicker, folded patches. As well as rocks, encrusting algae can coat shells and even other seaweed.

Encrusting algae are more common on exposed shores where the waves sweep away larger seaweeds. There are a number of similar species that require expertise to identify. Many grazing animals, such as limpets, eat encrusting algae.

Ceramium spp.

Size < 30cm tall
Distribution Rock pools and rocky shores

Ceramium algae are feathery red or purple algae that grow on rocks, in pools and also on other seaweeds or shells. If you look very closely, you will notice that each filament is very slightly striped. There is no obvious central stalk, instead *Ceramium* is highly branched and each branch gets slightly narrower towards the tip. Each tip is forked, but you probably need a magnifying glass or a powerful zoom camera to see this.

Genetically, there are actually many species of *Ceramium*, but they are extremely difficult for the naked eye to tell apart. As a group, they are common all over north-west Europe.

Each Ceramium *frond is forked.*

The delicate, feathery fronds of Ceramium.

Dense mounds of feathery red weed at low tide.

Feathery red weed grows in 'pom-poms' on other seaweeds.

Feathery Red Weed

Irish Feamainn dhearg chleiteach **Latin** *Polysiphonia* spp.

Size Variable

Distribution Widespread on middle and lower shore

Polysiphonia species are very difficult to tell apart without a microscope. All of them are red or reddish-brown and have fronds that are as fine as strands of hair. They often grow in tufts.

One species grows almost exclusively on knotted egg wrack (see page 86) and looks like a fluffy red pom-pom. This species (*Polysiphonia lanosa*) roots itself into the egg wrack with strong fibres. You won't usually find it attached to stones. On some shores it is difficult to see the egg wrack under the heavy coat of feathery red weed. When the tide comes in, the egg wrack floats up towards the surface and its feathery accessories are also lifted closer to the light.

Other species grow in rock pools, attached to shells, stones or other seaweeds.

The cylindrical fronds of black carrageen.

Multicoloured encrusting algae growing on black carrageen.

Black Carrageen

Irish Leaba phortáin **Latin** *Furcellaria lumbricalis*

Size < 30cm tall
Distribution Widespread

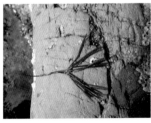

Black carrageen is usually red-brown.

Black carrageen has long, branching cylindrical fronds. Like many red seaweeds, it can vary in colour depending on how much light it receives. Usually it is more brown than red, and it can be green if bleached by sunlight. The tips are usually pointed, but in winter the reproductive bodies appear as plump, pale fruits. These drop off and the seaweed continues to grow from the tips. The base of the seaweed is often coated in coiled tube worms (see page 177) or in colourful encrusting algae.

Black carrageen has become rare in some areas of Europe where it has been heavily harvested, but it is still fairly common around Ireland.

It can be confused with another species, *Polyides rotundus*. They can be told apart by the way that they attach to rock – black carrageen clings to the substrate with a tangled mass of 'roots', not a fleshy disk.

Lomentaria articulata

Size < 10cm tall
Distribution Rock pools and low on rocky shores

Lomentaria is common all around Ireland and Great Britain, but in the south-west of Ireland, plants are larger than anywhere else. It varies from shiny red to brown. It is usually darker when it is dried out. The entire plant is hollow and constricted at regular intervals, making it resemble a string of sweets, sausages, or something created by a balloon artist! Branches appear at the constrictions. It often lives in fairly shaded spots underneath other larger seaweeds.

The fronds resemble strings of plump sausages.

Shiny mounds of Lomentaria.

Pepper dulse looks flattened.

Pepper Dulse

Irish Míobhán **Latin** *Osmundea pinnatifida*
Size < 15cm tall
Distribution Mid to low rocky shore

This red seaweed has a slightly cartoonish appearance with fronds shaped like flattened trees. It is reddish-brown, but if it grows on the upper shore, it may look bleached from sunlight and desiccation. It is fairly solid in texture and can survive all year round. Pepper dulse is smaller and tuftier when it grows higher on the shore. It can form quite extensive mats that provide shelter for small animals on rocky shores.

Pepper dulse is named for its distinctive, peppery taste. Traditionally, it was dried, ground and added as a flavouring to foods.

Sea beech 'leaves'.

Sea beech is translucent and delicate.

Sea Beech

Irish Feá mara **Latin** *Delesseria sanguinea*

Size < 30cm
Distribution Rocky shores and shady rock pools; mid to low shore

Sea beech is aptly named as it really does look like it has leaves. Underwater, these float like silk. They are usually bright red, translucent and delicate, with wavy edges. They attach to the rock with a thickened holdfast. Some divide into branches very close to the rock.

Each 'leaf' has an obvious midrib. In the winter, the delicate frond is lost and reproductive bodies grow along the midrib. Each plant can live for up to six years.

Sea beech prefers to live in deeper rock pools and shady areas. It occurs all around Ireland, as far south as Spain and as far north as Iceland and Norway.

Irish Moss/Carrageen

Irish Carraigín **Latin** *Chondrus crispus*
Size < 15cm tall
Distribution Mid to low rocky shore
Similar species False Irish moss

Irish moss growing in a rock pool.

Irish moss is quite delicate and bushy. The stipe (stem) and fronds are flat rather than rounded. It is quite a dark red, but the edges of the fronds can be paler. If you are a snorkeller or find Irish moss just under the surface on a sunny day, you might notice that the tips of the fronds have a bright petrol-like shimmer. The shape and appearance of Irish moss can vary depending where you find it. The main variation is in the width of the fronds. Irish moss often grows under larger brown seaweeds. You will see it all year round and it can live for up to six years.

This species and the easily confusable false Irish moss (see page 74) are gathered and sold as 'Irish moss'. These red weeds are the source of 'carrageenan', which is used in cosmetics and foods as a gelling or thickening agent.

Irish moss has a tough stipe and delicate fronds.

Irish moss can become bleached by the sunlight.

False Irish Moss

Irish Cluimhín Cáit **Latin** *Mastocarpus stellatus*
Size < 17cm tall
Distribution Mid to low rocky shore
Similar species Irish moss

False Irish moss grows in dense tufts. The fronds are dark reddish brown and are paler towards the ends where they thin out. Often confused with Irish moss, the two species grow in similar environments and you might find them growing side by side on the lower shore and in rock pools. Look at the stalk part of the frond for a channel. This channel is present in the false Irish moss, but not Irish moss. False Irish moss does not have the blue shimmer that is sometimes visible at the tips of Irish moss. However, you might notice small wart-like bumps on the tips of the fronds. These are the reproductive bodies, which are more obvious than on Irish moss.

False Irish moss can live for a number of years. It is often picked alongside Irish moss and sold as one product.

False Irish moss growing on the low shore.

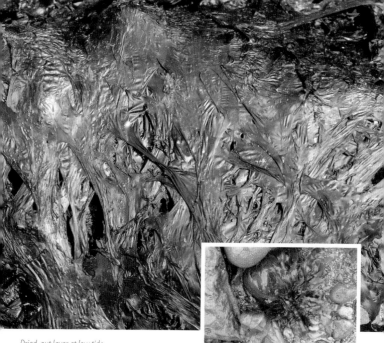

Dried-out laver at low tide.

Laver fronds are almost transparent.

Laver/Nori

Irish Sleabhac **Latin** *Porphyra* spp.

Size < 20cm long
Distribution Low rocky shore or on other seaweeds

Laver is almost transparent. Although it appears like cling film, it is quite gelatinous. Each frond is irregularly folded. The colour can vary from olive green to purple. As it dries, it often darkens. It can survive on rocks and amongst mussels high up on wave-washed shores. It can survive getting dried out during low tide. You might notice large clumps of laver growing in one area. It can also be abundant on built structures, such as piers and jetties.

Laver is traditionally eaten in 'laver bread' – fried cakes of dried laver mixed with oatmeal. There are many similar species that are difficult to tell apart on the shore, so here we have just referred to them as one. In Japan, similar species are referred to as nori. It is widely cultivated and is used as the wrapping for sushi.

Dillisk fronds can be opaque.

The smooth, leathery fronds of dillisk.

Dillisk

Irish Duileasc **Latin** *Palmaria palmata*

Size 20–30cm tall

Distribution Low rocky shore or on other seaweeds

Dillisk is common all over north-west Europe. In Ireland you will find it on most rocky shores, where it grows directly on the rocks or attached to larger seaweeds. The fronds are broad, flat and smooth, although the edges are irregularly shaped with unevenly spaced outgrowths. Although the shape can vary hugely, the overall outline widens from the base. Dillisk is a dark purplish red and is opaque.

Dillisk has been part of the Irish coastal diet for a long time. Traditionally, the plants that grow on the wilder, more exposed shores are sold as Creathnach and are more highly prized than the tougher plants from more sheltered shores. It has a good taste and texture for eating, but it should be dried rapidly after it is picked.

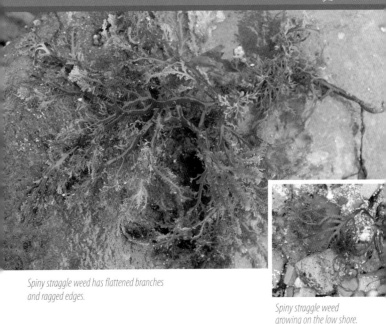

Spiny straggle weed has flattened branches and ragged edges.

Spiny straggle weed growing on the low shore.

Spiny Straggle Weed

Latin *Gelidium spinosum*
Size < 60cm
Distribution Low shore in rock pools

Although it is a red seaweed, spiny straggle weed often grows in rock pools where it becomes bleached yellow or green. It is obvious because of its ragged appearance. It has a flattened central frond that is up to a centimetre wide. From that, horizontal branches appear like spines or hairs. These are usually not much longer than the width of the central frond.

Because it grows on the lower shore, it can be pulled up by winter storms and you might find tangled clumps of it washed up on beaches.

It prefers the warmer water of the south and west coasts and is often hidden in shady patches underneath other algae. Agar, which is commonly used in laboratories for growing bacteria or fungi, is a jelly-like substance extracted from spiny straggle weed. This species and others in the same family are the subject of research because of their antibacterial properties.

Hairy Eyelash Weed

Latin *Calliblepharis jubata*
Size < 30cm long
Distribution Mid to low rocky shore and rock pools

Hairy eyelash weed washed up on shore.

The fronds of the hairy eyelash weed are long and pointed, and have many branches and narrow hairy outgrowths. They can be bright red or slightly yellowed. The fronds are much narrower than those of the eyelash weed (see page 87), and it grows higher up the shore. It feels quite tough, but hangs limply.

Hairy eyelash weed grows on rocks and on other seaweeds, especially coral weed (see page 65). It is most common in the south and west and is rarely found in the north-east.

Hairy eyelash weed is covered in fine outgrowths.

Hairy eyelash weed can look yellow in sunny rock pools.

Eyelash Weed

Irish Feamainn feabhra **Latin** *Calliblepharis ciliata*
Size < 30cm tall
Distribution Low rocky or sandy shore

Eyelash weed has a tiny holdfast and expands quickly from there into a broad, flat frond like a spatula. There are many flattened, frilly branches along the edges. These branches are irregularly sized and shaped. Sometimes the main frond is branched, but not always. Eyelash weed is slightly coarse-textured and not as shiny as many similar species.

Eyelash weed is a southern species that is less common on colder shores. It generally lives underwater, but you might find it in rock pools on the low shore or washed up after stormy weather.

The frilly branches of eyelash weed.

Eyelash weed can be very irregularly shaped.

The delicate red fronds of slender wart weed.

A tangled mass of slender wart weed washed up on shore.

Slender Wart Weed

Latin *Gracilaria gracilis*
Size < 50cm tall
Distribution Rock pools and low on sandy shores

Slender wart weed is a lot more attractive than the name suggests. The fronds are delicate and translucent and no more than the thickness of a coin in diameter. The colour can vary from brown to jellybean orange or red, depending on the season and desiccation. You are most likely to find it on sandy shores. It attaches itself to small rocks and stones and can become dislodged and wash ashore.

Slender wart weed and related species are commercially grown in many parts of the world as food and as the source of agar or other food products. Most species in this family are native to warm waters (such as ours) and are classed as invasive in colder places, such as the North Sea.

Channelled Wrack

Irish Caisíneach **Latin** *Pelvetia canaliculata*

Size 5–15cm long
Distribution Upper rocky shores

The fronds of the channelled wrack are curled at the edges to create the channel that it is named for. It grows in tufts of branched fronds. When the tide is out, the tufts hang down with the channelled side usually facing the rocks. The channel holds water, allowing this species to live on the upper shore without drying out. In fact, channelled wrack can survive spending up to 90 per cent of its time uncovered by the tide. It is officially a brown seaweed but can appear dark green.

Channelled wrack does not have the air bladders characteristic of some brown seaweeds, but sometimes swollen patches appear at the end of the fronds. These are fruit-like reproductive bodies.

The fronds curl in towards the rock to create a channel.

Channelled wrack grows in small tufts on the high shore.

Spiral wrack has no air bladders.

Spiral Wrack

Irish Casfheamainn   **Latin** *Fucus spiralis*

Size < 40cm long
Distribution Sheltered rocky shores
Similar species Bladder wrack

Spiral wrack occurs high up on the shore often just below channel wrack (see page 91). It can often form a band or zone where no other seaweed grows.

The fronds have a prominent midrib and no air bladders. The edges of the fronds are smooth, with regular branches. As the name suggests, this wrack grows in a twisted spiral.

Spiral wrack is common and widespread around Ireland. On more exposed shores a slightly different dwarf variety grows in tufts. The spiral shape may not be so obvious on the shorter fronds.

Horned Wrack

Latin *Fucus ceranoides*
Size < 60cm long
Distribution Estuaries and areas with some fresh water
Similar species Bladder wrack

Horned wrack is similar in colour and shape to the other wracks, but has no air bladders and the edges of the fronds are smooth. Instead of air bladders, some of the fronds are inflated either side of the prominent midrib – a little bit like long blisters.

Although it occurs throughout north-west Europe, it is only really common in brackish water where the salinity is low. It can be particularly abundant where fresh water flows onto the shore. In estuaries it grows attached to rocks and stones in the mid and low shore.

Fruiting bodies on horned wrack.

The inflated fronds of horned wrack.

Bladder Wrack

Irish Feamainn bhoilgíneach　**Latin** *Fucus vesiculosis*
Size 1m long
Distribution Mid shore
Similar species Serrated wrack, spiral wrack, horned wrack, egg wrack

Vibrant colours of washed-up bladderwrack.

Bladder wrack is the archetypal wrack. It is greeny-brown coloured and the air bladders appear in groups of two or three along the flattened fronds like bubble wrap. It occurs all around Ireland on sheltered and exposed shores. You can find it on the mid shore alongside egg wrack (see page 86) and above serrated wrack (see page 85).

All seaweeds, like land plants, need sunlight to photosynthesise. The air bladders in bladder wrack keep the fronds close to the surface of the water when the tide is in to maximise the amount of daylight that the plant receives. Because of this, wracks with air bladders can live further down the shore than those without. However, on wave-swept shores, these bladders are a disadvantage because they make the plant vulnerable to being washed away. As a result, bladder wrack can appear with few, or even no, air bladders, depending on the shore.

Bladder wrack attached to a stone on the low shore.

Air bladders help the bladder wrack to float.

The jagged edges of serrated wrack.

Serrated Wrack

Irish Mioránach **Latin** *Fucus serratus*

Size < 1m long
Distribution Mid to low shore

As its name suggests, the fronds of this brown alga are serrated all along their edges. They also have a very obvious midrib, like that of a leaf, running down the centre, and are quite rubbery. The end of each frond is forked. Serrated wrack can range from olive green to dark brown in colour. There are no air bladders, but sometimes rough patches appear at the tips; these are part of the reproductive cycle.

Serrated wrack grows low down the shore, where it can help to protect the shore from damage by strong waves, by slowing the flow of the water. It has a strong holdfast that prevents it from being washed away. It cannot survive long periods out of the water. This species of seaweed is often used in seaweed baths and as the source of some cosmetic ingredients.

Egg/Knotted Wrack

Irish Feamainn bhuí   **Latin** Ascophyllum nodosum

Size < 2m long
Distribution Mid shore
Similar species Bladder wrack

The translucent fruits of the egg wrack.

Knotted or egg wrack occurs on the high or mid shore in areas that are relatively sheltered. The fronds are longer and narrower than most wracks. The large air bladders swell at regular intervals like beads on a string. After the first year, one air bladder appears each year, so you can try to age the fronds that you find. Typically, knotted wrack lives for 6–17 years, depending on the shore.

Where the conditions are right, knotted wrack can blanket large areas of the shore. There is also an unattached variety of knotted wrack that drifts in tangled masses near the surface in sheltered areas, mostly on the west coast.

You may notice soft bunches of red algae growing on the fronds of knotted wrack. These are most likely the feathery red weed *Polysiphonia lanosa* (see page 68).

The long fronds often get wash up.

A tangled clump of egg wrack at low tide.

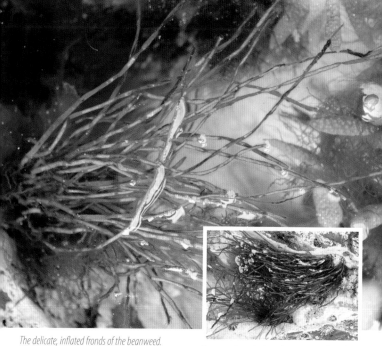

The delicate, inflated fronds of the beanweed.

Beanweed attached to a limpet in a rock pool.

Beanweed

Latin *Scytosiphon lomentaria*
Size < 40cm long
Distribution Mid shore and rock pools

Beanweed is a delicate brown seaweed. The fronds are long and narrow, and have no branches. They are hollow, but constricted at irregular intervals and they might be inflated or flattened. Beanweed is yellow or brown. It grows attached to rocks, limpets or other shells and is especially common on wave-exposed shores. Beanweed is an annual, meaning that it lives for only one year. You are most likely to see it in the spring and summer. The more mature the plant, the more constrictions it has on its fronds.

Pod weed growing in a rock pool.

Pod weed washed up on the beach.

Pod Weed

Irish Crúba préacháin **Latin** *Halidrys siliquosa*
Size < 130cm long
Distribution Rock pools and shallow shores
Similar species Wireweed, tuning fork weed

This pale brown or honey-coloured weed grows in long, irregularly forked strands. The main stem is flattened and forks in a zigzag pattern. The air bladders are shaped like pea pods and keep the fronds floating up near the surface of the water. The colour of the plant changes and darkens as it ages. Older plants also become more leathery.

Pod weed can become dominant in large, sunny rock pools. Plants regularly shed the outer layer of their 'skin' to rid themselves of other plants growing on them. In spite of this, some other seaweeds and animals still live on the outer surface of the weed.

Tuning Fork Weed

Latin *Bifurcaria bifurcata*
Size < 50cm long
Distribution Mid shore, mostly on the west coast
Similar species Pod weed

Tuning fork weed is named for the way that its cylindrical fronds repeatedly branch into two. It is olive brown with a smooth, shiny appearance. Elongated, cylindrical reproductive bodies occur at the tips of the fronds.

This is a southern species that prefers the warmer waters of the west coast. For unknown reasons, it is almost absent from the south coast. It is most commonly associated with limestone areas and is often found in the same places as the purple sea urchin (see page 200).

Tuning fork weed can be confused with pod weed (see page 88), which has pea-pod shaped air bladders and tends to branch in a more zigzag fashion.

Each frond forks in two.

Tuning fork weed in a midshore rock pool.

Wireweed is an invasive species.

Wireweed can cover the surface of rock pools.

Wireweed

Latin *Sargassum muticum*

Size < 3m
Distribution Midshore and rock pools
Similar species Beanweed

Wireweed is pale yellow-brown, the fronds are flattened and it has many spherical air bladders that are about the size of an apple pip. It often grows so long that it lies flat on the surface of the water. You are most likely to find it in rock pools on the south, south-west and north-east coasts, although it does occur in other patches and is becoming more common. It grows quickly in springtime and completely covers the surface of rock pools by late summer.

Wireweed is native to the Pacific, where it does not become very large and does not cause problems. However, it has been introduced to many parts of Europe, probably as a result of shipping. It can be highly invasive and competes with some of our native species. Wireweed can block light from rock pools, overgrow other algae, and impede boats and swimmers. It is now so common in Ireland that there is little we can do. It is recommended that boat owners ensure it does not get caught in outboard motors as this can allow fragments to spread and be dragged to other locations. On other coasts it has reached a balance with the native ecosystem over time. Hopefully, this will happen here too.

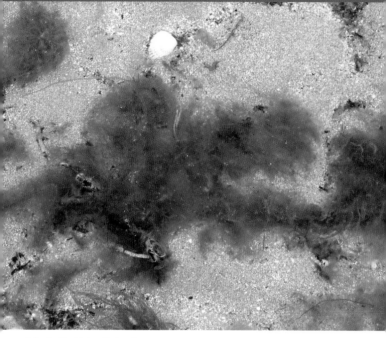

Tufts of maiden's hair on the low shore.

Maiden's Hair

Irish Folt bé **Latin** *Ectocarpus* spp.

Size < 30cm long
Distribution Mid shore and rock pools
Similar species *Polysiphonia* spp.

Maiden's hair is a very fine, branched seaweed that grows in tufts from the mid shore to below the low-tide mark. It can be brown or yellow and when the tide goes out it often just appears as a slightly slimy patch on the rock or sand. It is called maiden's hair because of its furry appearance under the water. Maiden's hair also grows on other seaweeds, much like the feathery red weed (see page 68). However, feathery red weed looks like a pom-pom or tuft even when the tide is out.

Water-filled oyster thief that has become detached and washed ashore.

Oyster thief can grow quite large.

Oyster Thief

Latin *Colpomenia peregrina*
Size Variable
Distribution Growing on other seaweed
Similar species Sea cauliflower

Oyster thief looks like a deflated brown balloon on the seashore. You might see it in rock pools or washed up, attached to coral weed (see page 65) or other algae. The surface of the oyster thief is thin and glossy and can be torn easily. When it is washed up, it often contains water that squirts out if you step on it. It is not a solid jelly texture like sea cauliflower (see page 93).

Oyster thief is an introduced species that is native to the Pacific Ocean. Its name comes from stories that it can attach itself to an oyster shell and grow until it becomes extremely buoyant and floats away with the oyster still attached.

Sea Cauliflower

Irish Bolgach **Latin** *Leathesia marina*
Size Variable
Distribution Rock pools and rocky shores
Similar species Oyster thief

Sea cauliflower is a slippery, jelly-like algae that grows in irregular golden-brown lumps that cling tightly to rocks or other hard surfaces. It is visible on the shore all year round, but it grows quickest in the summer months.

Sea cauliflower looks like oyster thief, but it is more solid to touch and does not grow into large hollow balloons like the oyster thief. It is also an introduced species.

A gelatinous mass of sea cauliflower.

Thong Weed

Irish Ríseach **Latin** *Himanthalia elongata*

Size <2m long
Distribution Low shore
Similar species Bootlace weed

There are two stages to the lifecycle of the thong weed that you might notice on the shore. Both of these stages are common on the lower shore, between the wracks and the kelps. The first stage is usually referred to as a 'button'. It looks a bit like a dark green mushroom with a funnel-shaped cap. This can be about 3cm across. The very long 'straps' that grow from the centre of this button are, in fact, the reproductive parts of the plant. These straps are slightly flattened – more like linguine than spaghetti! As these straps grow, they branch in two. After about a year the tips of the straps become spotted, which means they are ripe. After they have released their seed-like reproductive bodies into the water, they die (usually in autumn).

The underside of the buttons and the long straps often have many other plants and animals living on them. The upper side of the button, however, seems to have some kind of repellent that prevents this.

Thong weed was traditionally used with kelp in the potash industry in Ireland. Nowadays, it is sometimes harvested as a sea vegetable and sold as 'sea spaghetti'.

The long thong weed fronds are flattened, not round.

Thong weed growing on the low shore.

Bootlace weed feels very slippery.

Bootlace weed grows as long spaghetti-like fronds.

Bootlace Weed/ Mermaid's Tresses

Irish Ruálach **Latin** *Chorda filum*

Size <6m long
Distribution Low shore
Similar species Thong weed

Bootlace weed is also known as mermaid's tresses. It doesn't survive drying out, so it is rarely seen growing above the low-tide mark. However, you will notice the long, spaghetti-like strands floating upwards along the surface from where they grow in the sand or among pebbles. Bootlace weed prefers more sheltered areas than thong weed (see page 104). The very long, hollow fronds are covered in tiny hairs, so they appear fuzzy under the water. You might also notice lots of other plants and animals living on and among the fronds. If you are a swimmer, you may be familiar with the slimy texture of bootlace weed as you brush against it in the water.

The long frilly frond of Dabberlocks may look similar to sugar kelp. (Kerryann O'Farrell)

A charachteristic feature is the distinctive 'midrib' running down the centre of the frond. (Kerryann O'Farrell)

Dabberlocks

Irish Láracha **Latin** *Alaria esculenta*

Size < 1m

Distribution Low on rocky exposed shores

Dabberlocks is a pale olive brown or yellowish kelp that has long fronds that look like leaves. A prominent, pale midrib runs the length of each frond. These fronds can grow to about 4m long, but are more commonly about a metre long and about 8cm wide. Reproductive bodies appear on smaller structures close to the holdfast.

This species is also known as winged kelp, horsetail kelp and, more recently, Atlantic wakame. There are many attempts under way to cultivate dabberlocks for the Asian food market. It has also been a traditional source of food in Ireland. Dabberlocks is long-lived. Even though old growth may become damaged and tear away, new growth occurs at the base of the leaf-like frond.

Sugar Kelp

Irish Rufa **Latin** *Saccharina latissima*

Size < 4m long
Distribution Low shore
Similar species Dabberlocks

The rounded stipe of sugar kelp.

Sugar kelp, like the other kelp species, is only visible during the very lowest tides. However, it is common and can be abundant on sheltered rocky shores, or you might find it washed up on the tideline following storms.

The small holdfast and short, flexible stipe (stem) are less robust than some kelps. The frond can be very long. It is relatively delicate compared to some of the tougher kelps that you might see piled up on the shore. It is pale brown and slightly transparent. The edges of the frond are always frilly and the centre is wrinkled or dimpled. There is no obvious midrib.

When sugar kelp dries, a sweet-tasting powder forms on the frond. This powder is created by the sugars inside the frond coming to the surface as it dries out. It is commonly eaten and used as a sweetener in food and drinks.

Sugar kelp is also known as the poor-man's weather glass because, if you keep it out of the water, it goes crispy when the air is dry and softens again when the air is humid.

Sugar kelp fronds are less robust than other kelps.

Wrinkled fronds of sugar kelp.

The edge of the flattened stipe is frilly near the base.

Furbelows grows in an elaborate shape.

Furbelows/Sea Hedgehog

Irish Claíomh **Latin** *Saccorhiza polysychides*

Size < 4m
Distribution Low shore
Similar species Other kelps

The base of the stem, or 'sea hedgehog' is sometimes detached.

Furbelows is distinctive because of the flattened stipe (stem), unlike the tubular stems of other large kelps. This flattened stipe branches into caramel brown, straplike fronds. The holdfast is a hollow, bulbous shape with large warty bumps that give it the nickname 'sea hedgehog'. Above the hollow holdfast, the stipe often has a frilly appearance. It twists once, and then becomes smooth and straight.

Furbelows is very fast growing. It lives for only a year. Reproduction occurs in autumn or winter, after which the fronds decay and wash away. Eventually, the holdfast also detaches from the rocks and often washes ashore like a deflated ball. Because it is an annual, it occupies any available space in between the other kelps, but does not usually dominate the shore.

Oarweed

Irish Coirleach **Latin** *Laminaria digitata*
Size < 2m
Distribution Low shore
Similar species Other kelps

Oarweed is a glossy, smooth kelp. The tubular stipe (stem) is oval rather than circular and is very dark brown and flexible. The holdfast is dome-shaped. The stipe flattens and divides into up to 12 straplike fronds. These wear away at the tips as the plant ages, and grow again from the point where the fronds and the stipe meet.

The holdfast of oarweed provides habitat for many species. Oarweed is easily confused with strapweed (see page 101). They are easier to tell apart when the plants are older, but when young, the best way to differentiate them is by looking at the cross section of the stipe – is it oval or round? There is an increasing interest in harvesting oarweed along with other kelps. They have been traditionally harvested for food and ingredients for many years, but the introduction of mechanical harvesting has led to concerns about damaging marine ecosystems and rural communities.

The frond of oarweed.

Claw-like holdfast of oarweed.

Other seaweeds often colonise the rough strapweed stipe.

The stiff strapweed often washes ashore after storms.

Strapweed/Cuvie

Irish Ceann a'tslat **Latin** *Laminaria hyperborea*

Size < 3m tall
Distribution Low shore
Similar species Other kelps

Strapweed has a dark brown stipe (stem) that is rigid and often rough to touch. The fronds are caramel brown and shiny. The stipe is tubular and often washes ashore during the winter. Although it looks like a stick, it doesn't usually float. The holdfast is strong and claw-like with many branches. Strapweed usually occurs lower down the shore than oarweed. At a very low tide, you might notice the rigid stipes sticking up out of the water.

Once they have washed ashore, it can be difficult to tell the kelps apart. Strapweed is distinctive because it is more roughly textured and if you bend the stipe completely, it will snap. As with all kelps, they form a protective canopy below which many other algae and animals live and feed. Strapweed also provides places for fish and invertebrates to deposit eggs.

Strapweed reproduces over the winter and can live for up to ten years.

Crabs, Barnacles and their Relatives

It may seem strange that a family can include crabs with all their legs, their ability to move quickly, and their famously strong claws, and barnacles, with no legs, and no ability to move. They are both crustaceans and are also closely related to shrimps, lobsters, sandhoppers and land insects.

Crustaceans are covered in a hard external skeleton. They usually have a head with antennae, a thorax (middle) and an abdomen. These are often segmented into clear sections. The exoskeleton cannot grow, so they moult old shells and grow new ones to make room when their body grows. This means that some crabs seem 'fuller' than others when they are caught. Crustaceans usually spend a period of time as juveniles floating in the plankton, where they are food for many other animals, before they settle onto the sea floor and change into adults.

Crabs, lobsters and prawns

Crabs, lobsters, shrimps and prawns are all decapods, meaning that they have five pairs of legs. Lots of them have pincers or claws on the first pair. Many of these species are difficult to see from the shore, but you may find their shells on the sand. Some of the smaller crabs are common in rock pools or hiding under seaweed or rocks at low tide. Lobsters live in much deeper water. While crabs are usually shy, be careful of the sharp pincers; they'll be happy to use them under stress!

In many crab species, mating occurs just after the female has moulted in the winter. She then carries possibly millions of fertilised eggs for up to 30 days before they hatch.

Barnacles

It is hard to see the characteristic crustacean features in barnacles because the adult lives upside down inside an exoskeleton made of four or six small plates. Like most crustaceans, barnacles have many legs, which they stick out of the top of their shell to catch food from the water when the tide is in. Barnacles are characteristic of Irish rocky shores where they can survive the extreme forces of strong waves, long periods of low tide and (sometimes!) bright sunshine.

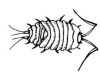

Insect-like crustaceans

Most of the small bug-like creatures you encounter on the shore, either in rock pools, under rocks, in sand or washed-up seaweed, are crustaceans – the isopods and amphipods. They are related to the woodlice you find in your garden. While they may not look so impressive, these little guys are vital in keeping our coasts clean because they are integral to the decomposition process of dead or decaying seaweed, plants and animals. Some species are parasitic and are found on jellyfish or fish.

Hermit Crab

Irish Faocha ghliomaigh **Latin** *Pagarus bernhardus*

Size 3–10cm
Distribution Widespread

Hermit crabs often live in the shells of periwinkles or dog whelks. If you see one of these shells moving quickly or 'scuttling' in a rock

Notice how one claw is bigger than the other.

pool or across the sand, it has probably been commandeered by a hermit crab. Unlike the other crabs, hermit crabs have soft, twisted bodies. At the end of this soft abdomen, there is a little hook that grips the inside of curved shells. If you disturb a hermit crab, it will pull the hard front part of the body into the shell along with its front claws and legs, but the claws are usually still visible on the underside of the shell. One of these claws is bigger than the other.

As the hermit crab grows, it must find a new, larger shell. It can take some time for the crab to find a shell that is big enough but not too heavy.

A hermit crab in a broken periwinkle shell.

The front claws of a hermit crab in a dog whelk shell.

Shore crabs are common around Ireland.

Notice the forward-pointing spines, the three blunt 'teeth' between the eyes, and the patterned shell.

Shore Crab

Irish Portán glas **Latin** *Carcinus maenas*
Size < 8cm
Distribution Widespread
Similar species Montagu's crab

This is the most common crab species on the shore. You will find them hiding under stones and seaweed on many types of shores, even in estuaries and rock pools.

Their shells are wider than they are long and are usually a dark brownish-green with patterned indentations. However, they can vary in colour. Between the eyes there are three blunt 'teeth', and four sharper, forward-facing hooks on either side of the eyes. The back legs are slightly flattened, but have pointed tips.

Shore crabs are predators and eat all kinds of worms, other crabs and shellfish.

The shore crab is a common native to Ireland and most of Europe, but it has spread to many other parts of the world where it is considered invasive.

The colour of shore crab shells can vary hugely.

This mating pair weren't happy about being disturbed.

The crinkled body of a Montagu's crab.

Montagu's crabs have heavy-looking claws.

The inside of a moulted shell.

Notice the hairy fringe on the back legs of this Risso's crab.

Montagu's Crab

Latin *Xantho hydrophilus*
Size < 7cm wide
Distribution Stony shores
Similar species Shore crab

Montagu's crab is yellow-brown, green or blue. The oval shape of its body could be confused with the edible crab or shore crab, but it has deeply ridged patterns that give it a crinkled look. The easiest way to tell these crabs apart is by the triangular 'teeth' on either side of the shell, which do not point forward like those of the shore crab (see page 105), and are more triangular than hooked. The area between the eyes is flattened. The front claws are large and heavy looking, with black tips. You will find them hiding under stones and rocks, often in the same places as broad-clawed porcelain crabs (see page 107).

Montagu's crab is a herbivore and can be common in areas with lots of seaweeds. There is another species, *Xantho pilipes*, or Risso's crab, which looks very similar but has a hairy fringe along the back of the body and on the legs.

Broad-clawed Porcelain Crab

Irish Portán poircealláin clúmhach **Latin** *Porcelana platycheles*
Size < 1.5cm
Distribution Gravel and stony shores

The large claws have a hairy coating.

The broad-clawed porcelain crab is a small crab whose body grows to only 1.5cm in length. The shell is mottled brown with a creamy-white underside. The front claws are large and flattened, which makes the crab look almost armour-plated. The back legs can be so small that they almost disappear. Underwater, you will notice the fine hairy covering on the claws, legs and body. The body is almost round and the antennae are long.

Broad-clawed porcelain crabs are mostly intertidal and you may find them hiding under rocks and within gravel at low tide. They pluck particles from the water to feed on. Despite their tiny size, the females take two years before they produce eggs.

The pale underside of a broad-clawed porcelain crab.

The claws of the porcelain crab are large compared to the body.

Note the blue markings and flattened back legs.

The velvet swimming crab has sharply pointed spines and bright red eyes.

Velvet Swimming Crab

Irish Luaineachán **Latin** *Necora puber*

Size < 9cm across

Distribution Widespread

The underside of a discarded shell.

If you come across a velvet swimming crab, you'll understand its name. The shell is covered in velvety hairs. Look for the dark blue lines along the legs, the many sharp 'teeth' around the edge of the body and the narrow spines between the bright red eyes. It has a ferocious appearance and can be quite aggressive. Like all swimming crabs, its back legs are flattened like paddles, which makes this species a strong swimmer.

Velvet swimming crabs eat brown seaweeds, smaller crabs, barnacles and other animals. They are fished commercially in some areas and exported to southern Europe where numbers are declining because of overfishing and disease.

Masked Crab

Irish Portán clismín **Latin** *Corystes cassivalaunus*

Size < 4cm long
Distribution Sandy shores

Masked crabs have elongated, almost oval-shaped shells that are longer than they are wide. The markings on the shell look almost like a face, hence the name. They are pale brown or yellow, and more delicate than most crab shells. Males have front legs about twice the length of their bodies. Females have much shorter front legs. Look for the distinctively long antennae. Between their eyes, they have two 'teeth'. There are also four 'teeth' on either side of their eyes.

Masked crabs burrow into the sand and feed on other burrowing animals. They burrow backwards and then knit their long antennae together to form a tube. They can then draw water down this tube.

The front legs of the male masked crab are long.

Edible Crab

Irish Portán dearg **Latin** *Cancer pagarus*
Size < 13cm wide
Distribution Widespread

The body, or carapace, of the edible crab is oval – it is much wider from side to side than it is from front to back. The edge of the carapace is smooth, with a wavy 'piecrust' edge. The upper body is uniformly orange, but the tips of the large claws are black.

Note the disctinctive 'pie crust' edge to their shells.

Edible crabs are common around Ireland, especially in sandy areas where they can dig to hunt or to hide. They live down to depths of 90m under water, but juveniles sometimes hide under rocks or seaweed closer to the shore. Edible crabs can live for up to 20 years.

Edible crabs are scavengers, but they also prey on live shellfish. The claws and white body meat are prized by fishermen who set baited crab 'pots' off shore.

Edible crabs are a distinctive orange-brown.

Even small juveniles are quite aggressive.

A spiny spider crab.

The front claws are narrow and pointed.

Spiny Spider Crab

Irish Portán faoilinne spionach **Latin** *Maja brachydactyla*

Size < 20cm long
Distribution All shores

The spiny outline of a spider crab.

Spiny spider crabs are the largest crabs on the Irish coast. Although they don't have the meaty claws of the edible crab (see page 110), they have large, rounded bodies and legs that can grow to 50cm long. They are orange-brown and their bodies are edged in short, blunt spikes. There are two prominent spines between their eyes. Their bumpy shells are often covered in algae. They live deep under water and you are unlikely to find one alive on the seashore.

Spiny spider crabs seem to be able to live on any type of seabed, although they don't like prolonged cold. Despite being commercially fished and exported to Europe, they are increasing in abundance in many areas, even in the cooler north.

Common prawns are well camouflaged in rock pools.

Moulted exoskeleton. Prawns moult in order to grow.

Common Prawn

Irish Cliocheán coiteann **Latin** *Palaemon serratus*

Size < 6cm long
Distribution Rock pools and low shore

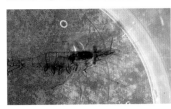

Common prawns have long yellow and blue claws.

Common prawns are almost transparent when they are alive, with red-brown lines encircling their bodies, and flattened tails a bit like a lobster's (their flesh becomes a familiar pinkish/white when they are cooked). They have beady eyes on stalks, long antennae and long front legs with small yellow and blue claws.

You might find groups of common prawns in rock pools and other areas that provide shelter. During the winter months, larger individuals move into deeper waters, possibly to avoid the cold. This dislike of cold water might be why there are fewer records of common prawns in the north-east of the island.

Females often carry eggs for about six weeks during the summer months before releasing them.

Common prawns eat algae and other crustaceans. There are a few different species of prawn that look similar, and you would need to examine them very closely to tell them apart.

Notice the diamond-shaped openings.

Acorn barnacles are divided into six plates.

Acorn Barnacle

Irish Garbhán carraige coiteann
Latin *Semibalanus balanoides*

Size < 1.5cm diameter
Distribution Mid to high on rocky shores
Similar species Australasian barnacle, stellate barnacle

The common acorn barnacle is characteristic of rocky Irish coasts. It is a northern species that is not found any further south than France. It is very easily confused with stellate barnacles (see page 124), and they often live on the same shores. Common acorn barnacles are larger and prefer to live a little further down the shore, but you might not notice where the division between the different species lies. The shell wall is divided into six plates, one of which is slightly bigger than the rest. They have a diamond-shaped aperture (opening). When space is limited and they crowd together, individuals can become quite tall. This makes them very painful to walk on with bare feet!

If they are not eaten by a dog whelk, a fish or another predator, they can live for up to eight years.

Stellate Barnacle

Irish Garbhán carraige réaltach **Latin** *Chthalamus* spp.

Size Approx. 1cm diameter
Distribution High on rocky shores
Similar species Australasian barnacle, acorn barnacle

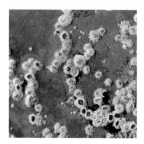

Note the bright blue colour of the open barnacles.

Two species of stellate barnacle are common on Irish coasts. Both of these species look very similar unless you have been trained to tell them apart. If you look closely, their volcano-shaped shell walls are divided into six white or grey plates that are all a similar size. Corrosion, algae or lichen might make these plates indistinguishable. They have oval-shaped apertures (openings).

One species of stellate barnacle is rarely found on Irish Sea coasts, but the other is common on all coasts. Stellate barnacles are most common high up the shore, close to the high-water mark.

Because they are small, they are less popular prey for dog whelks than other barnacles, but many species nip at the feeding arms that they extend when the tide is in. Stellate barnacles are a southern species so they enjoy the slightly warmer water carried close to Ireland by the North Atlantic Drift.

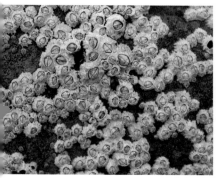

Stellate barnacle openings are roughly oval.

Stellate barnacles grow on the high shore where they are out of the water for a long time.

Australasian barnacles have four shell plates.

Note the pointed shape of the Australasian barnacle.

Australasian Barnacle

Irish Garbhán Astrálach   **Latin** *Austrominius modestus*

Size Approx. 1cm diameter
Distribution Mid to high on rocky shores
Similar species Acorn barnacle, stellate barnacle

Australasian barnacles are not nearly as common as the other barnacle species. They are not native but have become established in some areas, especially in the south-west. The main identifying feature is that the shell wall is divided into four (not six) plates.

All acorn barnacles also have four central plates that they open when the tide is in and they want to feed. Look closely at the shape of these plates: they are straight-sided and arrow-shaped in Australasian acorn barnacles (unlike the other acorn barnacle species).

Australasian acorn barnacles were first recorded in Ireland in 1957. They probably arrived here on ships. By the time they were recorded here, they were already well established around Great Britain and many other areas of Europe. Unlike the native species, Australasian acorn barnacles can reproduce all year round. They have also settled in estuaries and areas where native barnacles do not normally thrive.

The reproductive organ of a parasitic barnacle on a shore crab.

Parasitic Barnacle

Latin *Sacculina carcina*
Size 2.5cm wide
Distribution Not well studied, on bodies of swimming crabs

When you first notice the parasitic barnacle, you might think that you've found a crab that is brooding eggs. However, what you have found is the female reproductive organ of a parasite tucked into the abdomen of a shore crab or other swimming crab. It is creamy yellow and if you look carefully you will notice an opening on the upper side, opposite the crab's abdomen flap.

The crab could have been infected up to three years previously by the female parasite as it floated in the plankton. These females grow a network of rootlike filaments within the crab's body to absorb nutrients. Infected crabs become infertile and cannot moult. When the external stage of the parasite emerges, the host crab, whether male or female, cares for the parasite as if caring for its own eggs.

In some areas, half of the population of swimming crabs or more are infected by the parasitic barnacle.

Goose Barnacle

Irish Giúrann **Latin** *Lepas anatifera*

Size < 4cm long (shells)
Distribution Atlantic coasts

Like other barnacles, goose barnacles do not have one solid shell; instead, the body is encased in four blue-white plates. Each barnacle attaches itself to a hard surface with strong adhesive and a flexible stalk that can be up to 15cm long. If the shell plates are open, the flesh inside is orange-brown and you might see the long, feathery feeding arms.

Goose barnacles are not a seashore species but live on floating objects out at sea. These objects sometimes get washed ashore with the goose barnacles still attached. If they have been washed up for a long time, they are likely to be dried out and dead.

The long neck, beak-shaped shells and feathery feeding arms led people to think that goose barnacles were the embryonic life stage of the barnacle goose. Before the breeding grounds of these migrating visitors were found, it seemed possible that they started life in the ocean.

A colony of long-necked goose barnacles.

Goose barnacles grow on driftwood and other floating objects.

Sandhopper

Irish Dreancaid trá   **Latin** *Talitrus saltator*
Size < 2.5cm
Distribution High on sandy beaches

Sandhoppers burrow into the sand.

If you catch a sandhopper lying still, you will see it has a grey-white, almost translucent body, with one long antenna and many legs. You might also notice its black eyes. Sandhoppers are particularly common among decaying seaweed, especially the tough kelps, at the high-tide mark on sandy beaches. Other similar species are common among rocks and stones. Without a microscope, it is very difficult to tell the different species apart.

Sandhoppers usually spend the day buried in the sand. When disturbed, they can jump up to 30cm at a time. Sandhoppers are an essential part of the beach ecosystem. They are scavengers that clean up the sand. They, in turn, are eaten by larger animals.

Sandhoppers curl up when disturbed.

A gravel shore sandhopper.

Sea slaters live on piers and rocky surfaces.

They can vary in colour.

Sea Slater

Irish Cláirseach thrá **Latin** *Ligia oceanica*

Size < 3cm

Distribution Rocky shores and solid structures

Sea slaters are coastal cousins of woodlice, and look quite similar. They are olive green or grey and have slightly flattened, oval-shaped bodies. Their eyes are large and black. There are two long appendages that stick out from the back and look like a double tail.

Sea slaters usually hide in crevices or under stones during the day, so you are likely to find one only if you disturb it. At night, however, they emerge to feed on detritus, decaying seaweed, bits of plankton and anything else they can find. Like their relatives, the sandhoppers, they play an important role in cleaning up the shoreline. They often live hidden in the cracks of piers or other man-made structures and can survive for up to three years.

Pill Isopod

Latin *Sphaeromatidae*
Size < 1cm
Distribution Rocky shores

Pill isopods look like little capsule-shaped woodlice. They vary in colour from creamy white to olive green and can be patterned. They have large eyes and antennae on their head. Their back end is smooth, rounded and has leg-like appendages. Pill isopods can roll up into tight balls when disturbed. There are several similar species. All of them are southern species that prefer warmer shores.

You might find pill isopods in 'family' groups sheltering under stones on rocky shores. The young are brooded in internal pouches and usually hatch in late summer. They can live for around three years.

Pill isopods have two leg-like appendages on their back end.

Pill isopods burrow or curl up when they're disturbed.

Big-eye amphipods curl up when disturbed.

Note the bright green eyes and the long 'tail'.

Big-eye Amphipod

Latin *Hyperia galba*

Size < 1.5cm

Distribution Widespread, especially with jellyfish

Big-eye amphipods usually live alongside jellyfish.

Big-eye amphipods look like pale-coloured insects. Their bulbous eyes are bright green. The males have long antennae. The abdomen and tail is much narrower than the rest of the body, especially in females.

Big-eye amphipods are often associated with jellyfish, especially those that normally live further off the coast. They cling to a jellyfish and nibble at its body or at ripe eggs. They also eat the prey that the jellyfish catches. Big-eye amphipods that live like this usually have clear bodies, but when they swim independently their bodies are darker.

Snails, Mussels and their Relatives

Almost all of the shells that you find on Irish beaches belong to one of the most diverse groups of animals on the planet: the molluscs. On Irish shorelines these include the speedy octopus and squid (cephalopods), the slow-moving sea snails (gastropods) and chitons (polyplacophorans), and the sedentary blue mussel and oyster (bivalves). Many of Ireland's rocky shores are exposed to the wind and waves, which actually suits these hardy animals.

Despite their diversity, all molluscs share a number of defining features: the body has a head and a foot, and is at least partly covered by the mantle, which is like a thick cloak of skin. There is a space between the mantle and the rest of the body called the mantle cavity. In most marine molluscs, gills pump water in and out of this cavity to absorb the oxygen from it. Some molluscs are filter-feeders. In these species, the gills also pull in food. Most molluscs secrete a shell. This shell has three layers: a horny outer layer, a chalky middle layer and a pearly inner layer.

Molluscs have been historically important as a source of food for coastal communities. Irish people still have a taste for mussels and scallops, but we tend to shun the snails, now exporting them to other countries.

Snails, slugs and limpets

Sea slugs and snails are all gastropods, which means 'belly-footed' and refers to the large muscular foot on which the animals glide. Gastropod shells range from the dome shape of the common

limpet to the pointed spirals of the periwinkles and whelks. Shells provide protection from predators, heat and drying out during low tide. Because sea snails don't have external shells, it is uncommon to find them out of the water.

Gastropod shells have openings that require added protection. For this reason, limpets use their muscular foot to cling tightly to the rocks. Many of the snails have a hard disc called an operculum that they can shut like a trapdoor to cover the opening of their shells. You may also find periwinkles or whelks congregating in groups in damp, hidden areas of the shore, such as in crevices, under ledges and in seagrass beds. Despite all this protection, gastropods are eaten by birds, crabs, mammals and other molluscs.

Gastropods have a sharp, rasping tongue called a radula. Some, like the edible periwinkle and limpet, graze from the surface of the rocks using a scraping radula. Others, like the dog whelk, use their radula to drill through the shells of their prey.

Bivalves – open and shut

Bivalves, such as the blue mussel, have two shells that are attached at one point and can be opened or shut. They are all filter feeders: they strain food particles from the water as it flows across them. Many bivalves also have two siphons: one to carry water into the gills and one to release the water. Some species, including the tellin, have very long siphons which they use like vacuum cleaners to suck debris directly from the seabed.

Bivalves cannot glide like gastropods, but many burrow into the sand, and some, such as scallops, can even swim. Unlike the burrowing bivalves, mussels attach themselves to rocks using thick hairs called byssus threads. These are the 'beards' that we wash off mussels before eating them.

Other Molluscs

Surprisingly, chitons and cephalopods are also members of this family. Chitons are also known as coat-of-mail shells and can be found hugging tightly to the underside of rocks on the shore. Cephalopods include octopus, squid and cuttlefish. While we have these in Ireland, you do not often see them from the shore. The cephalopod you are most likely to encounter is the internal shell of cuttlefish (see page 49).

The delicate shell of a juvenile dog whelk.

Dog whelks lay yellow egg capsules in crevices and under stones.

Dog Whelk

Irish Cuachma chon
Latin *Nucella lapillus*

Size <4cm
Distribution Rocky shores
Similar species Common whelk, oyster drill, thick-lipped whelk

A striped dog whelk.

Dog whelks are common on rocky shores. They often congregate together under ledges or in crevices. Their shells spiral into a sharp point, but thicken and weather with age and become much smoother. Colours range from bright white to grey and brown, depending on their diet. Just inside the opening of the shell, small bumps like tiny teeth are sometimes visible. They look very similar to the common whelk, but are much smaller.

Dog whelks are predators; they drill into the shells of their prey, using a chemical to soften the shell as they go. After that, they inject the prey with a chemical to paralyse and begin to digest the body before they suck it out. If you find an empty shell with a very neat round hole in it, it is likely that it was the victim of a whelk.

Dog whelks stick their yellow eggs, which are the size of grape seeds, to the underside of rocks.

The toothy bumps and siphonal canal of adult dog whelks.

Dog whelks group together in damp, shady places during low tide.

Oyster Drill/Sting Winkle

Irish Feannadóir **Latin** Ocenebra erinacea
Size < 5cm
Distribution Low on rocky shores
Similar species Dog whelk, thick-lipped whelk

The opening of an oyster drill.

The oyster drill is also called a sting winkle. Its spiral shell has a very pointed spire and is highly decorated with ribs that stick out. It does not spiral smoothly – each swirl is very distinct. The shell is white, but it is often covered in algae and barnacles. It can grow larger than the dog whelk (see page 125), but is smaller than the common whelk (see page 129). It lives lower down the shore than the dog whelk.

Oyster drills are whelks, so they are predators. They drill a hole in the shell of their prey and inject it with a poison. They lay triangular yellow egg capsules on seagrass, algae and stones in the spring and summer. Each capsule contains around 300 eggs.

The ribbed shell of an oyster drill.

An oyster drill covered in algae.

Ridges run from top to bottom on thick-lipped whelk shells.

The edge of the opening is thick and curls outwards.

Thick-lipped Whelk

Irish Cuachma chon bhruasach **Latin** *Nassarius incrassatus*

Size < 1.2cm
Distribution Low on rocky shores
Similar species Dog whelk, oyster drill

The small thick-lipped whelk has a brown shell with rounded whorls that spiral into a sharp point. Ridges run down the length of the shell, but it does not have the squared patterning of the netted dog whelk (see page 125). The shell opening is symmetrically oval, and the outer lip is quite thick and curls outwards. You might notice a series of blunt 'teeth' on this edge.

Thick-lipped whelks are not as common high up on the shore as the dog whelk, but they are widespread. They are often associated with seagrass beds, where they lay their eggs.

Netted dog whelks are creamy brown with a criss-cross pattern.

Netted Dog Whelk

Irish Cuachma chon mhogallach   **Latin** *Hinia reticulata*

Size < 3cm

Distribution Sandy shores

Netted dog whelks live under the water on sandy shores.

Netted dog whelks are small and pale brown. They have criss-cross patterns that give the appearance of a net. Their pointed shells are more smooth-sided than other whelks. In older individuals, the opening is thickened and has 'teeth' on the inside of the outer edge.

Netted dog whelks are scavengers. They bury in the sand and then emerge to sniff out the carcasses of crabs, fish and other animals. Underwater, they can occur in high densities when feeding. You are most likely to find the empty shells washed up on the beach. Sometimes these are inhabited by hermit crabs (see page 104).

Common Whelk

Irish Cuachma **Latin** *Buccinum undatum*

Size Up to 12cm
Distribution Low-shore to subtidal on sandy or muddy shores
Similar species Dog whelk, oyster drill

Common whelks usually live in deeper waters or in deep rock pools on sandy and muddy shores. However, you might find their strong, spiralled white or grey shells washed up and empty. They are carnivorous and actively seek crabs, worms, bivalves and dead animals. The common whelk uses an organ called an osphradium, which it points in the direction of the current, to detect the smell of its prey. Once it has found a target, the whelk grasps its prey using its foot and then bores through the prey's shell using its sharp teeth. It then extracts and eats the body.

The egg cases of the common whelk are referred to as 'wash balls' and look like a mass of bubbles stuck together. You might even mistake them for old polystyrene or packaging material! The washed-up mass of eggs can be as big as a grapefruit.

Try putting the shell of a common whelk to your ear. Can you hear the sea?

The robust common whelk is much larger than the other whelks.

Common whelk egg mass washed ashore.

Mudsnails often congregate together and (inset) a tiny mudsnail on eggwrack..

Mudsnail/Laver Spire

Irish Seilide hidribiach **Latin** *Hydrobia ulvae*
Size < 0.5cm
Distribution Sandy or muddy shores

Mudsnails are very small, smaller than the nail on your little finger. They have swirling, spire-shaped shells, but the tip is usually quite blunt. The shell colour varies from white to brown. They often appear as small bumps just under the surface of sandy shores, below the high-tide mark. They are associated with tidal flats, estuaries and seagrass beds.

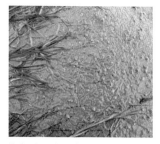

Mudsnails on the surface of a muddy shore.

You may notice large densities of mud snails climbing vertically on vegetation or debris. As the tide comes in, the mudsnails secrete a little raft made of mucous and they float in the water, feeding on detritus that gets trapped in this mucous. They also feed on particles along the surface of the sediment once they sink back down.

Mudsnails reach maturity after about a year. They can live for about two and half years.

Needle Whelk

Latin *Bittium reticulatum*
Size < 1cm
Distribution Widespread on the low shore
Similar species Mudsnail

Needle whelks have tiny, elongated shells. They are usually orange or brown and have clearly defined whorls that spiral up to the pointed tip. Ridges run horizontally and vertically along these whorls.

Needle whelks are particularly common where there is eelgrass (see page 22), but they can live on sandy or muddy shores, or among rocks and stones. You will usually find them close to the low-tide mark. They can live down to depths of 250m beneath the surface. They feed on a wide range of microorganisms.

Needle whelks are tiny, orange, and pointed.

Auger/Screw Shell

Irish Cuach coirn **Latin** Turritella communis
Size < 4cm
Distribution Sandy/muddy shores

Auger or screw shells are tall shells with clearly defined whorls that spiral up to a pointed tip. Each of these is delicately ridged. They are yellow-brown, but become pale towards the tip and as the shell ages. The colouring can be banded. The area around the shell opening is white or lilac.

Auger shells live buried horizontally in the sand or mud with their shell openings facing upwards. They breathe and feed by pulling in water from just above the sediment.

Auger shells lay clusters of egg capsules that they attach to the ground with a stalk. Each of these capsules contains up to 20 eggs.

Note the lilac colouring around the opening.

Auger shells are obviously coiled.

Edible periwinkles are the largest winkles on Irish shores.

The opening is teardrop shaped and often has zebra stripes.

Edible Periwinkle

Irish Gioradán **Latin** *Littorina littorea*

Size Up to 3cm
Distribution Widespread
Similar species Rough periwinkle

Edible periwinkles can vary in colour.

The edible periwinkle is very common at all shore heights on rocky shores, especially in crevices, among the seaweeds on which it grazes and on beds of eelgrass (see page 22). This is the largest of the winkles. The coiled shell has a pointed tip. It is usually dark grey or brown, often with stripes. Sometimes, the shell can be grey or even red. The snail-like body inside the shell is black. At low tide, they cover their vulnerable aperture (opening) with a hard disc called an operculum. This opening is teardrop-shaped, which makes it different from the smaller winkles.

Although it is uncommon to find periwinkles for sale in Ireland, they are picked and exported to markets on mainland Europe. They are grazing herbivores and are eaten by birds and crabs.

Rough periwinkles come in many different colours.

They often have obvious ridges or stripes.

Edible periwinkle (top), rough periwinkle (bottom): The opening of the rough periwinkle is shaped more like a D than the edible periwinkle and the snail is whiter.

Rough Periwinkle

Irish Faocha garbh
Latin *Littorina saxatilis*

Size < 18mm
Distribution Rocky shores
Similar species Juvenile edible periwinkles

The rough periwinkle is common around the coast of Ireland on rocky shores throughout the intertidal zone, especially in crevices, under stones and inside empty barnacle shells. Sometimes, it also lives on the base of plants on salt marshes. The shell of the rough periwinkle is plump, with a short spire. As the name suggests, the shell has a rough texture. The colour may vary from yellowish white, to green, red or brown. This species may be confused with small edible periwinkles (see page 133). However, a useful tip for distinguishing the two is by comparing their apertures (shell openings). The aperture of the rough periwinkle is large and shaped like a capital 'D', while that of the edible winkle has more of a teardrop shape.

Flat Periwinkle

Irish Faocha leathan **Latin** Littorina obtusata
Size < 1cm

The flat periwinkle is common, especially on seaweed. The colour of its delicate, coiled shell can vary from a well-camouflaged green or brown, to bright yellow and orange. Although the shell curls, it is not at all pointed. It is not unusual to find a wide range of shell colours on a single shore.

Flat periwinkle eggs on serrated wrack.

Flat periwinkles graze on many varieties of wrack (see the brown seaweed section), even the knotted egg wrack, which is inedible to most species.

Rather than broadcasting their eggs into the plankton, flat periwinkles lay eggs on seaweed or on rocks. These are white and kidney-shaped and are laid in a jelly mass.

Flat periwinkles graze on seaweed.

Flat periwinkle shells are not pointed and vary in colour.

Violet snail shells are delicate and easily broken.

The shell is darkest near the opening.

Violet Snail

Irish Gnamhán corcra **Latin** *Janthina* spp.

Size < 1cm
Distribution Rare, but could occur on any coast

There are a few species of violet snail and all of them have thin, delicate shells that are a similar shape to land snails but are a mix of pale lilac and strong purple, hence the name. The rounded shell is thinner than a periwinkle and breaks easily, but you may find them washed up on shores after strong winds.

Violet snails live their entire lives at sea. Instead of crawling around with their shells on top of them, they float, shell down, at the surface of the ocean. They stay afloat by reaching up out of the water and trapping air bubbles to make a little mucous raft. Their shells are much lighter than most sea snails as they do not need to protect themselves against waves hitting the shore. They have no eyes on the end of their tentacles and they feed on by-the-wind sailors (see page 207) and other floating creatures.

Flat Topshell

Irish Faochán Mhuire corcra   **Latin** *Gibbula umbilicalis*
Size < 2cm
Distribution Rocky shores
Similar species Other topshells

Flat topshells live on rocky shores and in rock pools. They are often under rocks or grazing on seaweed. They do not eat the seaweed itself, but feed on any detritus covering the surface. Flat topshells have silver or grey shells with blurred purple bands. They could be confused with other topshells, but the key is in their Latin name: *umbilicalis* refers to the small hole – like a bellybutton – on its underside near to the shell opening. This bellybutton is much larger than in similar species. The purple lines are also farther apart. As the name suggests, the shell is not sharply pointed. Nonetheless, the tip is often worn and silvery.

It is thought that flat topshells can live for more than eight years.

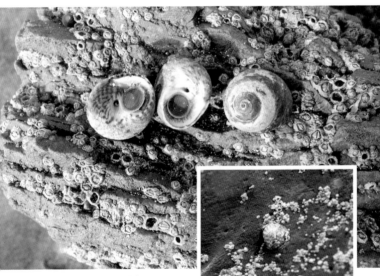

Flat topshells have a bellybutton hole next to the shell opening.

They have wide purple stripes; the tip of the shell is often worn and shiny.

The outer layer of toothed topshells is often worn away.

A small 'tooth' sticks out from the inner edge of the shell opening.

Toothed Topshell

Irish Faocha chíre **Latin** *Osilinus lineatus*
Size <3cm
Distribution Rocky shores
Similar species Flat topshell, grey topshell, turban topshell

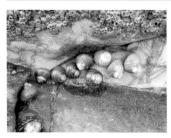

Toothed topshells have dark zigzag patterns.

The toothed topshell is common along the middle of moderately exposed rocky shores. The shell may be dark green, grey or black with brown or purple zigzag patterns. In older individuals, the outer layer of the shell may be worn off at the tip, revealing the pearly inner layer. The key to telling these topshells from the flat topshell (see page 137) is to look for the single protruding 'tooth' that sticks out into the shell opening.

The toothed topshell does not have a 'bellybutton' like the flat topshell. Both species have a similar zigzag pattern and pearly inner shell.

Grey Topshell

Irish Faochán Mhuire glas **Latin** *Gibbula cineraria*
Size 1.5cm tall
Distribution Low on sheltered rocky shores
Similar species Flat topshell, toothed topshell

The underside of a grey topshell

The grey topshell has a smoothly triangular shell that is grey but has many fine purple lines. The tip of the shell can be worn away and shiny. It might be easy to confuse this with other topshells. On the underside, there is a very small hole, or 'bellybutton' near the main opening. This is not as big as the bellybutton on the flat topshell (see page 137). The purple lines are also much narrower and continue all the way to the tip of the shell. The shell itself is also more triangular and smooth-sided than toothed or flat topshells.

Grey topshells are grazers and eat tiny microalgae and other particles. They do not have the hardened teeth that limpets have, so they cannot eat some of the tougher, large seaweeds or encrusting algae (see page 66).

The triangular outline of a grey topshell.

Painted topshells are triangular and brightly coloured.

The base of the shell is flat.

Painted Topshell

Irish Faochán Mhuire dathannach
Latin *Calliostoma zizyphinum*

Size < 3cm
Distribution Rocky shores

The pretty painted topshell is most common on seaweed-covered rocky shores from the extreme low-tide mark to 300m below tide. While you might not see live individuals without getting wet, the shells are often found washed up and empty on the shore.

The shell of the painted topshell is a straight-sided conical shape with a sharp point and a flat base. The colouration of this shell is highly decorative and can be pale pink, violet or yellowish with purple, red or brown markings. These attractive colours follow through to the body tissue, which is mottled with similar colours.

Turban Topshell

Latin *Gibbula magus*

Size < 3cm tall
Distribution Low on rocky or muddy shores
Similar species Flat topshell, toothed topshell

The turban topshell is much broader than it is tall. Unlike the other topshells, the outline of the shell is not smooth or rounded – it is more like a wedding cake, with angled steps between each layer. There are also little ridges on the upper surface of some of the layers. The background colour is a pale yellow with reddish markings. It has a large 'bellybutton' on the underside, beside the main opening.

This is a southern species that prefers warmer waters. It eats tiny particles that it grazes from the surface of rocks or sand.

Turban topshells are obviously coiled.

Turban topshells live on rocky or muddy shores.

Large Necklace Shell

Irish Bráisléad mór **Latin** *Euspira catena*
Size < 3.5cm tall
Distribution Low on sandy shores

The large necklace shell, or moon snail, has a cream or orange shell that is highly rounded and swirls into a blunt point. There is a single row of brown markings on the upper spirals. The main part of the shell is quite fat and the D-shaped opening is large. It may be striped. Beside the opening there is a large round 'bellybutton'. When moving, the body of the snail envelopes the shell as it moves along. This makes it very streamlined so that it can easily burrow into the sand to search for burrowing bivalves, which it preys on. It also prevents predators like starfish from being able to grip the shell easily.

Necklace shells get their name from the long coiled egg 'collars' that they lay in the sand. These contain large numbers of eggs. Some of the eggs hatch, others are 'nurse' eggs that provide food for the developing embryos.

Large necklace shells are sometimes called 'moonsnails'.

The 'bellybutton' and shell opening are both large.

The shell opening is straight and serrated.

The European cowrie is pink or orange with three brown spots

European Cowrie

Irish Fínicín eorpach **Latin** Trivia monacha
Size < 12mm long
Distribution Rocky shores

The European or spotted cowrie is most commonly found around the west coast of Ireland on the lower rocky shore. Live specimens are often found together with their prey: sea squirts. The empty shells may be more familiar as they are often found washed up on the shore.

This cowrie has a unique egg-shaped, thick and glossy shell with deep ridges and a long narrow aperture (opening). The rounded upper side of the shell is a pinkish-brown colour and has three characteristic spots. The flat underside is white. When the cowrie is active, its body tissue wraps up around a large portion of the shell and the brightly coloured head, tentacles and foot are visible.

Sea Hare

Irish Giorria mara **Latin** *Aplysia punctata*
Size Usually approx. 7cm. Can be up to 20cm
Distribution Lower shore or rock pools

The sea hare usually lives in shallow water on the lower shore or in rock pools. It is generally 7cm long, but can grow to 20cm. Sea hares vary in colour and may be green, brown, red or purple. This reflects the colour of the algae that they eat. They have grey and white blotches and sometimes have black spots and a black veining pattern along the body. The body is long and has a narrow foot. The sea hare has two long, slender tentacles on its head, which resemble the long ears on a hare. Sea hares have a transparent internal shell that can be seen through an opening in the mantle. When disturbed, the sea hare produces white and purple secretions.

An elegant sea hare in a rock pool.

A feathery common grey sea slug.

Eggs on the underside of a stone on the low shore.

Common Grey Sea Slug

Irish Bodalach glas **Latin** *Aeolidia papillosa*
Size < 12cm long
Distribution Widespread, low on rocky shores

Sea slugs are generally far more attractive than their close relatives that we find in our gardens. The common grey is widespread on rocky shores, but usually lives below the low-tide mark. They are a pale grey with many shaggy-looking outgrowths along either side. The eggs are white or pinkish and are laid in a characteristic mass on the undersides of stones. The egg mass is convoluted – a bit like the shape of an intestine – and is usually laid in a spiral. When they hatch, the larvae float in the plankton for a short time before they settle.

Adults eat a variety of sea anemones, especially the beadlet anemone (see page 212). The slug consumes the anemone's stinging cells and transports any undischarged cells through the gut and into the tips of the decorative frills on its body. It then uses these cells to defend itself against predators.

Common Limpet

Irish Bairneach coiteann   **Latin** *Patella vulgata*

Size Up to 6cm
Distribution Rocky shores
Similar species China limpet

Common limpets always return to the same spot when the tide goes out.

Alongside acorn barnacles and edible periwinkles, the common limpet is one of the best-known intertidal animals. The shells are conical, and the highest point is more or less central. Ridges radiate out from this point. The shell is usually white or grey, but can have a tortoiseshell pattern. The colour can vary if algae build up on it. When the tide is out, the limpet contracts its strong foot and clings tightly to the rock. If you try to pull it off, it will just cling more tightly. Look carefully in a rock pool and you may see a limpet moving about and grazing. It uses its sharp radula to scrape microorganisms and seaweeds from the rock. Sometimes you can even hear them scratching away.

When limpets move, they leave a trail that they follow when it is time to go back home. Limpets make a small depression or 'home scar' in the rock that their shell fits into tightly. This stops them from drying out at low tide. Limpets have been known to live for up to 17 years.

Common limpets are characteristic of Irish rocky shores.

Common limpets have creamy white bodies.

China limpets are usually flattened. The ridges alternate between single ridges and triple ridges.

China Limpet

Irish Bairneach **Latin** *Patella ulyssiponensis*
Size < 5cm long
Distribution Low on exposed rocky shores
Similar species Common limpet

The china limpet is very similar to the common limpet. However, there are some key differences. The shell of the china limpet is usually flatter – more like a little hill than a volcano; the highest point is off-centre towards the front of the shell; the ridges that run down the shell are usually much more pronounced, and you might be able to notice that they alternate between single ridges and triple ridges. China limpets never live on very sheltered shores; they live low down close to the low-tide mark or in rock pools, and they do not like fresh water, so you will not find them near rivers. The name comes from the glossy inside of the shell that is like porcelain china. They have a very similar lifestyle to the common limpet (see page 146). As the shells become worn with age, it can be even more difficult to differentiate the two species.

The iridescent blue stripes on a young blue-rayed limpet.

Young blue-rayed limpets are tiny and delicate.

The pearly inside of a blue-rayed limpet.

The blue rays wear away as the limpet ages.

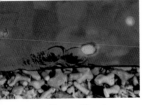

Blue-rayed limpets graze on kelp, leaving distinctive marks.

Blue-rayed Limpet

Irish Bairneach mín
Latin *Patina pellucida*

Size < 2cm
Distribution Exposed lower shores on brown seaweeds

The blue-rayed limpet lives around the Irish coast on exposed shores. It is found on the fronds and blades of brown seaweeds of the lower shore, including kelps, wracks and sea spaghetti.

The shell of this species is oval-shaped, smooth and translucent, with a brownish-yellow colour with iridescent blue rays that fan out from the head end. It is much smaller than the common limpet, growing up to a maximum of 2cm. As it ages, the shell thickens and the blue rays become less distinct.

The blue-rayed limpet creates charac-teristic holes in the surface of the seaweed on which it feeds.

Coat-of-Mail/Chiton

Irish Ciotán maille
Latin Lepicochitona cinereus
Size 4cm approx.
Distribution Low on rocky shores
Similar species There are various species, which are difficult to tell apart.

Coat-of-mail shells, or chitons, are a little similar to the outer shell of a woodlouse, but they have no legs, obvious head or antennae. They cling tightly to the underside of rocks or to shells. There are a few species, but all of them have a shell divided into about eight plates. These plates are all slightly pointed in the middle to form a central ridge. The shell is surrounded by a softer, fleshy girdle. Sometimes this girdle has small hairs or spines. Colours can vary hugely and they are often heavily patterned.

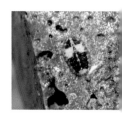

A black and white chiton.

A brightly coloured chiton.

You will rarely see the underside of a chiton, but the body is made up of a large foot, a mouth, an anus and up to 20 pairs of gills, which are tucked inside the girdle.

Because of their articulated shells, coat-of-mail shells can move over and cling to very irregular surfaces as they graze. If they are knocked from the rocks, they can curl up into a ball and be rolled around by the waves without their soft bodies being damaged.

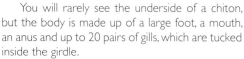

Chitons cling tightly to hard surfaces.

A chiton moving along a rock.

Common/Blue Mussel

Irish Diúilicín　**Latin** *Mytilus edulis*

⚠ **Caution:** Edible – but be careful

Size Up to 10cm
Distribution Rocky substrates
Similar species Horse mussel

The common mussel lives in water up to 10m deep and attaches itself to hard surfaces like rocks or even other mussels, using tough, sticky threads called byssus threads. They prefer exposed shores where currents bring plenty of food and prevent mussels from becoming smothered by sand and other particles. Common mussels have two smooth, oblong shells, which are usually purple, blue or dark brown, inside and out.

Mussels are ecologically important as they filter out floating particles in the water, resulting in clearer, cleaner waters. They also increase the area of hard surface available for other animals and seaweeds, resulting in increased biodiversity.

Common mussels are an economically important product of aquaculture in Ireland. If you choose to collect and eat mussels yourself, be very careful to avoid the summer months when there is a risk of red tide or toxic algal blooms that can cause severe poisoning. It is advisable to rinse the mussels through for a number of hours prior to cooking.

Blue mussels grow in dense 'beds'.

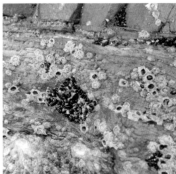

Juvenile mussels can use empty barnacles for shelter.

Horse mussels are blunter than edible blue mussels.

The inside shell is white.

Horse Mussel

Irish Diúilicín capaill **Latin** *Modiolus modiolus*
Size 10–20cm
Distribution All coasts
⚠ **Caution:** Many populations in decline
Similar species Blue mussel

Horse mussels can grow larger than the more familiar blue mussel. They darken as they age, becoming dark brown or black. They often have lighter yellow or brown stripes. If the shell is fresh, there might be a thin papery coating that peels away. The inside of the shell is pure white.

Horse mussels are long-lived (up to 25 years). They live in colonies on the seabed that create reefs for other creatures to inhabit. They also filter large quantities of water, keeping it clean and clear. These reefs can be easily destroyed by dredging or fishing with gear that drags along the sea floor.

European Oyster

Irish Oisre Eorpach coiteann **Latin** Ostrea edulis
Size Up to 11cm
Distribution Sandy, muddy or pebbled shallow coasts and estuaries
Similar species Pacific oyster

Older shells can appear scally and brittle.

European oyster shells are grey or white and very rough on the outside. The inner part is pearly. The two halves are different shapes – one of shells is flatter and fits inside the more cupped shell. Both shells are roughly oval shaped. The two halves are held together by an elastic ligament, which disappears over time. Older oyster shells may appear scaly and brittle.

European oysters have been eaten and farmed in Europe for many centuries. In some areas, oysters have been overexploited and even where they are farmed, disease can cause decreases in numbers.

The Pacific oyster (see page 153) looks quite similar to the common oyster and has been introduced accidentally to many areas. Pacific oysters outcompete the native European oyster, which has added to their decline.

The inside of one shell is cupped.

European oysters are white and almost circular.

This shell is deeply cupped with obvious ridges.

Pacific oysters sometimes have purple streaks.

Pacific Oyster

Irish Oisre an Aigéin Chiúin **Latin** *Crassostrea gigas*
Size Up to 18cm
Distribution Sandy, muddy or pebbled shallow coasts and estuaries
Similar species European oyster

Pacific oysters have elongated, oval shells with wavy ridges. On the outside, the shells can be white or brown, sometimes with purple streaks. Inside, the shells are pearly white. There is sometimes a mark left behind by the strong muscle that the oyster uses to keep the shells closed. This mark is often purple. One of the shells is deeply cupped

Note the elongated oval shape.

and has six or seven obvious ridges. The other shell is much flatter, but with an edge that fits perfectly to the ridges of the cupped shell.

Pacific oysters are natives of Japan and South-east Asia. They were brought to Europe intentionally for farming, but they have escaped and spread in many areas. They can overgrow native oyster reefs and reproduce more quickly than native European oysters (see page 152). They also prefer warmer waters, so will probably continue to flourish in Irish waters if sea temperatures continue to increase.

A pearly saddle oyster with the characteristic hole.

Shells are smooth and shiny.

Juveniles on the underside of a rock on the low shore.

Saddle oysters can become worn and lose their original shape.

Saddle Oyster

Irish Sligín slámach coiteann
Latin *Anomia ephippium*

Size < 6cm
Distribution Widespread

Saddle oyster shells are fairly common among shells along the tideline. They are roughly circular, but irregular and rarely flat. They are pearly white, silver, or lilac on the inside and can sparkle brightly on a sunny day. The bottom shell has a large hole. Saddle oysters cling tightly to rocks or other surfaces by using strong byssus threads that grow out through this hole. They cling so closely that the shell takes on the shape of whatever surface it has grown on. The upper shell is more dome-shaped. Overall, the shell is very thin and brittle. It is usually white, but can have a pink tinge. You might find saddle oysters growing on the sides or undersides of rocks on the middle shore and below.

Banded Wedge Shell

Irish Sliogán dinge bandach **Latin** *Donax vittatus*
Size Up to 3cm
Distribution Common throughout Irish sandy shores
Similar species Thin tellin

The curved outer edge is serrated.

The banded wedge shell lives between the mid shore and depths of up to 20m. It buries beneath the surface of sandy shores and bays. The triangular shell is shiny with bands of white, yellow, brown or purple running horizontally. The edge of the shell is serrated.

The banded wedge shell uses siphons to draw in water from the surface. As it sucks in this water, hairlike filters in its mouth extract food while the gills absorb oxygen. If disturbed or exposed, it extends its foot downwards to act as an anchor and pull itself deeper. At low tide, when the sediment is most frequently disturbed, banded wedge shells can leap from the surface and rebury themselves. This can attract predators, such as gulls.

Note the characteristic wedge shape.

Banded wedge shells vary in colour.

Tellins have a roughly oval shape and delicate shells.

Tellins

Irish Teillíneach **Latin** *Tellinidae*
Size < 2.5cm wide
Distribution Sandy shores
Similar species Banded wedge shell

Tellins have thin grey or white shells, often with pink or pale orange banding. They are ear-shaped, with a curved outer edge and a beak that is nearly central on the pointed edge. There are two common species that are very similar – the thin tellin and the Baltic tellin. Both are common and widespread throughout north-west Europe. The Baltic tellin is slightly more rounded than the thin tellin, and is more common in estuaries and mud.

Both species live buried in the sand. They extend two siphons up into the water and feed on particles that drift past. The tips of their siphons are sometimes eaten by flatfish, but they can survive this and regrow.

For such small shellfish, they have a fairly long lifespan, with individuals recorded to be ten years old.

Banded Carpet Shell

Irish Breallach croise bandach **Latin** *Tapes rhomboides*

Size < 6cm wide
Distribution Muddy sand or gravel shores
Similar species Pullet carpet shell, chequered carpet shell

Banded carpet shells are oval. They are creamy yellow on the outside and usually have purple or brown markings. Inside, the shells are shiny white. The edges are smooth. The beak at the hinge where the two shells join is towards the front end, so each shell is asymmetrical. Both shells have a series of very fine concentric lines running around the shell, but no horizontal lines radiating out from the beak.

Banded carpet shells are widespread and burrow into the ground from where they extend their feeding tubes to pull food out of the water.

The pearly inside of a banded carpet shell.

Notice the concentric lines and the smooth edges.

Pullet carpet shells burrow into sand or gravel.

Notice the rectangular shape. This pullet carpet shell became home to a stellate barnacle and a keel worm.

Pullet Carpet Shell

Latin *Venerupis corrugata*

Size < 5cm

Distribution Sandy or gravel shores

Similar species Banded carpet shell, chequered carpet shell

Pullet carpet shells are pale coloured, but are often tinged with brown or purple. The shell is textured with many tiny ridges that are very close together. There are no lines radiating out from the beak. The edge of the shell is smooth. The rounded 'beak', where the two shells join together, is towards the front of the shell. The overall shape is oval, except the edge furthest from this beak is quite angular and square. The banded carpet shell (see page 157) looks similar but is more elongated and curved.

Chequered Carpet Shell

Latin *Ruditapes decussatus*
Size < 7cm
Distribution Sandy or gravel shores
Similar species Banded carpet shell, pullet carpet shell

The two siphons are clearly visible.

Chequered carpet shells are roughly oval. The slightly pointy 'beak' is off-centre and points forwards. Concentric grooves run around the shell as well as the distinct lines that radiate out from the beak. The other carpet shells do not have these radiating lines. The outer shell is pale, sometimes with darker brown markings. The inside is shiny and sometimes has purple markings. Look inside a carpet shell: a distinctive mark shows where the animal was once attached to the shell. The scar in the chequered carpet shell has more of a 'zigzag' shape than the other carpet shells, which are more like an 'S'.

Chequered carpet shells are suspension feeders. They catch food from the water column by sucking in water with one siphon, gathering any food, and then releasing the filtered water from the other siphon. They are a southern species that reach their northern limit in Britain and Ireland.

Chequered carpet shells are criss-crossed by fine ridges.

Notice the shape of the scar left behind by the animal.

Blunt gapers have one very straight end.

The inside of a blunt gaper shell.

Blunt Gaper

Irish Breallach maol **Latin** *Mya truncata*
Size < 7.5cm wide
Distribution Muddy or sandy shores

Blunt gapers have strong, dirty-white shells that have a series of fine, concentric lines running along them. One end is obviously straightened or 'blunt' compared to the other, which is more rounded. You may find the two parts of the blunt gaper shell together, in which case you can look for the spoon-like projection that sticks out of one of the shells.

Blunt gapers live buried in muddy sand. They are common all over north-west Europe. They look very similar to otter shells (see page 161), but they are smaller and distinctly asymmetrical.

Otter Shell

Irish Sliogán dobharchú cioteann **Latin** *Lutraria lutraria*
Size < 15cm wide
Distribution Muddy sand or gravel shores

Otter shells are large and almost oval. If you find the two shells still attached, you'll notice that they don't quite meet each other the whole way around. If the shell is fresh, there is a thin brown coating on the outside that peels away. The shells can be white, pale orange, or brown, with a pattern of concentric lines.

Otter shells live buried up to 30cm in sand or gravel. They have long siphons that they can extend up to the seabed. When alive, otter shells remain more or less stationary their entire lives, digging deeper with age.

When they are fresh, you might be able to tell them apart by the papery brown coating on the otter shell and the flatter bottom edge, but this is very difficult as the shells age.

The common otter shell has nothing to do with otters. Its name originates from a spelling mistake! The biologist who first named it intended to call it *Lutaria* meaning silt, but he wrote *Lutraria* meaning otter.

The brown coating is still visible on this otter shell.

The inner shell is white.

Icelandic Cyprine

Irish Breallach quahog   **Latin** *Arctica islandica*
Size < 13cm
Distribution Sand at 5–500m depth

The Icelandic cyprine, or ocean quahog, is widely distributed throughout the north Atlantic Ocean. We often find their shells washed up on our shores. These shells are thick and oval-shaped with fine lines running horizontally. They have a brown, thick, flaky coating called a periostracum on the outside of the shell, which peels off once washed ashore.

Icelandic cyprines commonly live for more than 100 years. Growth rings on the inside of their shells help to determine the age of an individual. The oldest known individual was dredged off the coast of Iceland in 2006 and was found to be 507 years old. It was named Ming by *The Sunday Times* because, being born in circa 1499, it would have lived during the Ming dynasty.

The inside of an Icelandic cyprine shell.

The brown periostracum peeling away from the shell.

The outer edge of the shell is slightly ridged.

The ridged shell is not quite symmetrical.

Edible/ Common Cockle

Irish Ruacan **Latin** Cerastoderma edule

Size < 5cm

Distribution Mid to low sandy or muddy shores and estuaries

Similar species Prickly cockle

Common cockles can vary in colour depending on where they live.

The common cockle usually lives buried under the sand, but the empty shells are strong and are commonly found on beaches. Cockles can survive in areas of low salinity, so they are common in estuaries and in the tangled roots of seagrass beds. The shell is white or pale brown, with ridges that fan outwards and growth rings that run perpendicular to the ridges. Each growth ring represents a year, and cockles have been known to live up to nine years.

When the tide comes in, cockles extend their tube-like siphons to the surface to breathe and to feed on particles suspended in the water.

Cockles are still commercially gathered, just as in the days of Molly Malone. They can be dredged up with a rake. Oystercatchers are one of their many natural predators.

Common cockles can be abundant in some areas.

Prickly Cockle

Irish Ruacan garbh **Latin** *Acanthocardia echinata*
Size < 7cm
Distribution Low sandy, muddy or gravel shores
Similar species Common cockle

The prickly cockle usually lives further down the shore than its close relative, the common or edible cockle. It is rare to find this animal alive on the shore. You can tell if a bivalve is still alive if the two parts of the shell are tightly glued together, or if they clamp closed when you tap them. In the image, the cockle is 'gaping'. This is unusual to see. Its pink muscular foot is clearly visible inside. Although it is a similar size and shape to the common cockle, this species has tiny spikes along each of the shell ridges.

There are stories of prickly cockles leaping up to 20cm to escape from predators if disturbed under or out of the water.

A prickly cockle gaping open.

The strong ridges of a warty venus.

*The inner shell is usally white –
this one is discoloured.*

Warty Venus

Irish Maighdeog fhaithneach **Latin** *Venus verrucosa*

Size < 6cm wide
Distribution Low sandy, muddy or gravel shores
Similar species Banded Venus

The warty Venus has a strong, round shell covered in very raised circular ridges. Some of these ridges have an irregular 'warty' surface, especially near the outer edges. The pointed 'beak' is slightly off-centre. The outside of the shell is creamy or brown. The inside is white when it is fresh. The outer edge of the inside of the shell is slightly serrated.

The warty Venus is a southern species that prefers the south and west coasts of Ireland. It lives beneath the sand. If you find one with a perfectly round hole in the shell, it is likely that this particular animal became prey for a large necklace shell (see page 142).

The banded venus has a hooked beak and coloured rays.

Note the layered look of the banded venus shell.

Banded Venus

Irish Maighdeog bhandach **Latin** *Clausinella fasciata*

Size < 2.5cm wide
Distribution Low sandy, muddy or gravel shores
Similar species Warty Venus, rayed trough shell

The banded Venus has a robust, rounded shell. The beak points to one side as if beginning a spiral. The outer shell is usually pale with concentric growth rings visible between the prominent circular ridges. Darker markings fan out from the central beak, these are most visible towards the outer edge of the shell. The outer edge of the underside of the shell is slightly serrated, but only on the side that the beak points towards.

Banded Venus shells live low down on sandy shores all around north-west Europe. They do not bury themselves very deep but live just below the surface.

Northern Lucina

Latin *Lucinoma borealis*
Size < 4cm
Distribution Sandy or muddy shores

Note the straight scar at an angle on the inside of this northern lucina.

Northern Lucina shells are almost circular and not deeply cupped. The point of the shell is in the middle, but angled to the side. Northern Lucina are white and have finely textured ridges. Look inside the shell: you might notice a distinctive straight scar, which no other similar-looking shell has. For such a small shell, it can be quite thick and robust. Northern Lucina shells can be locally abundant in areas on all of Ireland's coasts.

The white, finely ridged surface of the Northern Lucina.

The inner shell is white.

Smooth Artemis

Irish Artaimis mhín **Latin** *Dosinia lupinus*
Size < 4cm
Distribution Sandy shores

Smooth artemis shells aren't actually very smooth, but are textured with very fine lines. They are white or yellow on the outside. The outer edge of the shell is smooth and circular. The shells are not deeply cupped. To tell them apart from similar shells, look at the inside of the shell and see if you can notice the sharp angle that is chopped into the otherwise circular scar left by the animal on the shell.

Smooth artemis bury deep into sand, gravel, or mud, so they can survive on very wave-swept or exposed shores. They occur all over the north east Atlantic, from Iceland to the Canary Islands.

The exterior of a smooth artemis sitting in a child's hand

Note the markings inside the shell

Rayed trough shells.

The inside of the delicate rayed trough shell.

Rayed Trough Shell

Irish Sliogán trach gathach **Latin** *Mactra stultorum*
Size < 5cm wide
Distribution Low sandy, muddy or gravel shores
Similar species Banded Venus

Rayed trough shells are delicate and thin. The blunt beak is more or less central, making the overall shape of each shell triangular with a curved base. The faint concentric growth rings are criss-crossed by darker lines that radiate out from where the two shells join. The inside of the shell is glossy and smooth. The outside is usually a pale colour and the rays are neutral buff or brown. Rayed trough shells prefer clean sand and can occur in large numbers offshore. Many of their shells will wash up on nearby coasts.

Great Scallop

Irish Muirín mór **Latin** *Pecten maximus*
Size < 15cm long
Distribution Sandy or gravel shores
Similar species Other scallops

If you imagine the stereotypical mermaid, it is the shells of the great scallop that would form her bikini top. Both shells of the great scallop are roughly circular with 16 or so ridges that radiate out from the pointed end. From the inside, these ridges are flat-bottomed, not wavy. There are also two straight-edged 'wings' that jut out from the pointed end. This is where the two shells are joined by a strong ligament. The upper shell is fairly flat, but the lower shell is deeply cupped. The shells are usually brown or yellow with white markings.

When great scallops are very small, they attach themselves to the substrate with strong threads. As adults, great scallops live buried in the sand, but can make a rapid escape if disturbed and can swim jerkily by flapping their two shells together. You will often find the strong shells washed up on the shore. Traditionally, scallops were fished for by diving or snorkelling for them. These days, in Ireland, the only licences for fishing scallops are given to dredge boats that scrape them up from the sea floor. They have been overfished in some areas.

One of the great scallop's shells is cupped.

Note the square ridges of the great scallop.

The colourful patterns of the variegated scallop.   *Both shells are cupped.*

Variegated/Black Scallop

Irish Cluaisín garbh   **Latin** *Chlamys varia*
Size < 6.5cm long
Distribution Sandy, gravel and stony shores
Similar species Other scallops

Variegated scallops are asymmetrical.

Variegated scallops are smaller than the great scallop and are more oval than round. They can be brown, red, yellow and patterned. Both shells are cupped. The 'ears' on either side of the beak are not equal. The many ribs that radiate out from the beak are narrow and close together. Some of these ridges have little blunt spikes sticking out from them. These are usually more obvious around the outer edge of the shell.

Variegated scallops use strong byssus threads to attach themselves to rocks and stones. They have been recorded to live for ten years on the west coast.

Variegated scallops are often associated with sponges that live on their shells. The sponge feeds on the small particles that the scallop draws towards it, and the scallop gains protection from predators, such as starfish.

A distorted humpback scallop.

Inner shell.

Humpback Scallop

Latin *Crassadoma pusio*
Size < 3.5cm long
Distribution Rocky shores
Similar species Other scallops

Humpback scallops cling tightly to rocks and become distorted as they grow. They can be white, red, brown or orange. The two 'ears' on either side of the shell are not equal. The many ridges on the shell are delicate. Some of these ribs have small spikes on them.

When humpback scallops first mature, they are usually male. They then become female after they first spawn.

Razorshells

Irish Scian mhara chuar **Latin** *Ensis siliqua/Ensis ensis*
Size Up to 20cm
Distribution Low-water mark of sandy shores

A pod razorshell.

It is common to find empty razorshells washed up on the shore. They are elongated and curve inwards. The two shells are joined on one of the long edges. The outside of the shell often has a flaky brown layer. They are common on sheltered, gently sloping sandy or muddy shores. When alive, the two sides of the shell house a muscular body and live upright buried in the sand. The pod razorshell (*Ensis siliqua*) has tough, straight shells. The curved razorshell (*Ensis ensis*) is slightly smaller and has more delicate shells that curve slightly into a banana shape.

Razorshells, also known as razor clams, are commercially fished in the northern Atlantic. You can find them by looking for a keyhole shape in the sand when the tide is very far out. Sprinkle a little sea salt into these holes and wait for the strong jet of water to squirt out. Sensing the salt, they will then think the tide is coming in, so they will rise up to the surface and you may catch a glimpse of the animal alive.

A curved razorshell.

Common Piddock

Irish Pideog   **Latin** *Pholas dactylus*
Size <12cm
Distribution Soft rock

A common piddock inside the hole it has bored into a rock.

This oblong bivalve has a dull white or grey shell that feels quite brittle. Concentric ridges run across the length and radiating lines fan out from the hinge. The overall texture is rough, like a nail file. The rounded beak is at one end of the shell.

The common piddock lives in soft rock, such as sandstone, as well as clay or peat. It bores a hole into the rock and lives in this. They live on the lower shore and are most common around the south-west of Ireland.

The common piddock is forever locked in its burrow but has siphons, which are twice the length of the shell, that extend to the surface to feed. Common piddocks have phosphorescent capabilities and can glow in the dark with a green-blue light.

Exterior of a common piddock.

Inside shell.

 # Worms

Don't say 'ew!!!' The marine worms you will encounter around the coast of Ireland are highly variable in their appearance and lifestyles. Some are beautiful, others otherworldly and, yes, some are your typical slimy, wormy-type worms. All of them are an important part of a healthy coastal environment.

As they have no shells, seashore worms have all developed ways of protecting their soft bodies. Some worms build protective tubes and never move. These worms are often filter feeders, keeping coastal waters clear. Their tubes also provide support and protection for other species. Other worms burrow into the sand and are usually deposit feeders that clean the sand. Others hide under rocks and stones for protection. These worms are mobile and are often scavengers that keep the coast clean as they go. Marine worms reproduce in a range of ways: some of them can break off a part of themselves to form a clone, some are hermaphrodites (i.e. they don't have separate males and females), and some have separate males and females.

Importantly, worms are a food source for larger creatures further up the food chain, such as crabs, fish, and birds. Some people use marine worms as bait when fishing.

So next time you go the beach, give the worms a chance and you might be surprised at what you find!

Coiled tubeworms live in tiny, white tubes.

Coiled Tubeworm

Irish Tiúbphéist chorntha **Latin** *Spirorbis spirorbis*
Size < 4mm
Distribution Fronds of brown seaweed of the lower shore

The coiled tubeworm is permanently encased in a smooth, white coiled tube that is no more than 3–4mm in diameter. It is common on rocky shores all around Ireland, where it attaches to the fronds of low-shore brown seaweeds, such as serrated wrack (see page 85), bladder wrack (see page 84) and kelps.

Coiled tube worms brood their young inside their tube, releasing the larvae when they are almost fully developed. These larvae spend just a few hours in the plankton before settling permanently.

Keel Worm

Irish Cílphéist **Latin** *Pomatoceros triqueter*
Size < 25mm long
Distribution Rocks and shells

When you first see a keel worm, you might think that it is just a white squiggle on a rock, and not a living creature. The unassuming keel worm lives inside a calcium-rich white tube that sticks to a rock, a shell or even the top of a crab. It never leaves this tube.

The keel worm is sometimes seen as a pest because it coats buoys, boats and marinas. In the early 1990s the keel worm even caused large losses in scallop production in Bantry Bay, County Cork.

Marks left behind by keelworm tubes.

Keelworms build their elongated tubes on rocks and other solid surfaces.

The frayed ends of sand masons with their tubes buried in the sand.

Sand Mason

Irish Péist fheadáin trá
Latin Lanice conchilega

Size <30cm
Distribution Low on sand and gravel shores

The sand mason lives in sand between the mid shore and 1,700m below sea level. You will notice the upright tube made of sand grains and shell particles which the sand mason has glued together. The frayed end of this tube sticks out above the ground. You might also see these tubes fixed along the undersides of rocks. Inside this tube, the sand mason uses its crown of white tentacles to trap food from the surrounding water.

Sand masons may live individually or in populations of thousands per square metre. The tubes can form a habitat for other animals, protecting them from predators.

The full length of a sand mason tube.

Empty sand mason tubes broken after a storm.

Honeycomb Worm

Irish Péist mhilteogach **Latin** *Sabellaria alveolata*
Size 3–10cm; tube: up to 1m long
Distribution Low on rocky parts of the shore

Found on the north, south and west coasts of Ireland, honeycomb worms live inside tubes that they build by gluing together small fragments of shell and sand. The worms live in colonies, forming reefs of tubes with a honeycomb structure. The tiny worm inside each tube has a crown of spines and feathery tentacles that it uses to trap plankton from the water.

Delicate and beautiful – honeycomb reefs.

The honeycomb reefs are a protected habitat because they provide a place to live for other plants and animals. They are vulnerable to storm damage and cold weather. However, a major threat is human activity – including trampling of the enticing, crunchy reefs by excited rock poolers!

The purple body of a honeycomb worm.

The distinctive shape of honeycomb tubes.

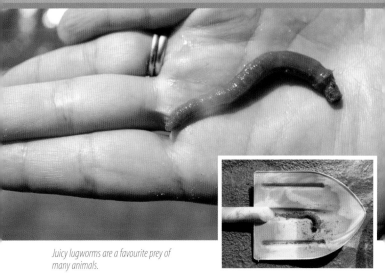

Juicy lugworms are a favourite prey of many animals.

A lugworm dug from under the sand.

Lugworm

Irish Lugach **Latin** *Arenicola marina*
Size < 20cm
Distribution High to low shore in sand and mud

A curled lugworm cast.

Lugworms live from the mid shore to below the low-tide mark in sand and muddy sand. Lugworms' burrows are easily identified by the swirly worm-shaped 'casts' that they create – these are made of defecated sand. They build U-shaped burrows that are between 20–40cm deep to escape from the extreme changes in salt levels as the tide goes in and out. Look also for a 'blow hole' dip in the sand – this is the head end of the burrow. The worm is somewhere in the middle. Lugworms are highly prized by anglers who use them as bait.

They are preyed on by flatfish and wading birds, which snip off their tails.

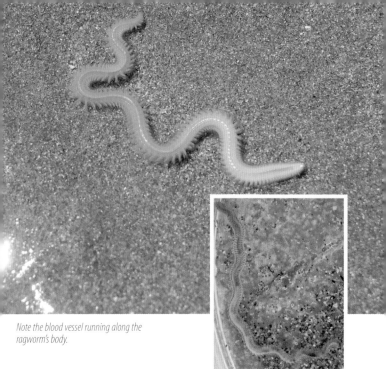

Note the blood vessel running along the ragworm's body.

A ragworm with its many legs.

Ragworm

Irish Raga coiteann **Latin** Hediste diversicolor

Size < 12cm
Distribution Muddy or stony shores

Ragworms live in muddy shores in burrows shaped like a U or a J. They are very common in estuaries. Sometimes they also burrow along the underside of stones.

A ragworm's body looks flattened and has a clear blood vessel running down the back. It has hundreds of pairs of hairlike legs, which it uses for crawling or swimming.

Ragworms are omnivorous – they eat other animals, they scavenge and they graze on the mud. They are an important food for many Irish wading birds.

Scale Worm

Irish Péist ghainneach **Latin** *Polynoidae*
Size 3–7cm long
Distribution Low on muddy or stony shores

Scale worms are fast-moving and active worms. Their upper bodies appear broader and more flattened than most typical worms. This is because of the grey, brown, blue, yellow or red scales that coat their upper surface. From the underneath, they look more like a ragworm. There are a few species, many of which are widespread.

Most of the species that have been studied are carnivorous; some are active hunters. They usually have separate males and females. Some have been observed brooding their eggs under their scales for a number of weeks after they are fertilised.

The underside.

The armour-plated body of a scale worm.

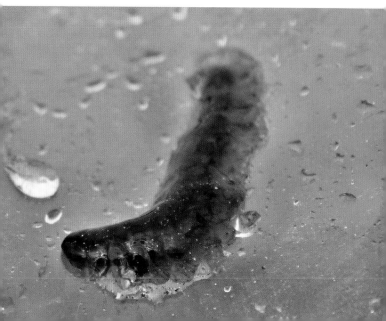

A green-leaf worm hiding among juvenile mussels.

Green-leaf worms are scavengers.

The jade-coloured masses contain the eggs of the green-leaf worm.

Green-leaf Worm

Irish Rámhach glas
Latin *Eulalia viridis*

Size 5–15cm
Distribution Crevices, mud and gravel

The striking green-leaf worm lives in crevices, among barnacles or mussels, on kelps and sometimes under water on hard rocks or gravel. It lives all around the coast of Ireland. This worm is a distinct bottle-green colour and has a flattened body.

It breeds between July and August, producing green jellyish egg masses that it attaches to seaweed. The green-leaf worm is a scavenger that mostly feeds on dead and decaying animals.

Green-leaf worm egg masses rolled in sand on the low shore.

Bootlace Worm

Latin *Lineus longissimus*
Size < 15m
Distribution Low shore

Bootlace worms are long, shiny, coiled and wriggly. They become black when they're older, but can be olive or brown. If you can identify the head end, you might notice that it is spade shaped. The head is often the palest part of the body. It is possible for bootlace worms to grow to many metres long. They are usually about half a centimetre wide. Watching them, you might wonder how they keep from getting their incredibly long bodies in a knot!

They usually live under stones or seaweed or buried in mud. If you pick up a bootlace worm, it might produce lots of smelly mucus. They are different from our earthworms because their bodies are not segmented.

Bootlace worms can grow many metres long.

A younger bootlace worm.

# Sponges and Sea Squirts

Sponges often fill damp crevices on the low shore where they do not risk drying out. They come in a range of shapes and colours and look a bit like lichens or algae. In fact, they are animals. There is a huge range of sponges, and scientists are still discovering new species today, especially in the very deep ocean. In this section we will cover just some of the most common on the shore.

Some sponges are irregularly shaped and encrusted onto rocks. Others are shaped more like vases and live in clusters under the water. The overall body structure of all of them is similar. Small openings, or pores, in the surface of the body 'inhale' water, and larger openings 'exhale'. Inside, there is a cavity through which the water moves. In its simplest form, this cavity is lined with cells that move the water around continuously so that any food particles can be absorbed. In more complex structures, there is a system of channels through which the water travels, and sometimes even a form of skeleton. Some sponges bore holes into rocks and animal shells, and live in them.

If a sponge is broken down into tiny fragments, these fragments can form new sponges. They can also reproduce sexually and often brood larvae inside them before releasing them out into the plankton. Sponges are food for a variety of sea slugs and other grazing animals.

Sea squirts belong to a different family, called Ascidians. Ascidians are very simple forms of chordates, or animals with some kind of spine. Although the adult animals do not look like they belong in this group, the larvae display some kind of chordate characteristics. Ascidians are all marine, and they live from the low-tide mark down to the deep sea. They are widespread and adapted to a range of coastal environments. They feed in a similar way to the sponges, by drawing in water, moving it around their bodies and expelling it through another opening. When they are disturbed, they can squirt out a jet of water.

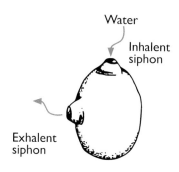

Water

Inhalent siphon

Exhalent siphon

Breadcrumb Sponge

Irish Spúinse grabhrógach **Latin** *Halichondria panicea*
Size Thin sheet to 20cm thick
Distribution Low tide to 500m depth, in rock pools

Breadcrumb sponges are yellow or orange in shadier locations.

At low tide you will find the breadcrumb sponge in crevices and rock pools. As the name suggests, this strange creature looks and feels like a crust of bread covered in volcano chimneys. These chimneys are, in fact, pores used for excreting a smelly substance which deters predators. Some people think the breadcrumb sponge smells like smoke – why not have a sniff?

It is very variable in its appearance. It may be pale green or orangey yellow in colour. In shallow, light-filled pools the green colour dominates because the sponge absorbs algae into its tissues. The algae use light to produce sugars for the sponge (photosynthesis). In the shade, and in deeper water, these algae are not present, so the sponge is yellow. Also, the shape and size of the breadcrumb sponge can vary a lot. If looking in rock pools, you will most likely see it forming a thin mat with small volcanoes all over. However, this sponge can also form large cushions with branches and large chimneys.

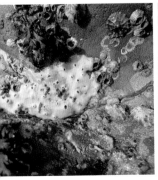

The openings and bread-crust texture are clear on this green breadcrumb sponge.

The size of the openings can vary.

The crumb-of-bread sponge has a grainy texture.

Crumb-of-bread Sponge

Latin *Hymeniacidon perlevis*

Size <20cm across
Distribution Exposed rocks, seaweeds and gravel

The crumb-of-bread sponge lives on the mid shore to below the low-tide mark on a variety of surfaces from rocks and seaweeds to muddy gravel. It prefers silty waters. It grows in various forms, depending on the exposure of its home. You will most likely see it growing in thin, blood-red sheets between the mid and low shore, with a texture similar to fine breadcrumbs. From the low shore and beyond, this sponge grows in orangey or pinkish-red cushions or turrets.

This sponge has a slightly sweet smell. Have a sniff – what do you think?

European Sea Squirt

Irish Ascaid choiteann
Latin *Ascidiella aspersa*

Size Up to 130mm long
Distribution Lower intertidal and to a depth of 80m.

Translucent European sea squirts.

Sea squirts are usually filled with water.

The peculiar-looking European sea squirt forms dense clusters on rocks and man-made structures, such as boat hulls and docks. They have an oval body and look a little bit like a peeled grape as they are transparent with a rough outer layer. They attach their left side to a solid surface.

The European sea squirt is a pest in some areas, where they grow densely on boats and piers. They can also overcrowd beds of commercial scallops, mussels and oysters.

Sea squirts can grow together in colonies.

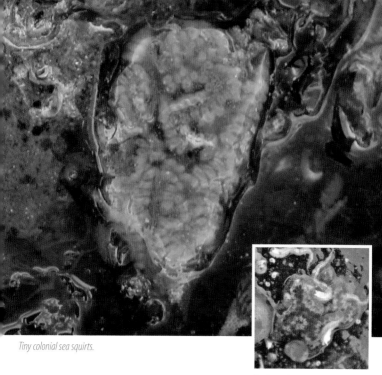

Tiny colonial sea squirts.

A colony of tiny sea squirts under a low-shore rock.

Colonial Sea Squirt

Irish Ascaid réaltach (and others)   **Latin** *Botryllus* spp.

Size < 15cm across
Distribution On solid surfaces on the low shore, especially west and south coasts

Colonial sea squirts include the star ascidian (*Botryllus scholsseri*) and other species. These are very small and form gelatinous mats across solid surfaces. Individual squirts (zooids) are embedded within this jelly. In the star ascidian, these individuals are arranged in groups around exhalant openings, resulting in the star shape. In others, such as *Botryllus leachii*, the individuals are arranged along an elongated exhalant opening.

Colours vary depending on the species. They can be blue, red, yellow, brown or orange.

Urchins and Starfish

Starfish and urchins belong to the group *echinodermata*. 'Echinoderm' means 'spiny-skinned' in Latin. Even though some echinoderms do not have noticeably spiny skin, they all have some obvious features in common, which will help you to distinguish this group from any others.

The body of all echinoderms, be it a starfish or an urchin, can be divided into five equal segments. Amazingly, each segment contains an entire set of internal organs. This means that starfish can cast off an arm to form a new individual, and it is why you might see a starfish looking perfectly happy despite missing several arms. This five-part structure is called pentamerous radial symmetry.

If you look closely at the underside of a starfish or urchin, you will see its many tentacle-like tube feet. The feet work like suction cups, which are controlled by the creature's advanced circulatory system. When the tube feet press against a surface, water is pulled out of them, causing the feet to attach to a hard surface, such as a rock, shell, or seaweed, by suction. Next time you see a starfish in a rock pool, don't pick it up straight away, but watch how it glides effortlessly across the rocks and seaweeds, thanks to its many tube feet.

In addition to the tube feet on the underside of starfish and urchins, you will see the central mouth. The echinoderms on Irish coasts are generally carnivorous or deposit feeders. Carnivorous species of starfish often feed on bivalves, using their strong arms to pull open the shells of their prey. Once the shell is open, they extend their stomach out of their bodies, envelope the prey, liquefy its body, and suck the food and stomach back inside! Echinoderms do not have eyes to help them locate their prey. Instead, some species have light-sensitive parts, which allow them to sense shadows. Others have chemoreceptors which allow them to 'smell' their prey.

Echinoderms are truly fascinating creatures: complex, beautiful and a little bit weird! That's a lot to think about next time you pick up an urchin shell or watch a starfish.

Common Starfish

Irish Crosóg mhara choiteann   **Latin** *Asteria rubens*
Size < 50cm across
Distribution Low shore

Notice the 'tube feet' on the underside.

Typical colouring.

The body of these five-legged starfish can vary from pinkish orange to brown. They have pale bumps and a pale underside. They live on all kinds of shores, but you are most likely to find them washed up, hiding among seaweed, or maybe in rock pools. You might hear stories of beaches being covered in these starfish after rough weather. It's common to find this species with one or more legs missing. These legs can regrow.

On the underside of each of the five legs, the common starfish has hundreds of tiny feet that each end in a sucker. The starfish uses these to walk and to feed.

Common starfish feed on small bivalves, including mussels, and other small creatures, including other starfish.

A common starfish.

A tiny green cushion star.

Cushion stars can also be yellow.

Cushion Star

Irish Crosóg fhaoilinne **Latin** *Asterina gibbosa*
Size About 5cm across
Distribution All coasts

The cushion star is a small starfish with five short arms that are not as separate from the body as the arms of other starfish. The body is dome-shaped and looks soft and cushiony. While cushion stars are quite common on and under stones and seaweeds, their colouring makes them difficult to spot. They are usually pale brown or green, but

The underside of a cushion star.

can be yellow, cream or orange. The upper part of the body is a uniform colour, but covered in short, stiff spines.

Cushion stars all start life as males, but as they get to about four years old, they become females. These females lay up to 1,000 orange eggs in crevices or the undersides of rocks in early summer. Cushion stars can live for about seven years.

Brittlestar

Irish Crosóg bhroisc
Latin *Phiothrix fragilis/Ophiura ophiura/Amphipholis squamata*
Size Central disc < 3cm
Distribution All coasts

As their name suggest, brittlestars are delicate creatures. Their central disc is solid, with a five-rayed pattern. They are generally very well camouflaged into their surroundings. Most brittlestars you find in the intertidal zone are very small and difficult to identify to species level. While the small brittlestar (*Amphipholis squamata*) is small for its whole life, the common (*Phiothrix fragilis*) and sand brittlestars (*Ophiura ophiura*) can grow much larger if they live deeper underwater.

The small and common brittlestars are often found under rocks at low tide and sometimes in the turf created by the 'roots' of coralline red algae. The sand brittlestar is more commonly found on sandy shores.

Deeper under water, common brittlestars can form dense mats of up to 10,000 individuals per square metre.

A delicate brittlestar.

Brittlestars on the shore are usually very small.

Fragile sea potato shells.

Some of the spines are still visible on this sea potato.

Sea Potato/Heart Urchin

Irish Croídín buí **Latin** *Echinocardium cordatum*

Size < 8cm long
Distribution Widespread on sandy shores

The sea potato or heart urchin is most familiar as a pale, delicate, heart-shaped shell washed up on shore once the animal has died. Sea potatoes can be the size of a large new potato. When the

animal is alive, the shell is covered in dense, furry-looking brown spines. However, they generally live buried in the sand, so it is rare to see them alive.

Sea potatoes are deposit feeders – they use their tube feet to pick up particles from the sand. They live on all coasts of Ireland.

Sea potatoes are easily broken.

An intact common urchin
without its spines.

The underside of a common urchin.

Common/Edible Urchin

Irish Cuán mara coiteann **Latin** *Echinus esculentus*
Size < 16cm across
Distribution Rocky shores and kelp on the west coast
Similar species Green urchin

The common urchin usually lives underwater, but you might also find it in rock pools and among seaweed at low tide. When alive, the body ranges from purple to green and is covered in short, dense spines. When washed up dead, these spines have usually fallen off, but the shell has little bumps like pores where the spines were. If the shell is intact, the five pale lines that divide the shell will be visible. The bottom part of the shell is flattened and you might be able to see the mouthparts inside the hole on the underside.

The common urchin grazes on algae and small invertebrate animals. Underwater, they use their tube feet to grip to rocks and to move. The productive organs are a delicacy in many countries, where they are sold as 'roe'. Commercial harvesting has caused local extinctions in some areas.

Green Urchin

Irish Cuán mara glas **Latin** *Psammechinus miliaris*

Size 5cm
Distribution Low on rocky shores and rock pools
Similar species Edible urchin

Green urchins are small and are slightly flattened, unlike the larger edible urchin which is almost spherical. Their tests (body shells) are green, and their spines are also green but with purple tips. They are widespread, but difficult to find because they hide themselves with pieces of shells, seaweeds or other camouflage. They use their tube feet to hold on to these disguises. It is not clear whether this is to trick would-be predators, to prevent sunburn or for some other reason.

Green urchins appear slightly flattened.

Their broken shells are common on the shore.

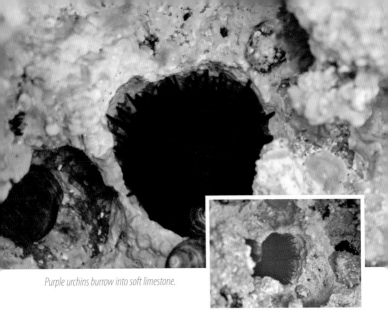

Purple urchins burrow into soft limestone.

The spines of the purple urchin are just visible.

Black/Purple Sea Urchin

Irish Cuán mara dubh **Latin** *Paracentrotus lividus*
Size < 10cm across
Distribution West and south-west coasts

The black or purple sea urchin is much darker in colour than the common or edible urchin. It has extremely strong, short spines that it grinds against the rock to make deep holes in limestone areas. You may find individuals trapped inside these depressions that they have created as they grow. Once inside, they use the upper spines to capture food.

This species has become extinct from many stretches of the Irish coast in recent years. This is usually blamed on overfishing by divers selling to the European market.

The black or purple urchin is one of the species that usually lives in warmer water, but can survive on the west coast of Ireland because of the warm currents that travel up from the Gulf of Mexico. However, there is at least one different species, also sometimes called the black urchin, that lives further south in the Atlantic and the Mediterranean. This has much longer spines than our black or purple urchin.

Jellyfish and other Stingers

Jellyfish are not the most popular seashore creatures. In spite of their stings, they are often mesmerisingly beautiful and although we don't know a lot about some of them, they are a natural part of our coastal ecosystem.

Large numbers of jellyfish in one area are called blooms. Blooms around the Irish coast in recent years have been well publicised and sometimes problematic. They can cause hysteria in the summer months when they float inshore close to beaches popular with swimmers. There have been recent stories about jellyfish numbers increasing around Ireland, and there seems to be a change in the species that we commonly see. The blame for this has been put on overfishing and climate change. However, as they are very difficult things to count, it is not clear whether there really has been an increase. In the early twentieth century, the botanist Séamus Mac an Iomaire wrote 'The sea is full of jellyfish in the summer.' If this was the case a century ago, perhaps the number of jellyfish on our coasts hasn't increased. We may simply be more aware of them, or maybe some species are becoming more common than they used to be. If there has been a rise, it could have implications not only for recreation and tourism, but for aquaculture and fisheries.

Jellyfish belong to a family called cnidarians (pronounced 'nidarian' – the 'c' is silent). The cnidarians all have fairly simple bodies with an outer skin and inner organs, which are separated by a layer of jelly. The inner organs are connected to the outside by a single mouth cavity, which is usually surrounded by tentacles. These tentacles often have stinging cells. When these cells are stimulated, they eject a tiny thread. This thread either sticks to the target, or injects a poison into the target.

Medusas are the true jellyfish as we think of them – umbrella shaped, gelatinous and with long dangling tentacles. These free-swimming jellyfish are not seashore animals, but you will find them washed up after storms or high tides in the summer and autumn. This section also includes their close relatives, anemones – brightly coloured and exotic jelly blobs that cling to rocks or emerge from the sand on all our shores. Related to the anemones are the hydroids, which cannot swim or move unaided. Hydroids often form colonies of many individual polyps. These colonies can be quite complex, with each polyp providing a different function. Some cnidarians have the ability to create light or phosphorescence, which can be seen from the shore at night time, especially in autumn.

Common/Moon Jellyfish

Irish Smugairle róin **Latin** *Aurelia aurita*

Size < 25cm across
Distribution Widespread and sometimes abundant

This pale, translucent jellyfish is the most common species washed up on Irish shores. Look for the four lilac horseshoe shapes clearly visible through the domed body. These are the reproductive parts. When it is floating, four feeding arms and many short tentacles dangle into the water.

Moon jellyfish eat plankton as they drift through the water. They are eaten by sunfish, leatherback turtles and seabirds. They usually live for about six months, during which time they reproduce frequently. They can occur in huge swarms but they are harmless to humans. The Irish name for this species translates as 'seal vomit'.

A common or moon jellyfish.

The short tentacles dangle in the water when afloat.

The frilly tentacles of a compass jellyfish.

Compass Jellyfish

Irish Smugairle an chompáis **Latin** *Chrysaora hysoscella*

⚠ **Caution:** Can sting

Size < 30cm across
Distribution Widespread but especially south and west coasts

A compass jellyfish.

The compass jellyfish has distinctive brown markings that radiate out from the centre of the translucent, dome-shaped body. The pale outer tentacles catch plankton from the water and transfer it to the long arms. These four arms surround the mouth parts. They are long and delicate with varying shades of brown. They are always much longer than the width of the body.

They are common between May and September and can live for about a year. The large, mature individuals that you see in the summer months are last year's young.

The sting can be quite shocking and painful, but it should not cause any long-term damage to skin. The best treatment is to wash with vinegar and apply heat.

Mauve Stinger

Irish Scálachaí **Latin** *Pelagia noctiluca*

⚠ **Caution:** Painful sting

Size < 10cm
Distribution Atlantic coasts

Mauve stingers are small, but can wash up in large numbers.

You can tell a lot about mauve stingers from their name – the inner part of their thick, translucent umbrella is mauve or brown, and the umbrella and tentacles contain cells that can deliver a painful sting. The thick, frilly 'mouth' arms are quite short, but mauve stingers also have eight very fine tentacles that can extend up to 3m.

The Latin name, *pelagia*, refers to the oceanic or pelagic habits of this jellyfish. It is not common in coastal waters, but occasionally washes up on shore in late summer, sometimes in very large numbers. Blooms of mauve stingers have been blamed for killing large numbers of farmed salmon on the west coast. *Noctiluca* refers to the ability of the mauve stinger to light up or glow in the dark if it is disturbed.

The feeding arms of a mauve stinger.

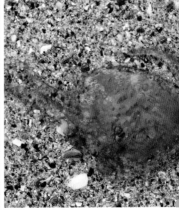

Mauve stingers can be brown or purple.

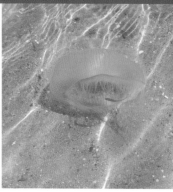

Many-ribbed jellyfish on the shore.

Many-ribbed jellyfish in water.

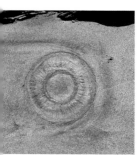

The pattern left in the sand by a dried-out many-ribbed jellyfish.

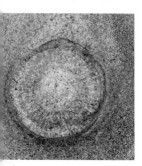

A many-ribbed jellyfish with some colouring.

Many-ribbed Jellyfish

Latin *Aequorea forskalea*
Size < 17cm
Distribution All shores

The many-ribbed jellyfish is completely translucent and without any colouration or obvious tentacles. There is a clear central circle, from which fine lines radiate outwards. It is also called the glass or crystal jellyfish because of its shiny, clear appearance. Technically, there is more than one species around Ireland, but they are extremely similar. They have a slightly different life cycle, but look very like true jellyfish.

Even though many-ribbed jellyfish are common on Irish shores, they are often mistaken for other species bleached and dried out, so they are under-studied. Often, all you will see of them is the indentation left in the sand once the jellyfish has dried out. They can become cling-wrap thin if they have been out of water for some time.

By-the-wind Sailor

Irish Smugairle na gaoithe **Latin** *Velella velella*

Size < 10cm across
Distribution Atlantic coasts

By-the-wind sailors sometimes wash up in large numbers.

Each by-the-wind sailor is in fact a colony of tiny predatory animals called hydrozoa. They are closely related to jellyfish. The 'body' is bottle blue and translucent. A 'sail' runs the length of the body and sticks up to catch the wind above the water. Within the body, there is a float, or sac of air. Large groups often travel together and can wash up on beaches in huge numbers following strong onshore winds.

The by-the-wind sailor is carnivorous and its mouthparts on the underside of the body catch and consume plankton. The poisons in the short tentacles are generally harmless to humans, although there is a slight risk of irritation.

The upright 'sails' of by-the-wind sailors.

By-the-wind sailors are a striking blue.

A Portuguese man-o'-war.

The bright blue tentacles can be very long.

Portuguese Man-o'-war

Irish Smugairle an tseoil **Latin** *Physalia physalis*

⚠ **Caution:** Painful sting

Size < 30cm across
Distribution Atlantic coasts

Like by-the-wind sailors, Portuguese men-o'-war float along the ocean surface with their tentacles dangling down into the water. These tentacles carry a very powerful sting and should not be touched.

While most of the body is translucent, the gaudy pink crest and bottle-blue tentacles are unmistakable. When alive, its gas-filled float moves to catch the best wind. Try blowing on or fanning the body – if it's alive, it will move.

Also similar to by-the-wind sailors, they are in fact a colony of tiny animals. Each of these has a particular role to play – controlling the float, feeding or breeding.

Portuguese men-o'-war travel in groups and usually live in warm waters, but they can wash up on Atlantic coasts in large numbers following south-west winds.

Sea Beard

Latin *Nemertesia antennina*
Size < 25cm tall
Distribution All sandy shores

Each of the stiff orange strands of the sea beard is a hydroid colony. They grow together in clumps that are matted together at the base by a tangle of 'roots'. Each colony is only a few millimetres wide. You might find other plants or animals living amongst the strands.

Sea beard lives anchored in sand under the water. You will only find it on the shore after it has been washed up, usually following a storm. When it is alive, each little colony is covered in delicate feathery hairs that catch food in the passing current.

A spiky sea beard colony.

Sea fir growing on kelp.

Sea fir is made up of tiny triangular organisms.

Sea Fir

Latin *Dynamena pumila*
Size < 5cm tall
Distribution On seaweed or rock

Sea fir appears as strings of downward-pointing arrows growing on seaweed or rocks. The strings are pale brown or yellowish and occur as a series of stems, each about 5cm long, that grow from what looks like a thread.

Depending on the shore, sea fir might grow very obviously on the tips of large algae or it may be hidden in more sheltered places, such as between the holdfasts of wracks. It also grows in estuaries and places where there is some fresh water.

Helter-skelter Hydroid/Whiteweed

Latin *Hydrallmania falcata/Sertularia cupressina*
Size < 35cm tall
Distribution Sand/pebble shores

The difference between helter-skelter hydroids is debated and sometimes they are listed as one species. If you find it washed up on the shore, it will look like a long, tapering tail with bushy branches that spiral around the main stem at intervals. The stem is dark and the branches are brown. Like other hydroids, even though this looks like a plant, it is made up of many tiny individual animals that group together. These hydroid colonies usually live in deep water, but it is possible to find them on the very low shore where there is firm sand or pebbles to attach to.

There is a small traditional industry around gathering, drying and dyeing these hydroids for aquaria or other decorative purposes.

The helter-skelter hydroid.

Beadlet Anemone

Irish Bundún coirníneach **Latin** *Actinia equina*

Size 2–7cm across
Distribution Mid or low rocky shores
Similar species Strawberry anemone

Beadlet anemones don't like to live too close to their neighbours.

This anemone is common in Irish rock pools and you might see it at low tide on rocky coasts with its tentacles retracted into the body, which looks like a shiny blob of jelly. The colours can range from strong green to red or dark purple. The slimy coating helps to protect the anemone from drying out at low tide. When the tide comes in, the tentacles emerge to catch food from the passing water. Tiny blue spots on the tentacles contain stinging cells.

You don't often see two anemones right next to each other, as they are not good neighbours. When they come into contact, they use their stinging cells to fight until one eventually moves away.

Both sexes can have broods of young, but we know very little about how they reproduce. They can live for up to three years.

A beadlet anemone partially buried in sand.

Beadlet anemones can retract their tentacles.

A strawberry anemone with tentacles retracted.

Strawberry anemones have red tentacles.

Strawberry Anemone

Latin *Actinia fragacea*

Size < 10cm across
Distribution Mid or low rocky shores
Similar species Beadlet anemone

The strawberry anemone is widely distributed, but a little less common and much bigger than the beadlet anemone. It has a similar base colour, but has striking bright green spots all over the stalk, like the pips in the skin of a strawberry. Its tentacles are also similar in colour to those of the beadlet anemone. Older books may describe them as a single species. They are

Strawberry anemones can be highly decorative.

adaptable creatures that occur everywhere between Norway and west Africa, the Azores, the Canaries and Cape Verde, usually on rocky shores, but sometimes buried in sand.

Strawberry anemones typically attach to the underside or to vertical sides of rocks, so they can be hard to find. However, at low tide, their colours jump out from the rocks. They can withdraw their tentacles and look like the big bellies of a fairy-tale monster!

Some snakelock anemones have striking green and purple colouring.

A grey snakelocks anemone.

Snakelocks Anemone

Irish Bundún nathairiúil
Latin *Anemonia viridis*

Size < 5cm across
Distribution Mid or low rocky shores

Snakelocks anemones are a similar size to beadlet anemones and live in rock pools and fairly high on the shore. However, their colour ranges from a pale mauve-grey to Day-Glo green with purple tips. Another feature that differentiates them is that they cannot withdraw their tentacles at low tide, so they are always visible. Their tentacles are also longer and more active than those of the beadlet anemone.

The colours can be so bright that they look almost unnatural. Similar to tropical corals, the range of colours comes from tiny algae that live inside the tissues of the anemone. These algae require light to survive, so you will not find such brightly coloured snakelocks anemones in deep or shaded water. The anemone and the algae form a symbiotic relationship where they each provide nutrients or shelter for the other.

The snakelocks anemone can sting and kill relatively large fish with its long, waving tentacles.

Snackelocks anemones cannot fully retract their long tentacles.

A snakelocks anemone feeding on a mauve stinger.

Gem/Wartlet Anemone

Irish Bundún na seod   **Latin** *Aulactinia verrucosa*

Size < 3cm across
Distribution Low shore and rock pools

Unlike many of the brighter anemone species, the gem anemone is quite well camouflaged against pebbles and coralline algae (see page 65). The column is pale pinkish grey and can extend to about 8cm high. It has characteristic warty bumps along its length. The tentacles are transparent but have grey-green stripes. When it retracts its tentacles, it forms a little ball with pale lines that radiate out from the centre and make it look like a small urchin (see page 198) without its spines.

Gem anemones are a southern species at the northern limit of their range in Ireland. They like sunny rock pools and sometimes group together at the bottom.

Retracted gem anemones resemble urchins.

Gem anemones have striped tentacles.

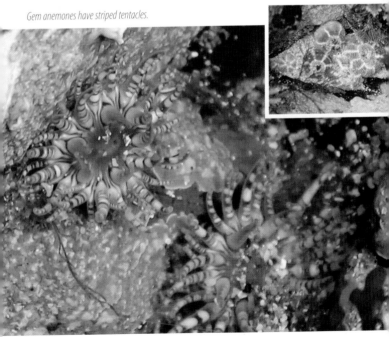

Daisy anemones crowded into a rock pool.

Daisy anemones can flatten out like a disk.

Daisy Anemone

Irish Nóinín mara **Latin** *Cereus pedunculatus*
Size < 4cm across
Distribution Mid or low rocky shores

Daisy anemones have much shorter tentacles than many of the other anemones. They also have wide mouths and a gap of a few millimetres where there are no tentacles. They always have at least 200 tentacles, but can have up to 700, so what they lack in length they make up for in numbers! The tentacles are usually grey and mottled with cream or light brown.

The trumpet-shaped column can be orange or brown, sometimes with a purplish tinge, and can grow to 12cm tall. Underwater, daisy anemones live buried in sand with only the tentacles above ground. The mouth parts and tentacles may be lying flat at the bottom of a rock pool, or there might be a number of them crowded together in a frilly mass. Daisy anemones prefer warmer water.

Sagartia elegans

Size < 3cm across
Distribution Mid to low shore rock pools and crevices

A characteristically mottled column of Sagartia elegans.

The colouring of *Sagartia elegans* is very varied. The tentacles are often white or transparent, but the background colour around the mouth can be red, brown, orange or white. The column is generally a grey-green colour with a number of white suckers dotted from the middle to the end closest to the tentacles. The middle of the column looks slightly pinched. If you disturb this anemone underwater, you might see the stinging threads being discharged from the tentacles.

You might find large numbers of these anemones together, especially on rocky coasts, but possibly on sandy shores also.

An adult specimen.

A white-tentacled Sagartia elegans.

 # Fish

Even though Irish waters are home to a huge variety of fish, there is not much diversity in what you are likely to find regularly in rock pools or very shallow water. There are a few that spend their entire lives very close to shore, and some have even developed the ability to spend the hours of low tide out of the water, as long as they are in a damp and shady place.

All of the fish described here are bony fish, unlike the sharks, skates and rays, which have skeletons made of cartilage. Fish use gills to breathe, but these are covered by a bony plate, which also differentiates them from sharks. We often think of fish as scaly, but scales can get rubbed off, damaged and infected if they rub against stones. Therefore, some shore fish have slippery skin that helps them to move against rocks.

To swim, fish have fins with rays that they can control very precisely. These fins come in sets – the dorsal fin runs along the back and can be separated into two parts; the pectoral fins are on either side of the body, like little hands; the pelvic fin is underneath the body just behind the head; and the anal fin is on the underside near the tail. The tail itself is also a fin.

Fish use an organ called a swim bladder to control their buoyancy in the water (so that they don't sink or pop to the surface). Swim bladders are filled with gas, and they can control it to move up or down in the water.

Most fish have very good hearing and eyesight. Unlike us, the eyes of many fish enable them to see clearly both in and out of the water. In addition to all of the usual senses, fish also have a 'lateral line' that is extremely sensitive to vibrations, pressure changes and even electronic activity. In some shore fish, this is reduced because of their wave-battered and very changeable environment.

Fish are important predators in the ocean food web; they are also preyed upon by birds, seals, jellyfish, whales, dolphins and, most of all, by humans.

In general, fish are an extremely diverse and highly developed group of animals. Some are solitary, others move in groups and have complex social structures. Some species also have elaborate mating rituals that include 'dances', 'songs' that are produced by the male's swim bladder, and creating underwater structures to attract females.

Important Features

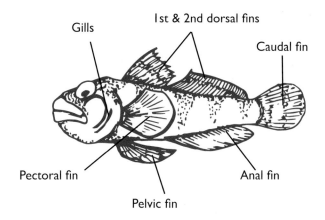

Gills

1st & 2nd dorsal fins

Caudal fin

Pectoral fin

Pelvic fin

Anal fin

A common blenny propped up on its pectoral fins.

Common blennies often live in rock pools.

Common Blenny/Shanny

Irish Ceannruán **Latin** *Lipophrys pholis*

Size < 16cm long
Distribution Rock pools and the low shore, especially Atlantic coasts

Common blennies can survive some time out of the water.

The common blenny is khaki-green to black and very patterned. It has large, protruding eyes and wide lips. It can prop itself up on its pelvic fins. The pectoral (chest) fins are shaped like fans, are transparent and have olive-green spines. The body is round and elongated. There is one long, continuous spiny fin along the back and a long anal fin on the bottom.

This is the fish you are most likely to see in rock pools or in shallow water. When there is somewhere to hide, they will dart away quickly as soon as you approach and sometimes all you will see is a puff of sand. However, you might get a better look if one is stuck in a small rock pool at low tide. You can even find them hiding in damp patches under stones or seaweed out of the water. There are reports that some individuals return to the same 'home' rock pool when the tide goes out.

Common blennies eat barnacles and small periwinkles. Larger individuals also eat seaweed. They can live to 14, but usually live to about five years of age.

Sand Goby

Irish Mac siobháin gainimh **Latin** *Gobius minutus*
Size < 10cm
Distribution Sandy or muddy-bottomed estuaries, salt marshes and coastal waters

The sand goby is small, pale brown/grey in colour, with large eyes at the front of the head. It is well camouflaged against pale and sandy surfaces. It lives in soft sandy or muddy substrates in estuaries, salt marshes and along the coast. It tolerates a wide variation in salinity and temperature.

It is suspected that the sand goby is migratory, moving to deeper, warmer waters in the winter.

This fish can live for up to two years in Atlantic waters. It feeds on small worms and crustaceans.

A well-camouflaged sand goby.

A two-spotted goby (probably a female).

Two-spotted Goby

Irish Mac siobháin buí **Latin** *Gobiusculus flavescens*

Size < 6cm

Distribution Intertidal to 20m depth in pools and shallow water among seaweeds

The two-spotted goby is quite different from other gobies that you might come across. If you look closely you will notice that the eyes on the two-spotted goby are on either side of the head rather than at the front. Also, unlike other gobies, the two-spotted goby is often found hovering in small shoals in the water column amongst kelps or seagrass, or over seaweed-covered rocks. Their name is derived from the spot at the base of the tail. Males have a second spot on their sides, just behind their fin. They are red to green in colour with bluish markings along their sides. During the breeding season, the males become much more brightly coloured and may even be difficult to recognise.

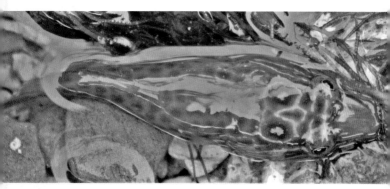

The iridescent markings on a Cornish sucker.

Cornish Sucker/Shore Clingfish

Irish Súmaire Cornach **Latin** *Lepadogaster lepadogaster*
Size <8cm
Distribution Rock pools and under rocks

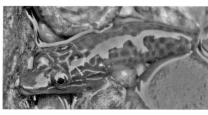

A Cornish sucker hiding among stones.

The wedge-shaped Cornish sucker is easily identified by its broad triangular head and its 'duck-billed' snout. The bright markings on the back vary in colour, but are unmistakable and look like eyes with glasses. The overall colour can also vary, but the body is always smooth and glossy as it has no scales. The fins at the pelvis form a sucking disk to allow the fish to cling to rocks, under which it sometimes lives.

Golden-coloured eggs are laid under rocks and are guarded by either the mother or father.

Lesser Sand Eel

Irish An chorr ghainimh bheag   **Latin** *Ammodytes tobianus*
Size < 20cm
Distribution Underwater on sandy shores

Thin, silvery lesser sand eels swim in fast-moving schools on sandy shores. They can dart into the sand once they sense your presence. They are yellowish-green in colour along their back and have silver bellies. Their lower jaw is longer than the upper and is pointed.

Females lay 4,000–20,000 eggs in the sand, where they stick to individual sand grains.

They spend their time either buried in sand or swimming in large schools. Through the winter, they hibernate buried 20–50cm below the sand.

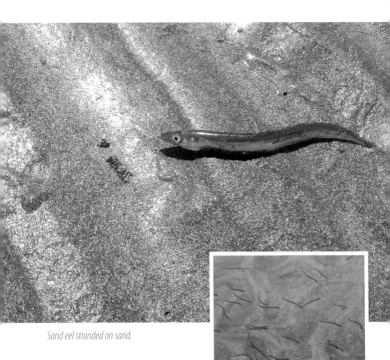

Sand eel stranded on sand.

Lesser sand eels usually move in schools.

Worm pipefish have elongated snouts.

Worm pipefish shelter under stones.

Worm Pipefish

Irish Pis an ribe **Latin** *Nerophis lumbriciformis*

Size < 15cm long

Distribution Sheltered rocky shores, especially south and west coasts

The worm pipefish is closely related to seahorses. It has a very long and slender dark green or black body. Its mouth is shaped like a short snout, similar to that of a seahorse. The underside of the body has pale markings. It has no obvious fins and moves like a snake or eel.

The worm pipefish is a sea-floor species that usually lives under rocks and seaweed on sheltered shores. It eats tiny crab-like plankton and very small fish.

They have been recorded breeding throughout the summer. Similar to seahorses, the female transfers up to 150 eggs to the male, who fertilises and carries the eggs until they hatch.

There are other larger pipefish species that you might also find on Irish seashores.

Five-bearded Rockling

Irish Donnán cúig ribe **Latin** *Ciliata mustela*
Size < 25 cm long
Distribution Low tide to 20m depth

The five-bearded rockling is easily recognised by the five barbels around its mouth: two above each nostril and one underneath the mouth. It also has recognisably long dorsal and anal fins. It is dark brown along its back and reddish black blending into pale grey on its tummy. This fish lives in rock pools and just below the low shore, preferring rocky bottoms but also living on sandy, muddy and shell gravel bottoms. These fish are predatory, mostly hunting shrimp, crabs and small fish. However, they often fall prey to terns and gulls. The five-bearded rockling is known to have a homing habit, returning to the same rock pool when the tide goes out.

The five-bearded rockling has a distintive beard around its mouth.

Acknowledgements

Special thanks to my parents, Maurice and Barbara Taylor for the support and time that they've given to this project – it was worth it for the sandy picnics! I'm grateful to my grandad, Bart O'Connor, for encouraging me to change direction, and to the many good friends who have been supportive, helpful and understanding while I've been entirely obsessed with seashore creatures.

Thanks also to Sam, Holly, Katy, Ellen and Megan Galvin; Katie and Mia O'Farrell; Nicola White; Roger Ahern; Maria and Anna Garagouni; and James McNena for keeping me company on photo trips to various seashores – I hope that you enjoyed it as much as I did.

Lucy

Many thanks to my family. Your ongoing encouragement, enthusiasm and the generous time invested in helping me made all the difference, especially on those rainy days when I dragged you to the beach on a mission to get a picture of some elusive creature or other. A special mention to my sisters, Pia and Lissi, for their impressive rock-pooling skills. If only I was such an expert at your age!

I'm very grateful to David Brandon for his support, immense patience and constant presence throughout this project, and for listening to constant chatter about my newest favourite seashore creature.

Finally, thanks to Lucy for the adventure. It was special.

Emma

Lucy and Emma would both like to thank all at The Collins Press, for guiding us through the exciting process of writing our first book.

References

Challinor, H., Murphy Wickens, S., Clark, J., Murphy, A. *A Beginner's Guide to Ireland's Seashore*. 2003. Sherkin Island Marine Station, Cork, Ireland.

Fish, J. D. and Fish, S. *A Student's Guide to the Seashore*. 2011. Cambridge University Press, Cambridge, England.

Gibson, C. *Pocket Nature: Seashore*. 2011. Dorling Kindersley, London, England.

Hook, P. *A Concise Guide to the Seashore*. 2008. Parragon Books Ltd, Bath, England.

Preston-Mafham, K. and R. *Seashore*. 2004. HarperCollins Publishers Ltd., London, England.

Preston-Mafham, K. *Seashore of Britain and Europe*. 2010. HarperCollins Publishers Ltd., London, England.

Mac an Iomaire, S. *Shores of Connemara* (translated by Padraic de Bhaldraithe). 2000. Tír Eolas, Kinvara, County Galway, Ireland.

Sterry, Paul. *Complete Guide to Irish Wildlife*. 2010. HarperCollins Publishers Ltd, London, England.

Trewhella, S., Hatcher, J. *The Essential Guide to Beachcombing and the Strandline*. 2016. Wild Nature Press, Plymouth, England.

Whelan, Paul. *Lichens of Ireland*. 2011. The Collins Press, Cork, Ireland.

Useful Links

Ainmneacha Plandaí is Ainmhithe (acmhainn.ie): www.acmhainn.ie/tearmai/plandai.htm

Atlantic Irish Seaweeds: www.atlanticirishseaweed.com/

Great Eggcase Hunt: www.sharktrust.org/en/great_eggcase_hunt

Ireland's Lichens: **www.lichens.ie**

Irish Lichens: **www.irishlichens.ie**

IT Sligo Seashell Guide: **http://staffweb.itsligo.ie/staff/dcotton/Sea_Shells.html**

Irish Wildlife Trust: www.iwt.ie

Marine Life Identification Network: **www.marlin.ac.uk**

The Seaweed Site: **www.seaweed.ie/**

Wildflowers of Ireland: www.wildflowersofireland.net

World Register of Marine Species: **www.marinespecies.org**

Index of English species names

Index of Latin species names

Index of Irish species names

General index